In Love with a Gentleman

In Love with a Gentleman

Elisa Ellen

Translated by Terry Laster

This is a work of fiction. Names, characters, organizations, places, events, and incidents are either products of the author's imagination or are used fictitiously.

Text copyright © 2013 Elisa Ellen

Translation copyright © 2015 Terry Laster

All rights reserved.

No part of this book may be reproduced, or stored in a retrieval system, or transmitted in any form or by any means, electronic, mechanical, photocopying, recording, or otherwise, without express written permission of the publisher.

Previously published as *Verliebt in einen Gentleman* in Germany by the author in 2013. Translated from German by Terry Laster.

First published in English by AmazonCrossing in 2015.

Published by AmazonCrossing, Seattle

www.apub.com

Amazon, the Amazon logo, and AmazonCrossing are trademarks of Amazon.com, Inc., or its affiliates.

ISBN-13: 9781477828793

ISBN-10: 1477828796

Cover design by Shasti O'Leary-Soudant

Library of Congress Control Number: 2014919889

Printed in the United States of America

Chapter 1

"Tell me, what do people wear to the casino?"

The peacefulness of teatime bursts like a soap bubble.

My parents look up at the same time—my mother from her knitting and my father from his sudoku. They look shocked, as if I've said something terrible.

My mother seems to consider what to say. Apparently, my question has caught her off guard.

"To the casino? Mmm . . ." she finally says. "Well, I think a little black dress, or whatever you call it, would be appropriate. But don't ask me, I've never been to one."

My father just shakes his head and returns to his numbers puzzle. I imagine he is thinking his daughter is out of her mind again. The best thing he can do is pretend he didn't hear me.

My mother returns to knitting her socks, then asks mildly, "Why do you ask?"

"I'm going to the casino tomorrow," I say. "I was just thinking about what I should wear."

My father looks up from his puzzle again and furrows his brow. "To the casino? Are you kidding?"

"No," I answer. "I'm going to the casino in Hohensyburg tomorrow evening. Cross your fingers I'll get to ride in a stretch limo!"

My father puts down his pen and fixes me with a stern look. "Who are you running around with, Lea?"

"Don't worry so much," I say over my shoulder as I dash upstairs to my room. I don't want to get in a discussion with him about my trip to the casino. Right now there are much more important things to do: I need an outfit. Little black dress. Hmm.

I'm home for the weekend from Münster, where I go to school. My parents live in Bielefeld; my father is a retired teacher, and my mother is a homemaker heavily involved in community work.

I throw open the doors to my closet and look inside. The closet in my childhood bedroom is cluttered with old clothes; if I'm lucky, I'll find something that will work. I pull at a bit of black cloth peeking out from a stack of clothing. As if I'd released the one thing keeping everything packed inside, at least twenty garments fly out, landing on the floor. Great. The black dress is somewhere in the pile. I kneel down and rummage through the mountain of fabric until I find the dress. It's a lightweight little thing with spaghetti straps. I bought it in Istanbul, where I'd spent a semester.

Did I really need this in Istanbul? Oh yeah. I think dreamily of the great nights I'd spent with my fellow international students in the city's many discos. I sniff the dress. It still smells vaguely of an impossibly exotic perfume that I used at that time. It was called something like "The Secret of the Desert." One of my girlfriends back then referred to it jokingly as "The Secret of the Deserted," which was unfair. Although I liked to party, I preferred to sleep off my hangovers alone.

I take off my jeans and T-shirt and slip on my dress. Not bad. I turn in front of the full-length mirror. I haven't put on any weight since the last time I'd worn it, at least two years ago. But seeing the straps of my white bra doesn't work. I look through my drawer for a black strapless bra and pull on sheer black stockings. Wow. I should wear clothes like this more often. I look really good.

Now for the shoes. That's a little more complicated. I still have the black dancing shoes I bought for a flamenco class I took in my first semester at the university. The heels are about two inches high. Reasonable. Comfortable. Elegant. But wait! Didn't I buy high heels during my semester in England?

I find them deep in my closet and look skeptically at the heels. They are wickedly high. In England, there were a number of occasions when high heels for women and ties for men were a necessity. I'd bought these shoes, but because I was terrified of falling flat on my face, I looked like I was walking on eggshells when I wore them. I also towered over my dates, irritating both of us. Over the course of the evening, I usually ended up removing the high heels and dancing in stockings. Of course, the stockings ran in an instant. I suspect the stocking industry is in cahoots with the high heel industry.

I squeeze my feet into the black heels and stand in front of the mirror. I look amazingly chic and sexy. Maybe too much?

I snatch up the flamenco shoes and totter back downstairs to my parents. "I need some advice. Which shoes are better, the high heels or the flamenco shoes?"

My mother looks up and is so startled that a stitch drops off her knitting needle. "Darn it!" she curses as she tries to recover the stitch.

Now I look at my father.

"Agreed, Elsa. Darn it!" he says. He wrinkles his forehead. "You're not leaving the house like that, are you? Forgive me for saying this, but you look like you belong to the oldest profession in the world."

In my mother's eyes, however, I see something that kind of looks like admiration.

"You look extremely seductive, Lea," she sighs. "Oh, what I would have given to be so beautiful at your age!"

"But you were," says my father.

"Oh, no, Wilhelm," my mother replies. "I was such a proper little gray mouse. I wasn't allowed to look so chic. My father would have had a seizure."

"I'll have one, too," my father says. He throws down his pencil impatiently and tries to sound authoritative. "Lea, I forbid you to go anywhere in that outfit!"

I ignore him and hold up the flamenco shoes, asking my mother, "Which shoes do you like better?"

My mother tilts her head to the side, eyeing them critically. "I like both, but I'm afraid if you wear those insanely high heels, you'll ending up breaking your neck."

"Yes," I say, "but the other shoes are a little too conservative, don't you think?"

"In that outfit, you wouldn't look conservative if you wore sneakers," my father says grumpily.

"Yes," says my mother, "the high heels are better. Picture perfect."

I could have hugged her. I sometimes get the feeling she likes it when I dress up, because she wasn't able to as a young woman.

"Just a second," my mom says. "I have something for you." She jumps up and leaves the room. I hear her climb up the steps to her bedroom.

What the heck? My toes are already hurting like the devil so I sit down in the chair. To relieve the pressure even more, I bring my knees up under my chin.

My father says sullenly, "Now the whole world can see under your dress."

I angle my knees a bit and softly drum my fingers on the tabletop—I just finished polishing my nails.

My father shakes his head and continues working on his sudoku.

A minute later, my mother is back in the room with a small velvet pouch in her hands. She throws it to me. "Here. Catch!"

Something rattles inside. It falls to the floor, and I bend over to pick it up.

"I can see under your skirt again," my father growls.

I consider the pouch curiously. What could it be? I open it up and look inside. Something sparkly catches my eye. I pour the contents into my palm. It's a pair of heavy chandelier clip-on earrings.

"Wow," I say, thrilled. "Where did you get these? They're awesome!"

The earrings are like the ones actresses wear to the Oscars, except they probably wear real gems. These are definitely rhinestones—otherwise they would be worth at least a million dollars and we wouldn't be living in a small semidetached house on the outskirts of Bielefeld.

I lift up the earrings and hold them to the light. They glitter and sparkle like a fireworks display.

"Try them on," my mother says, out of breath from the quick hike up and down the stairs.

I position myself in front of the nearby hall mirror, carefully clipping the pendants on my earlobes. They almost touch my bare shoulders. I swing my head slightly. They tinkle and gleam in the light.

"They go great with my outfit," I say. "Where did you get such sexy earrings?"

My father looks at my mother curiously. Apparently, he is asking himself the same question.

My mother throws my father a quick glance and turns red. "Oh, um, I got them on eBay. I thought it would be nice to have something sparkly for the opera or for a concert. When I got them, I was shocked to see how big they are. I thought they'd be smaller—and a bit more discreet."

"Well, they are definitely not discreet," my father remarks, looking grim. He doesn't like it when my mother wears earrings at all, so I can understand why she wouldn't have dared to wear them in my father's presence.

I pirouette and look at myself in the mirror again. "Hurray! I'm really looking forward to tomorrow. Thanks, Mama." I give her a little peck on the cheek and climb the stairs to my room again.

I pause at the landing, where I loved to perch as a child, secretly eavesdropping on the adult world after I was supposed to be in bed. Now I hear my father say, "The things you allow, Elsa. I stand by what I said: Lea looks like a hooker in that outfit."

I lean forward, cocking my ears.

My mother replies, "What do I allow, Wilhelm? What's so bad about Lea having a happy-go-lucky student life—especially after what she's been through?"

My father grunts reluctantly in acknowledgment. Although I can't see him from where I'm standing, I can imagine his facial expression. "That has nothing to do with it. I thought her past experiences would make her a more mature, reasonable person."

"Oh, and mature, reasonable people never have any fun?" my mother retorts. "That's ridiculous! Well, I'm glad she's so happy and cheerful. If she were serious and withdrawn, I would be worried."

I gulp. I know exactly what they're alluding to, but I shove it quickly into the recesses of my brain, where it usually sits safe and sound. Must they rehash it over and over again? They must need more time to process it than I did. I suppose that a younger person is better able to come to grips with things like that than adults—even if the younger person was the one who was most affected.

My father just grunts again and says something unintelligible. He falls quiet, and when I hear my mother's knitting needles clicking again, I tiptoe through my door and close it softly behind me.

The next evening I am back in my shared apartment in Münster, waiting to be picked up. My roommates, Marc and Lisa, eye me as I stroll into the communal kitchen wearing my little black dress. Lisa finishes her cappuccino with a gulp, and Marc, who's washing the dishes, splashes water out of a glass, soaking his shirt.

"Hey, gorgeous!" he says. "Where are you going? The Miss Germany pageant?"

Lisa looks a bit peeved. She's got a secret crush on Marc. "Isn't your dress just a bit skimpy for early September?" she asks pointedly.

"Oh, I don't think so," I answer nonchalantly. "It definitely won't be too skimpy for a stretch limo."

Lisa's jaw drops. As if on command, someone honks from the street. Marc goes to the window, looks down, and squints.

"I'll be damned!" he exclaims. "An actual stretch limo is waiting down there! Man, I'd give anything to ride with you in one of those!"

Lisa sniffs. "I wouldn't. Way too vulgar." But I can see that her eyes say something entirely different.

The doorbell rings.

"Bye, everyone," I say, waving before I run into the hallway and rush downstairs. As I pass the hallway mirror, I can see my earrings sparkle in the dim light. I'm young and feel great, overjoyed to be heading out for an exciting evening.

At the curb, a chauffeur wearing a uniform and cap holds open the door of a snow-white luxury limo. I duck my head down and slide in. Inside I find six very cheerful and, I suspect, already-tipsy students— female students, to be exact, with Tom sitting among them. Tom is a Facebook friend of mine. I'm actually not sure how we know each other—I think I may have met him at a party.

It's Tom's twenty-fifth birthday, and because his parents are quite rich (I think his father is an attorney or something like that), they've treated him to a night out at the Hohensyburg Casino with his friends. They also threw in the stretch limo. He'd announced on Facebook that he'd choose seven beautiful girls to ride with him. I'd thrown my name in the hat on a whim.

I think it's a bit weird to surround yourself with random beautiful strangers like that, but when are you going to be twenty-five again? Let him have his fun. I sit down in the seat next to Tom and look around. The chauffeur is back behind the steering wheel and starts the engine. It purrs so quietly that it sounds like an electric car. I look up at my apartment window. Lisa and Marc are staring down at us in disbelief. Ha-ha! Life is so beautiful!

The car is packed tight with long legs, bare shoulders, and cleavage. The air reeks of heavy perfume. The other girls obviously devoted themselves to the same question—what does one wear to the casino?—with the same results. Tom's all gussied up, too. He's wearing an elegant tuxedo with highly polished patent leather shoes.

He holds up a bottle of sparkling wine, and a brunette girl—I think I saw her once in a lecture on English literature—passes around the champagne glasses. The cork pops out of the champagne bottle and hits the driver on the neck. He touches his neck, rubbing it where the cork hit. Everybody giggles, and the birthday boy roars with laughter.

"Sorry," Tom says, leaning forward. "Wasn't on purpose. Won't happen again."

Without turning around, the driver mutters something and calmly continues driving.

Tom fills each of our glasses.

"Drink quickly, before it spills," says the brunette. I think her name is Carla.

"No!" a blonde beauty next to me says. "First we have to sing!"

So we all take a deep breath and sing "Happy Birthday" so loudly that the limo's windows rattle. Tom grins happily, then clinks our glasses. We drink down the bubbly brew.

Another bottle is opened, and everyone drinks another round. Needless to say, we're all in high spirits. The jokes fly through the air. Everyone has an anecdote about some other birthday party or a university party or a cranky professor. The landscape whizzes past us.

Occasionally lights flash from houses, streetlights, or neon signs, and then it's dark again as we drive past forests or meadows.

Suddenly, I feel a hand on my thigh. It creeps up higher, little by little. It's Tom's hand. I don't want to make a scene, but I really don't like this. I take Tom's arm by his tuxedo sleeve, lift it up, and put his hand back on his own leg.

Tom glares at me angrily, then says to another girl, "Hey, Carla, how about switching seats with Lea? I'd like to sit next to each of you beautiful girls before we arrive at the casino."

I'm only too happy to swap with Carla. We have to climb over each other to switch places. Secretly, I'm thinking, *Ah, so that's how it is. We're not just decorative accessories, but subject to being groped, too.* I no longer have such a high opinion of Tom.

As I drop into my new seat, I casually look toward the front. I catch the eyes of the chauffeur through the rearview mirror. I blush a bit. Did he see what happened? I stare out the window. I doubt anyone could see anything in this dark car.

About an hour later, we drive up a steep hill. The old walls of the Hohensyburg Castle soar above us. The limo swings around the castle ruins and stops in front of an ultramodern glass building. It's lit up like a giant lantern, illuminating the whole area. I've never been inside a casino, and I'm tingling with excitement.

We all climb out of the limo, and the cool night air embraces us instantly. Tom exchanges a few words with the driver, who restarts the engine and pulls into the parking lot a few hundred yards away.

Inside the building, it's warm and bright, with music playing from somewhere. An elegantly dressed staff member welcomes us and checks our IDs. A group of Tom's friends, who arrived in their own cars, joins us. I look around. They're Tom's fellow students, and, because he studies medicine and I'm an English major, I don't know any of them. Honestly, I don't know if I want to get to know them. All too often, the best students in school are nerds, and Tom's friends bear this out.

They're med students and look lost in a casino. They're dressed up, but it looks like most of them are wearing their confirmation suits for the occasion. I sigh. Uh-oh, this is going to suck! Oh well. I intend to have a good time this evening, anyway. Somehow, I'll make this work . . .

An hour later I am sitting on a bar stool, bored to death. I didn't realize that this isn't a hosted party and recklessly left my wallet at home. Some partygoers flit over to the gambling tables to try their luck. I watch for a while, but it's not that exciting if you're not gambling yourself. Others drift into the restaurant to get a bite to eat.

I feel a bit like Cinderella, although I don't think I look the part. No lie—in the last half hour, at least ten middle-aged men approached me, asking if they could buy me a drink. I politely refused each time, and each gentleman staggered away, shoulders drooping.

But I'm dying of thirst. Tom, our cocky host, has approved only one glass of white Italian champagne for each partygoer—no more, no less. To be honest, I feel really, really terrible. I would be the perfect model for a drugstore poster. The title would be "Lea's Condition at the Casino." Under the title would be a picture of me in my great outfit, an arrow pointing at my throat with the word "Thirsty." Another arrow would point at my belly with the words "Very hungry because she hasn't eaten dinner and was on the road for over an hour." Two arrows would point at my earlobes with "Traumatized by very heavy and too-tight clip-on earrings." And two more would point at my feet with "In extreme pain due to too-tight shoes with heels that are far too high." Perhaps a final arrow would point at my heart or my head: "Tired, disappointed, just wants to go home."

What am I doing here? What the hell possessed me to participate in this event? My father was right. If I were more sensible, I wouldn't have put myself in this stupid situation. Whatever. Something must be done. I absolutely must get out of these damned torture-shoes. I look around. Would anyone care if I just slip them off?

I kick one shoe to the floor. Almost immediately, a middle-aged couple walks by. The woman nudges her husband and points at me, not even very discreetly. He grins. I imagine they are saying, "Look at the woman at the bar with only one shoe. Probably already tossed back one too many." They smirk at one another.

A moment later, another gentleman, definitely on the wrong side of forty, hurries over to me. "Excuse me," he says. "You've lost your shoe. May I . . . ?"

Well, this certainly wasn't what I intended. Pulling off my shoe was supposed to improve my situation, not complicate it.

"No, thanks," I say coolly, and jump off my stool to slip on my torture-shoe again.

I have only one choice: I'll go outside and take off my shoes there. My feet will be a little cold, but the way my toes feel right now, cold would be a blessing. I find the exit and step out into the night. I unclip my giant earrings, throw them into my handbag, and rub my painful earlobes. Ah, I feel so much better already. Then I slip both my shoes off. My thankful feet melt immediately. *I am not going to put these shoes back on again, even if that means I have to stay out here the whole night,* I think glumly.

I can still hear the music from the casino; it's muffled, as if somebody turned down the volume knob on a radio. Inside, it smells of people, perfume, food, and alcohol. But out here, it's beautiful. The air smells earthy and autumnal. I throw my head back. Dry leaves rustle in the treetops, and stars twinkle in the black night sky.

After a while, I begin to pace back and forth. My feet are freezing cold, and if I stop, it feels like they will freeze solid. My aching feet bring me to the parking lot. Maybe I can wait in the limo until we go home? Hopefully the chauffeur is waiting until Tom and his troops decide they want to go back to Münster.

I'm in luck! I find the stretch limo and see that the light's on inside. Maybe the chauffeur will let me sit in the backseat for a little while. I wouldn't have to stay there the whole time—just long enough to warm up a bit.

I look through the window. He has taken off his hat and laid it on the passenger seat, revealing a shock of short blonde hair. He's balancing his open laptop on his knees and is focused on the screen, completely oblivious to my presence. I drum on the passenger-side window with my freshly manicured nails.

He winces and looks up. When he sees me, he immediately presses a button and the window rolls down. "Yes?" he asks. "What can I do for you, miss?"

I rub my cold upper arms and look at him pleadingly. Lisa was right. The dress is definitely too skimpy for September. "Excuse me, sir. Would it be too much to ask to sit in the car?"

He rolls up the window again, reaches for the door handle, and pushes open the front passenger door. "No problem," he says. "Come on in, miss."

I breathe a sigh of relief. Actually, what I really want is to sprawl out on the backseat, but it doesn't really matter. I drop gratefully into the passenger seat and close the door.

The chauffeur sees I'm barefoot and carrying my shoes in my hand. "Miss, if you're Cinderella, then you're a very prudent Cinderella," he says, grinning. "After all, you didn't lose your shoe."

I look at my shoes and smile. "True," I say, "but I wasn't running away. I made a very deliberate retreat."

"What, you didn't dance with your prince?" he asks.

I sputter indignantly. "Ha! As if there was anyone even remotely resembling a prince in there—only a great big bunch of toads."

The chauffeur apparently finds this very amusing, because he laughs loudly.

I examine his profile. He's very handsome when he laughs; he has beautiful teeth and nice laugh lines at the corners of his eyes. Without his cap, he looks young, and I realize he's not much older than I am.

My stomach rumbles audibly. "Excuse me, sir," I say, embarrassed. "I'm starving."

The chauffeur laughs again, but I don't laugh along. My empty stomach is making it very hard for me to be cheerful. "You don't happen to have anything in here, do you? Maybe some crackers or a piece of candy?" I ask.

"I'm sorry, miss," he says, shrugging. "I had a sandwich, but I already ate it a while ago."

"Some water maybe?" I know I sound like a cranky toddler, but in the face of starvation and dehydration, I waive all dignity.

The chauffeur furrows his brow. "Miss, are you saying they didn't give you anything to eat or drink in such a swanky place?"

I nod and admit that I'd assumed Tom was paying for the food and drink and left my wallet at home.

The chauffeur shakes his head in disbelief. "Well, isn't that something. Nice host! How dare he show off with a limo, then leave his guests high and dry."

I nod vigorously. I see it exactly the same way.

The chauffeur looks at the clock on the dashboard. He seems to be thinking. Then he says, "Let me make a suggestion. It's only ten thirty. I don't think they'll need my services before twelve thirty. If you promise not to say anything, we can drive into town and see if we can find a place to eat."

A glimmer of hope warms my heart. I smile broadly. "There's only one problem," I say.

"And that is?"

"I don't have a cent to my name."

He waves it off. "It's okay. I'll loan you the money, and we'll settle up in Münster. Buckle up, let's get going."

The heating system kicks in almost as soon as the car starts. It's toasty warm. I wiggle my toes appreciatively and lean back on the softly cushioned seat. I suddenly think to myself, *Actually, you could be a little less trusting.* The seemingly helpful driver could be a rapist, driving deep into the forest to attack me. But when I turn and examine the man, I realize my concerns are probably unfounded. He certainly looks like a nice guy.

I decide to make small talk to lighten up the atmosphere. "How long have you worked as a chauffeur?" I ask.

"Since tonight at seven thirty," he answers.

I hesitate a bit. "What? You're completely new to this job?"

He shakes his head. "No, not really. I drive occasionally, mostly on the weekends. I'm a student and earn a little money part-time."

I'm surprised. So, that's it! I thought I was supposed to play the role of fine lady from a genteel background, but it turns out that we're both just students. Maybe we've even passed each other on campus. Who knows?

"So, if you don't mind my asking, sir, what are you studying?"

He gives me a sideways glance. "I propose we stop being so formal, but only if that's okay with you . . . miss. If we had met in the cafeteria, we wouldn't talk to each other like that."

"Okay, that's a good idea," I reply. "Well, what are you studying?"

"I'm in my senior year of studying information technology. And you?"

"I'm studying English and history."

"So you want to be a teacher?"

"I hope so—if it works out. But information technology sounds very exciting, too. What will you do with it?"

He shrugs. "We'll see. First, I've got to complete my degree. It's a lot of fun."

"Was that what you were doing on your laptop?"

"Yes, I have an assignment due tomorrow."

"Oh boy, I'm keeping you from your work. That's not good," I say. I suddenly feel bad.

"True, but I don't have the opportunity to meet Cinderella every day. Sometimes a person needs to be flexible." He smiles.

We stop in front of an Italian restaurant. Little lanterns light up the window ledges. It looks like they're still open. The chauffeur turns off the motor and pulls the parking brake.

"By the way," he says, "my name is Jens."

"And I'm Lea."

"Well, let's go in, Lea, and see if we can find something to eat."

Jens gets out, and before I can find the door handle, he appears by my window and opens the passenger door.

"Thank you! Such great service."

"Force of habit," he replies.

As I move to get out of the car, I realize that I'm barefoot.

"Crap, I have to put these things back on."

"Oh nonsense!" says Jens. "I don't think anyone will notice you don't have any shoes on."

I place my feet on the pebble-covered ground. "Ouch, I'm getting a free foot massage here."

"Wait a minute," Jens says. "I need to change, then I'll help you to the door."

He slips out of his uniform jacket and throws it past me onto the driver's seat. Then he grabs a gray sweater out from under my seat and pulls it over his white shirt. He looks like a normal guy now. I realize he's quite burly and not very tall. Well, it's a good thing I'm not wearing my heels, or I would tower over him. He offers me his arm. I gratefully accept and cling to him with both hands as we walk into the restaurant. He feels strong and stable through the sweater.

The restaurant is busy, which I interpret as a good sign. The food must be good. The people here aren't dressed as glamorously as those at the casino, but it's a good-looking crowd. And it smells delicious—like tomatoes, pizza crust, and garlic. I'm dizzy with hunger.

The waiter leads us to a two-person table in the corner. Of course, Jens was right; no one notices that I don't have any shoes on. Still, it feels a bit odd to stroll inside a restaurant in stocking feet.

"Something to drink?" The waiter whips out his order pad and looks at me questioningly. I'm relieved he's taking our orders right away.

"Oh, yes," I say. "Please bring me a large pilsner!"

Jens looks at me and smiles. "That bad, huh?"

"Worse than bad," I reply.

He orders a cola for himself.

I'm so hungry I'd like to get everything on the menu, but I order the tortellini in a cream gorgonzola sauce. My mouth starts to water even as I'm ordering. Jens orders a pizza.

A few minutes later, the waiter places our drinks in front of us, and I don't hesitate before taking a long, deep gulp of my beer. Divine! I feel like a burning house that's finally been extinguished.

Jens watches me with an amused look on his face. "The only thing that's missing is steam rising out of your throat," he says.

I put down the glass and catch my breath. "You have no idea how thankful I am. You've saved my life. If I had to wait any longer for a drink, I guarantee you I would have died of dehydration. They could have taken me right to the morgue."

"I can't believe that a pretty girl like you couldn't get a drink at the casino," he says.

I can feel my face darken. "Men aren't content to see me drinking by myself. I would have to talk with them—and who knows what else."

Jens smiles. "Yeah, I already got the impression that you're very intent on keeping your honor and dignity intact."

I know immediately what he's alluding to, and my blush deepens. "Oh, so you think it's all right for a host to feel up his guests?"

Jens shakes his head. "No, of course not. I found your response to be very appropriate. Too bad for Tom, though. He forfeited his chance with the prettiest girl from the get-go. It was quite foolish of him."

I tilt my head to the side a bit and look at him. Is he flirting with me? And if so, what do I think of it? He definitely makes a nice impression, but unfortunately, he's not my type at all. He's too approachable and down-to-earth, like a huggable teddy bear. I like men who look dashing, with dark hair and mysterious eyes. I prefer men who are a little sad, as if they have some sort of deep, dark secret. My dream man also has to be tall and slender with broad shoulders. No, Jens doesn't fit the bill at all.

Our food comes just then, sparing me from having to respond to his comment. The tortellini are fantastic, and not only because I'm starving to death. They're still piping hot, so I have to be careful not to bolt down my food too quickly.

After my first bite, I put down my fork and take another sip of beer. "I'm so lucky," I say cheerfully. "This night's turned from being a total flop to being quite nice."

Jens looks deeply into my eyes—a little too deeply for my taste—and says, "I think so, too."

I avert my eyes and concentrate on my food.

"Weren't you wearing some glittery earrings on the way to the casino?" Jens asks.

Hmm, he noticed that. "Yeah, but they were just as brutal as my shoes. I had to take them off."

Jens looks at me. "Right. Your ears are still totally red." He reaches across the table and softly touches my earlobe.

I pull my head back quickly, although I can't say that his touch is unpleasant. His genuinely sympathetic words make me feel better.

"I know what the problem is," he says.

I almost choke on the tortellini. "Excuse me?" I can't help laughing.

Jens smiles. "Well, not personally, but I have three sisters. They occasionally wear clip-on earrings, too. They always have to adjust them."

"Oh," I say, "so how does that work?"

"Well," says Jens, "you just need a little know-how and a pocketknife."

I rummage through my purse. I find what I'm looking for—a small pocketknife with a nail file and tiny scissors. My aunt gave it to me for my birthday.

"Something like this?" I ask.

"Exactly."

I pull the earrings out of my bag and lay them on the table with the knife. Jens flips open the blade, then works the tip gently into the spring mechanism of one earring. As he works, he pulls in his chin and pushes out his lower lip. He looks quite focused and cute, like a child trying hard to paint a beautiful picture. I would like to have a brother who does things like this for me.

"Okay," says Jens. "Try it out."

I clip the earring onto my right ear. It sits perfectly, not too tight and not too loose. I shake my head a bit, but the earring holds.

"Awesome," I say. "You did a good job. Can you fix the other one, too?"

"Of course."

As Jens focuses again on his handiwork, I look around the room. It's nicely decorated: wine bottles are arranged on shelves with tasteful, flickering lanterns placed between them. Italian love songs play in the background. The guests are cheerful and chat contentedly in the way people do when they've just eaten a delicious meal. I'm so happy we ended up here. My food is soon gone, and I feel so warm, full, and content I don't envy the other girls at the casino one bit.

"Darn!"

My attention is abruptly drawn back to Jens. The earring lies next to its silver clasp in the palm of his hand.

"This has never happened to me before," Jens says contritely. "I broke the mechanism. Bummer! I didn't mean to do that."

He looks so sad I have to laugh. "Don't worry, Jens. These earrings aren't very valuable. Did you think they were real diamonds?"

"No, of course not! But that doesn't mean that they aren't worth something to you." He still looks very sorry.

"It doesn't matter," I say, then laugh. "I can wear just one. It still looks quite fashionable. Look." I shake my head so the earring sparkles as it sways back and forth.

Jens admires it, shaking his head at the same time. "I don't know what to make of you," he says.

What does he mean by that? I furrow my brow.

"If I'd ruined one of my sisters' earrings, they would have screamed bloody murder. At the very least, they would have strangled me. But you just laugh it off as if it doesn't bother you at all."

I shrug. "Why should I be upset? There are more important things in life."

"Yes," says Jens, "but it's not just about the earrings. I was watching you this evening."

"Right. Through the rearview mirror," I say with mock severity.

He smiles. "Yes, I admit it. I liked you right from the start. There is something about you—how do I describe it?" He thinks a moment, then says, "All seven of you in the group were intent on amusing yourselves. However, the other six seemed a bit forced. They weren't just eager to have fun. I couldn't help thinking they were aiming to reach some sort of crazy, over-the-top party goal."

I look at him skeptically. "And you were able to observe all that through the rearview mirror?"

"You'd be surprised at the things I can observe. People interest me. Anyway, you were quite different. From the very beginning, you seemed relaxed and calm, as if you were just having fun."

"I was!" I say. "I found the whole undertaking rather amusing. What a crazy concept—riding in a stretch limo to the casino with seven good-looking girls! I like stuff like that."

The waiter asks if we want another drink, and Jens looks at his wristwatch. "Man, time flies. But I think we have a little more time before we need to be back. Would you like anything else?"

I nod and order a glass of red wine; Jens orders another soda. After the waiter leaves, Jens asks, "What were we talking about?"

"I said that I enjoy this kind of adventure. What about it?"

"It's not just that you enjoy it," says Jens. "Just think about how the evening progressed. First, your host touches you."

"Feels me up," I correct him.

"Right. But instead of getting upset, you stay totally cool and confident. Then, after traveling over sixty miles from Münster to Hohensyburg just so the birthday boy can make his grand entrance as a big shot, surrounded by beautiful women, he leaves you and doesn't give a damn about your comfort. What kind of an idiot does that?"

"A big one," I say. "But I still don't know what you're trying to tell me."

The waiter brings our drinks. We raise our glasses and toast each other, then take a sip. The wine is good and warms me up from the top of my head to the tips of my toes, which had become a bit chilly again on the restaurant floor.

"You forgot to mention the foot and earlobe pain, if we're talking about the list of disasters," I say.

Jens sets down his glass and says, "At the risk of repeating myself, I've known a lot of women."

"Oh," I say with a smile, "that's pretty impressive."

Jens blushes slightly. "No, I didn't mean it like that. I meant I have three sisters and they're all very different. You might think they're not even related. Yet I know for a fact that, confronted with a similar situation, all three would freak out and go on the warpath. They would have been completely inconsolable for the rest of the evening. And who could blame them?"

He tilts his head to the side and looks at me very sweetly. "It's different with you. You look like you're enjoying yourself now—as much as the moment when you first stepped into the limousine. How do you do that?"

"It's not such an amazing feat," I say. "I'm sitting here in a supernice restaurant in pleasant company. I feel great. I'm not pretending—I'm genuinely enjoying myself."

But Jens looks at me as if I'm the eighth wonder of the world. "I don't really think you understand what I'm getting at. Let me put it another way. You seem to be completely relaxed, as if nothing at all could disturb you. I find that fascinating. What's your secret?"

Hmm. How do I respond to that? "Maybe it's because I think there's no point in reacting to bad situations by screaming bloody murder. What good would come of it? It would only make a bad situation worse."

"I'm impressed," Jens says. "Apparently, your serenity is authentic and not a pretense. It's true, you're right. If you'd come to the limo and knocked on the window, and I had seen a woman who was totally loaded, with a face that looked like a month of wet Sundays, then I wouldn't have let you in."

I burst out laughing. "Ha! You would have been capable of sending me away?"

"Hello! You forget I was busy working on my laptop. I didn't need some crazy bitch dumping her bad mood on me."

"But you didn't know what I'd do," I say.

"I did know, because I'd already been watching you. Anyway, you didn't seem angry; you just looked kind of helpless."

I grin. "Awesome. My tactic worked."

Jens says, almost a little longingly, "I'd like to know your secret."

"The secret behind my success," I quip. But I don't want to tell him my secret. I don't know him well enough. I'm not going to share that with someone I've only known for a few hours.

So, I change the subject. "From what I can tell, I think you would be better off studying psychology. You've obviously got a soft spot for it."

The distraction works. Jens begins to tell me about information technology, moving the conversation in a direction that is much more palatable to me. We chat about school and our professors, and we discover that we have a couple acquaintances in common.

It's getting late, and the crowd in the restaurant is thinning out. Jens looks at his wristwatch and winces. "Oh, now it's good and late." He beckons to the waiter and pays the bill.

"If you wait a moment when you drop me off, I can run inside for my wallet and pay you back," I say.

But Jens grabs the receipt off the table and rips it up on the spot. "No," he says, "let's just leave it at that. You're my guest. It was a really nice evening, and thank you for sharing it with me."

Embarrassed, I protest, "But that's not right. That wasn't our deal."

"It's okay," Jens says. He offers me the crook of his arm and asks, "May I escort Cinderella to her carriage?"

"With pleasure," I say. "Let's hope it hasn't turned into a pumpkin."

As we walk out of the restaurant into the cool autumn night, I think how strange life is. If someone had told me yesterday that I'd go out to an Italian restaurant with a chauffeur in a white stretch limo—and barefoot, too—I would have never believed them. How wonderful that life sometimes presents such funny twists and surprises. I chuckle lightly to myself.

Jens glances at me. "You see?" he says. "You're doing it again. You laugh because you have such a zest for life. I bet people are very envious of you."

We arrive at the car, and I look at him. "But there's no reason everyone can't be like me. You can't deny that."

Jens opens the passenger door for me. "I don't think most people have it in them. I don't know—maybe people have just forgotten how to live?"

I consider this. Yes, maybe that's right. I find his thoughts on the subject kind of touching. I don't think I know many young men who would concern themselves with such things. Without heels, I'm just about as tall as he is. I lean toward him and place a gentle kiss on his cheek. It's a bit prickly. It's probably been a while since he last shaved.

"Thank you for saving my life, and thank you for the lovely meal," I say. I sit down in the passenger seat and buckle up.

Jens just smiles. He hurries around to the other side of the car, opens the door, and strips off the gray sweater. It has a warm, pleasant, manly fragrance. He slips into his suit jacket, puts the cap back on his head, and gets behind the wheel.

"Home, James—and a shilling extra if you make it in ten minutes," I joke.

"Very funny," says Jens, but he doesn't sound the least bit perturbed.

On the ride back to the casino, we're both quiet. Maybe it's because we want to enjoy the calm before the storm. Soon the clucking hens and their proud rooster will take over the limousine again.

Just before we reach the casino, Jens pulls over to the curb. He turns to me and says, "I would like to see you again, Lea."

"Then it has to be within the next week, because it won't work after that," I say.

He frowns. "Why? Are you really Cinderella? Are you going back to doing chores for your wicked stepmother?"

I smile. "No. It's not that bad. I'm leaving town next weekend."

His face brightens. "That's no problem. We can get together after that."

I shake my head. "You'd have to be very patient."

"Why?" he asks.

"I'm going to England next weekend. I won't be back for a year."

Jens doesn't act like his sisters; he doesn't scream bloody murder, and he doesn't turn red, but he looks sad and disappointed.

"Crap!" he says. "I finally meet a really amazing girl, and then this! I'm cursed."

Silently, he puts the car in gear and drives the last few yards to the casino. He hasn't even turned off the engine when his cell phone rings. It's Tom, calling to let him know that he's ready to go.

"You're at least going to give me your number, right?" Jens asks.

"It doesn't make sense, I'll have a different number in England," I say. "I think we should leave it at this. Long-distance relationships aren't my thing. They're doomed from the outset. I think we should go our separate ways. It was a lovely evening, and I'll think of it often. Hopefully you will, too. Thank you for everything."

Even if Jens had responded, I wouldn't have been able to hear him, because just then the girls tear open the doors and tumble into the car. They reek of alcohol. Tom settles in between two of them, stretches out his legs, and begins to snore almost instantly. The girls find this insanely funny, giggling and shrieking. I stay in the front passenger seat. No one seems to notice. Nobody seems to miss me, either. *If I hadn't already been sitting here, they would have driven back to Münster without me*, I think, a bit peeved.

Jens turns on the navigation system and puts the car in drive. The girls settle down after a while, but Jens has to stop once, so that one girl can throw up. Then the limo smoothly continues on its way, purring gently. Occasionally the female voice of the navigation system gives a direction. Otherwise, it's warm and silent in the car.

At some point, the limo stops and I open my eyes. Confused, I realize that I fell asleep. My head is on Jens's shoulder.

"End of the line, Lea," he says gently. "You're home."

It takes me a second to come to my senses. Then I pick up my shoes and purse. I find my keys and get out of the car. Jens, still the perfect chauffeur, holds my door open for me.

"Is it the end of the line for us, too?" he asks quietly.

"I'm afraid so," I mumble. I touch his stubbly chin, then hurry to my front door. Less than ten minutes later, I lie down in bed and fall asleep instantly.

Chapter 2

The following week, I'm so busy with travel planning, packing, and running errands, I hardly think of Jens at all. My room is rented immediately by a female student from Portugal. I free up space in my closet by stuffing everything in large duffel bags and dragging them all up to the attic. When I come across my black high heels, I think of Hohensyburg. I was lucky such a disastrous evening had ended so well. Unfortunately, Jens wasn't as happy with the outcome. I know he fell for me, but I'm sure he'll forget all about me soon enough.

I search my heart a little. Was I interested in him at all? My answer is definitely no. I'm even a little glad that I have a bona fide excuse for not seeing him again. He's simply not my type, but he's such a nice guy that it would have really been tough for me to tell him that.

I look at my shoes, slightly perplexed. What should I do with these things? Should I take them to England? Then I remember that I'm going to a very small English village. There won't be any wild discos or lavish parties where I'd need them. I throw the shoes into a duffel bag and take it up to the attic with the rest of my belongings.

I'm heading to England for a year to work as an assistant teacher at a comprehensive school, the equivalent of a public high school.

Although I was very diligent about studying English and got very good grades, my actual language skills are not very impressive. My hope is that a year abroad will change that. Also, I had no say in choosing a school—your assignment is always a surprise. I was assigned to a school in Gatingstone, about an hour's drive northeast of London in Essex County. Although I've been assured that traveling to London is a no-brainer—many villagers commute to London daily—I figure a reputable teacher probably shouldn't be hanging out in trendy London clubs on a regular basis. No, I'll be better off hanging out with my books in the evenings. Anyway, over the course of the next year, I have to finish my entire required-reading list for the Cambridge exam.

I did Google Gatingstone, of course. The village has about thirty-five hundred residents, and I saw a few nice pictures of cute little houses and a red-brick mansion. I imagine the village is very old; it's said that Queen Elizabeth I once stayed there overnight. Judging by the description of Gatingstone, it seems they roll up the sidewalks way before midnight. Oh, and the student body is quite diverse. There's a large car factory nearby, and the factory's international staff from Germany, France, and Spain send their children to the school where I'll be teaching.

Instead of my torture-shoes, I pack several pairs of sensible flats as well as a few pairs of jeans. I'm not sure whether a teacher in England can wear jeans to work, but presumably I'll have some free time. I vacillate over what else to pack. Winter boots or not? I'm bringing my luggage on the train, so my suitcase can't be too heavy. Perhaps I can buy things I need when I'm there . . . But since assistant teachers are not well paid, it's probably best to bring anything I need.

So much to think about! What will the accommodations be like? The headmaster made arrangements for me. He wrote in an e-mail that I'll be staying in an older couple's house. However, because my landlords will be on vacation when I arrive, I'll stay with a student's family for the first two weeks. What if it turns out to be a nightmare?

What if I'm unhappy with where I'm staying? Oh, it'll be okay. My indomitable optimism chases away my concerns. I'm excited about my trip to England.

A few days later, I find myself on a ferry from Calais to Dover. I decided against traveling through the Chunnel. Although my friends assured me that it is the fastest and cheapest way to travel, the concept scares me. Whizzing deep into the bosom of Mother Earth in a tunnel underneath the English Channel? How scary is that? A person needs nerves of steel for that kind of thing. Alternatively, I could have booked a flight, but then I couldn't take all the luggage I need. Besides, I like the idea of taking such a monumental journey—a whole year in another country—in a more traditional way.

I store my bags in the overhead bins and stay out on the deck for the duration of the crossing. I'm too excited to sit still. The sea is calm, and the sun is shining. I lean on the railing and look over to the English mainland. Chatty travel companions and parents with small children, who are all running around and playing, surround me. The wind blows my hair and clothes. Now and then I turn my head so the wind can blow against my face. The White Cliffs of Dover appear in the distance. It's the first time that I've traveled by ferry to England, and I am amazed by how impressive the cliffs look. I had no idea they soar so high. Along the top of the cliffs, I can see tiny points moving up and down. Apparently, these are people looking down at us. I wonder if there's a railing up there. I hope so.

As the ferry comes into port, I quickly pick up my bags and get in line with the other passengers who are waiting to go ashore. The tranquility that I enjoyed on the deck ends quickly once I'm off the ferry. People are scurrying everywhere, and officials stand around, wanting something from everyone. I just want to get away, find my train to London, and move on. Almost an hour later, I'm finally able to catch my train. It's evening rush hour, and the train is full to bursting. Scraps of conversation in English swirl around me. I try to understand, but so many people are talking at once I can't make sense of anything.

Lugging my heavy bags, I move through the packed train and find an open seat. An obese man is standing in the middle of the aisle, blocking my way like a cork in the neck of a wine bottle. We're at a standstill. Two slim girls try to push past us. I squeeze myself into a compartment. Inside, the passengers give me dirty looks.

The fat man hisses at me, "How can you be so stupid and travel with such heavy luggage at this time of day? Completely thoughtless."

I bite my tongue so I won't say, *How can you be so thoughtless and bring your big, fat ass on the train during rush hour?* Of course, I resist the temptation. I don't want people to chalk me up as just another rude German. My accent would be a dead giveaway.

Our train stops at Victoria Station and bursts open like a piece of ripe fruit. My fellow passengers and I spill out onto the platform. I pull my suitcases clumsily behind me. I also have a shoulder bag with a strap that's constantly slipping off my shoulder. Every time it slips off, I have to stop, put down my suitcases, and fix the strap. Then I can go again. Why do English train stations smell so strange? They reek of tar and carbolic soap, a special cleaning agent probably prescribed by law for all public buildings—cheap and pungent.

The London Underground's concourses are never ending. I walk a long distance, tired and exhausted. Finally I find the train to Colchester and an unoccupied compartment, too. I'm half dead from exhaustion. I drop into the seat and look around. In contrast to the train from Dover to London, you can't move between compartments. Each compartment has two benches that face each other and a door on the right and left. I notice with concern that there's no way to go from compartment to compartment. It's locked, and you're trapped like a rat. What do you do if somebody boards and tries to rob you or even worse? This is even scarier than whizzing along in a train under the English Channel. But I don't want to think about it. I'm so tired. I close my eyes and lean my head back against the cushion. It's already dark. An elderly couple boards the train, muttering very quietly and peacefully. Their voices blend in with the steady rattle of the train's wheels.

After a while, I open my eyes. We've stopped. The pair gets off the train, and I'm all alone in the compartment. A glance at the clock and a station sign confirms that I've almost arrived at my destination in Brantwood, where my host will pick me up.

I check to make sure my luggage is within easy reach. I'm worried that I'll forget something in the rush to get off the train. The train begins to slow down again. I look out the window and see the sign saying Brantwood. I get up and stretch, then pull the strap of my shoulder bag on. The train stops, its brakes squealing loudly. I reach for the door handle—and find nothing. There is no door handle.

It's like a nightmare. I know the train will move on again soon, and I have no idea how to get out of the compartment! I bang on the window. Someone standing on the station platform gestures that I should open the window, which I do with lightning speed. At least that works.

The man reaches through the small open window. He finds a tiny lever—I swear it's really tiny—and pushes it to one side. The door swings open, and I'm free. Trembling, I reach for my suitcases, but he picks them up with his strong hands and swings them on down to the platform. He stands in front of me. He is big and broad shouldered with dark hair.

"Thank you," I say, my voice quivering.

He raises a hand to his forehead and salutes. There is something like amusement in his dark eyes. *You must be stupid not to be able to open a compartment door*, his look seems to say. Then he turns around and disappears into the darkness.

I stand on the platform. I'm all alone. The station is deserted, and there is no one to ask for help. Where are my hosts? What do I do if no one arrives to pick me up? I drag my suitcases in front of the small railway station and sit on one of them. There's a red telephone box. I wonder whether I should try to call the Seafields, my provisional hosts.

While I'm rummaging through my purse for their phone number, a large Volvo stops in front of the station. Its doors burst open. A tall, slender woman with short red hair and a teenage girl with long hair and dark eyebrows rush toward me.

"You're Lea?" the woman asks breathlessly.

"Yes," I say.

"Oh, I hope you're not too upset that we're late! I had to pick up my daughter, Linda, from sports practice." She nods in the direction of the girl, then holds out her hand. "I'm Melissa Seafield."

I shake her hand and say, "Nice to meet you, Mrs. Seafield."

She has a warm, sparkly laugh. "For God's sake, please don't call me that! Call me Melissa. Get in. We're going to Powlands Farm. I'm sure you're completely exhausted and hungry, you poor thing!"

We stow my bags in the trunk and drive off. About half an hour later, we stop in front of a Low Country house. The windows are lit, and it looks warm and inviting. The front door opens, and a small dog with delicate limbs dashes out and dances around us, barking happily. Melissa and Linda roll my suitcases into the house, and inside I see sturdy furniture, dark oak floors, fine Persian rugs, and antique-looking oil paintings. Before I know it, I'm nestled on an extremely soft sofa, spooning warm soup into my mouth between bites of crispy toast. Melissa and Linda each sit in a chair and admire me, as though they've never met someone from another country.

"Do you like it?" Melissa asks.

I nod. The green soup tastes delicious, even though I have no idea what's in it.

"Is this pea soup?" I guess.

Melissa laughs her sparkly laugh. "No, it's not pea soup. It's watercress!"

Watercress. Aha. Which tree does that grow on? I decide not to ask, not wanting to appear foolish.

A man enters the living room. He has the same dark eyebrows as Linda.

"This is Morris, my husband," Melissa says. "Morris, this is Lea, our guest from Germany."

Morris shakes my hand. "How was your trip?" he asks.

I say truthfully, "Extremely exhausting. The worst part was that I almost missed my stop." I tell them about my futile search for the door handle and how a stranger helped me at the last minute.

"Oh, how terrible," Melissa says sympathetically. "It's true—the door handles are actually very hard to find. Don't you think, Morris?"

Morris mumbles something unintelligible. He's bent over the fireplace, stoking the cozy fire. I feel pleasantly warm. Though I try hard not to be rude, I can't keep my eyes open.

"You should go to bed," Melissa says resolutely, noticing my exhaustion. "Come on. Let me show you the guest room."

I get up and shuffle up the creaky wooden stairs behind her. She opens the door to the guest room. It's decorated with tasteful green-ivy wallpaper, and there's a large four-poster bed. Melissa shows me the bathroom, then goes back downstairs. Within ten minutes, I am fast asleep.

The next morning, the sunlight shining through the white tulle curtains wakes me up. I stretch and get out of bed. I want to look out the window and see where I am in the daylight. What's out there, anyway? I take a step—and almost fall on my face.

I realize that the floor in my room is sharply slanted toward the window. If I were to put a ball on the wooden planks, it would definitely roll down. Carefully, I step forward, push aside the curtains, and look out. I see a pristine landscape: stubbly yellow fields scattered among groups of small dark trees and in the distance a picturesque windmill, its blades turning gently in the wind. I sigh. It's so beautiful!

I get dressed quickly and hurry downstairs. It's Sunday, and I wonder whether my hosts are already up. Indeed. In the country kitchen, Melissa's cooking on a huge cast-iron stove. Morris is at the breakfast table, rustling through his newspaper.

"Good morning," Melissa says. "Do you like goat yogurt?"

Do I like goat yogurt? Hmm. Good question. I've never had it.

Two minutes later, I'm sitting at the breakfast table, eating goat yogurt. It's the best yogurt I've ever tasted. It's light, creamy, and smooth—and tastes a little like it has a hint of amaretto in it.

I tell this to Melissa, who laughs and says, "That's because the yogurt is so fresh. I only made it yesterday."

I suppose that this amazing woman, with her infectious laugh and quiet husband, keeps a goat, which she cares for and milks. This is astounding to me. The house is so elegant and dignified a goat doesn't fit into the picture. What other surprises await me here?

For starters, there is the family's younger son, Edwin. He's ten years old and attends a so-called prep school—a preparatory school for one of the most expensive and prestigious private boarding schools in the country. His seventeen-year-old brother, Andrew, already attends that boarding school and will graduate soon. Linda, on the other hand, attends the comprehensive school, where I'm going to start teaching tomorrow. I ask Linda why she doesn't also go to the boarding school. Melissa replies, with some embarrassment, that because boarding schools are insanely expensive, it's not unusual to send only the family's male offspring. The girls go to a regular school because it's more affordable. I think to myself, *That's understandable, but by no means fair*. But I say nothing.

After breakfast, Edwin is thrilled to have someone he can show off the entire farm and its surrounding environment to. He takes me to a neighboring farm, where there are two Shire horses in a paddock. I've never seen such massive horses. The head of a Shire horse is as big as a medium-sized sheep. Its hooves are the diameter of a pie plate! I stay well away from the fence, but Edwin is fearless. He grabs the animals by their manes, pats their ears, and strokes their noses.

Then we go back to the farm. The old stuccoed farmhouse is painted pink and looks slightly askew, set amid flowering perennials. Although I'm not used to seeing a pink house—in fact, I've never seen a pink house before—it just looks like it should be pink. Any other color just wouldn't fit. I follow Edwin to the garden, where he shoos the geese aside as they honk excitedly. He leads me to the slightly overgrown rear part of the property. The goat is tied up here, determined to nibble all the grass within reach. As we approach, she raises her head and eyes us peacefully as she chews. Then she dedicates herself to eating again.

Edwin grabs a shovel and starts to dig into a mound of earth. What is this boy doing?

Panting with effort, he says, "This mound is the farm's old garbage dump."

And why do we want to mess around with this? I wonder.

"It's over four hundred years old!" he continues, undeterred. "You mustn't think of it as just a garbage dump. People used to throw everything into holes in their gardens. For centuries this is where they tossed things they could no longer use."

His shovel clatters against something, and he bends down to pick it up. He turns it in his hand and holds it against the light. It's green.

"Look," he says, "an old glass bottle! Maybe they kept oil or some kind of medicine in it."

He hands it to me. The bottle looks quaint and very old. The glass is solid and thick, and feels heavy in my hand. It was probably handblown.

Edwin throws down the shovel. "You can keep it. It's a museum piece. Let's go inside, and I'll show you everything I've found."

At the house, we bend over a small chest. He has more glass bottles, empty cream containers with barely legible print, porcelain shards, and even a dog tag.

"They probably buried the whole dog there," Edwin says.

A chill runs down my spine. "As long as it was just a dog," I joke. "Who knows who or what else they may have buried there?"

Sunday flies by in no time.

In the evening, Linda and Edwin jump on bikes and offer me one. We cycle far into the countryside. We cycle past low wood-frame houses and houses that are colorfully stuccoed like the farmhouse. A farmer is burning stubble in his field. We stop and watch the dancing flames eat up the ground. The air is filled with the spicy scent of autumn and burning vegetation. I love this area. Only after it's become dark and cool do we cycle back to Powlands Farm. The geese greet us with their excited chatter.

After dinner, we sit down together in front of the TV. On one show, Germans in spiked helmets strut about, clicking their heels together and holding out their arms, yelling, "*Achtung*!" They all have pointed Kaiser Wilhelm beards. Culturally and historically, none of it's really accurate, but it's amusing.

My hosts look a little embarrassed. "I hope you don't mind," Edwin says.

I smile. "No, not at all. It's funny to see how you view us Germans." They smile with relief. Morris says, "We know you're not like that." "Well, I should hope not!" I exclaim.

Morris continues, "But it is kind of fun to imagine you are."

Hmm, I think, *probably because the English are proud to have won both wars.* I suppose it's a relatively harmless pleasure for Morris to make fun of his European neighbors. I wonder whether my new students expect me to wear a spiked helmet tomorrow.

The next morning Linda and I walk side by side along the road to school. I'm wearing gray wool pants and a green cardigan over a white blouse. Linda confirmed that I'll definitely pass for a teacher. She's wearing the school uniform: a dark-blue skirt, a yellow blouse, and a dark-blue V-neck sweater.

"What do you do if you don't like yellow?" I ask Linda.

Linda shakes her head darkly. "You can't do anything. These colors are mandatory. The yellow makes me want to puke. The boys are lucky. They have light-blue shirts and look a thousand times better. I'm looking forward to the sixth form. Then we can wear whatever we want." The sixth form in England is like senior year.

About twenty minutes after we left the farm, we reach the village, walking past small shops and homes. Linda leads me onto a side street. Lots of cars are pulling up, driven by parents dropping off their children; many are laughing and chatting. I catch sight of a modern building with a flat roof behind a fence: Gatingstone School. My heart beats faster. I feel like a kid on the first day of school, or on a visit to the dentist.

"I'll take you to the teachers' lounge," Linda says. "Then I have to go to class. Do you want to meet this afternoon and walk back together?"

I only nod because I'm too nervous to speak.

Linda leaves me in front of the teachers' lounge, my heart beating wildly. What's next? Who do I need to talk to? Apparently, I'm standing in the way, because the next thing I know, someone bumps into me.

"Whoops," says a voice. "Sorry! Are you new? Do you know where your classroom is?"

I turn around. A man is standing in front of me, and I swear I've seen him before. But how can that be? Who would I know in Gatingstone?

His dark eyes examine me from top to bottom. "Maybe you're looking for the door handle?" he asks.

Now it sinks in, and I laugh freely. "No," I reply, "not at the moment."

He frowns. "So, you're looking for your classroom. What grade are you in?"

Again, I laugh. "There appears to be a misunderstanding. I'm not a pupil; I'm a teacher."

The man looks at me, dumbfounded. "And you expect me to believe that?"

I admit I do look pretty young, and, strictly speaking, it hasn't been that long since I was a student myself. The drawback to my youthful looks is that it's hard for anybody to take me seriously. I start to explain this, but luckily my salvation comes in the form of an older gentleman rushing toward me. He looks quite elegant, with his graying temples and light-colored suit.

"You must be Ms. König!" the older gentleman says. "I've been looking for you! Welcome to our school. Did you have a nice trip? How are your accommodations? Come along, I'll show you to the language department's teachers' lounge. Your colleagues are looking forward to meeting you!"

He takes me by the elbow and leads me away. I look over my shoulder—I really would like to know the name of the man who helped me at the train station and what he's doing here, but he has disappeared.

As it turns out, the older gentleman is Mr. Henley, the head of the modern languages department. He brings me to a small teachers' lounge, where I meet the other language teachers. They shake my hand or nod at me pleasantly.

I'm paired with a German-language teacher, who will show me the ropes. I follow her into a classroom, where there are thirty children dressed in blue, light blue, and yellow. They are trying their best to master the German language. I'm hopeful that I'll eventually be able to take over the entire one-hour lesson myself.

After the class ends, we return to the teachers' lounge, where we find Mr. Henley waiting for me. Next to him is a young woman with very rosy cheeks and smooth, black bobbed hair.

"This is Catherine." Mr. Henley introduces us. "She hails from Brittany and is the assistant teacher for French."

Catherine and I look at one another, and we hit it off instantly. She's shy, but her smile is warm and friendly. I think we both feel a little overwhelmed by everything. Neither of us knows exactly what's expected of us, and whether we'll succeed in our work or be happy doing it. Mr. Henley is responsible for looking after us, so he seems to notice the instant camaraderie between Catherine and me with relief.

"Take a little time to get to know each other," he says, then rushes off to his next class.

Catherine and I sit down at a table, and before we know it, we're deep in conversation. She tells me about her home in a small fishing village and her two sisters, who miss her. She's staying with a police officer and his family in town. I tell her about the Seafields and their children. I'm charmed by Catherine's lovely, distinctive French accent. When she speaks English, she often omits an *h* sound when she needs one or puts one where it doesn't belong.

Catherine looks at the wall clock. "I need to be in a class in 'alf an hour." She makes "hour" sound like it begins with "how." I wonder if I also have such a strong accent. Well, that's the reason why we're here in England—to improve our language skills.

We make plans to eat lunch together in the school cafeteria and meet up at exactly one o'clock, after we're done sitting in on our respective classes. With ninety students gathered all at once in the large cafeteria, the noise is deafening. The students are noisy, almost hyper, shouting across the tables at each other. Once Catherine and I finally pick up our food at the counter and find a free table, we try to talk about our classes, but we can barely hear each other. We end up yelling as if we're sitting in a nightclub with music blaring.

The food is nothing special, and I watch the students, especially the boys, ignore the main dish, which is actually the most nutritious part of the meal, and eat a bowl full of French fries instead. I wonder if their parents know they're eating junk food, and if so, do they care? I try to ask Catherine's opinion, but she can't hear me over the din. She shrugs.

When we're finished eating, we flee from the noise into the hallway.

Catherine asks, "See you tonight?"

"Sure, but where?" I answer.

Catherine smiles at me broadly. "In Brantwood!"

"Excuse me?"

"The course for the Cambridge Certificate of Proficiency in English."

Now it's coming back to me. The course was mentioned during my registration for my year as an assistant. It provides proof of English proficiency and is an important certification when applying for a job. I'd enrolled in the course but simply forgot about it with all the excitement of travel.

"Oh, yes, of course," I say. "What time is the course, and where is it exactly?" I'm embarrassed to admit I don't have the information.

"It's at the adult-education school in Brantwood," says Catherine. "You know what? Let's take the bus together—it'll be fun."

"Great," I say. "I look forward to it. I'll meet you at the bus stop."

"Between you and me," Catherine adds, "I find it pretty boring to spend evenings in front of the TV with my hosts. I look forward to getting to know the other language assistants in this corner of England."

"I agree," I say. I think to myself that the Seafields aren't that boring; I would be perfectly happy watching another film with strange Germans wearing pointed helmets.

At the end of the school day, Mr. Henley presents me with my schedule. It seems reasonable enough. I'll have to attend about twelve lessons per week, or two to three hours per day. Students, in comparison, work their fingers to the bone. When Linda and I meet after school to walk home together, she's tired and relatively reticent, which I can understand. The comprehensive school goes all day and can be long and exhausting.

We walk along the street, past shops and houses. When we finally reach the open meadow, a question occurs to me. I ask Linda, "There's a teacher at school who I've seen before, when I arrived at Brantwood."

Linda frowns. "Brantwood? Who are you talking about?"

I describe him to her—tall, broad shouldered, dark eyes, quite handsome.

Linda stops and ponders. "Hmm. Was he older? If so, then perhaps it's Mr. Jones. He's the physics teacher. But he's fat, not broad shouldered."

I insist. "No, this guy is athletically built and pretty young. I'd guess he's about twenty-eight."

"Ah," Linda says, as if a lightbulb suddenly turned on. "I know who you mean. How stupid of me not to think of him right away! You mean Ethan Derby. He's the worst around here. He teaches physical education and history, and all the girls are crazy about him. They say that a brokenhearted student almost committed suicide over him two years ago." Linda blushes, as though she's not entirely immune to the charms of Ethan Derby herself.

"Yes, the description fits," I say. I think about his dark eyes, which gazed at me in amusement at the station, then gave me the once-over this morning in front of the teachers' lounge.

"Don't fall for him," Linda adds, sounding like my father. "He's a total womanizer. He only wants your body, not your heart."

I break into a fit of laughter upon hearing her melodramatic warning. "Thanks for the warning! How do you come up with such priceless words of wisdom?"

But Linda's expression remains serious. "Listen to me, Lea. Don't tempt fate and lose your heart and your independence here in Gatingstone."

Again, it sounds so melodramatic that I laugh uproariously. "Okay, whatever," I say. "Do you read dime-store novels in your spare time, Linda?"

"Go ahead and laugh," Linda says. "You'll see soon enough that I'm right."

By the time we finish dinner, it's pitch-black outside and raining in torrents. While the Seafields make themselves comfortable in front of the TV, I go up to the guest room and pull my pocket umbrella out of my suitcase. I'd been warned that I wouldn't be able to go a week without an umbrella here in east England. How right they were!

I hang a purse with my pen, paper, and wallet over my shoulder and pull on my anorak.

"Bye!" I shout through the TV-room door. It looks so cozy in there. Morris has again made a nice fire in the fireplace, and Melissa's tasteful lamps and comfortable furniture look even more inviting than they did yesterday after my exhausting trip.

"Have fun!" Melissa shouts back.

As if, I think. I push through the front door into the darkness. The bus stop is only about five minutes away, but by the time I get there, the driving rain has already soaked my pants. I think about just going back home, but I can't let Catherine down. What will she think if I don't show up? And I really want to get this Cambridge certificate thing. I can't possibly miss the first class.

Luckily, it's not long before the bus approaches. I immediately jump on the first step. I want to shake out my rain-soaked umbrella, but the automatic door closes with a hiss of compressed air. The only problem is, I'm in and the umbrella is out. In a bit of a panic, I lose my grip and the umbrella slips out of my hands. The wind catches it, and it's gone! I jump over to a window and can see my umbrella dancing away from the bus in the wind. The whole situation is so funny that I'm overcome with violent giggling. I stand there, clinging to a pole, bent over with laughter.

After a while, I search for a handkerchief in my jacket and wipe away my tears of laughter. I see Catherine sitting in the back of the bus. I try to keep my balance as I walk toward her; the other passengers follow me with amused glances. Only after I slide into the seat next to my new friend do I feel a pair of dark eyes fixed on me. The womanizer, Mr. Derby, is sitting several rows in front of us. He turned around to watch me, but when our eyes meet, he turns to the front again without even acknowledging me.

That kind of rankles me. It's the third time we've seen each other, and we've even exchanged a few words. He could at least have the courtesy to smile at me. Whatever. I guess it's not that important. I turn to Catherine, who is sitting next to a girl with a tangle of long hair and very eye-catching earrings.

"Hi, Lea," she says with a Spanish accent. "Catherine was just telling me about you. My name is Inez; I'm from Barcelona. I'm an assistant teacher at Chelmsford." Chelmsford is another school in the area.

During the twenty-minute bus ride to Brantwood, the three of us share pretty much our entire life stories. By the time we get off in front of the adult-education school—what we call "evening college"—we're thick as thieves and looking forward to the evening. Only later, as we are trying to concentrate on the exercise sheet our teacher passed out, does it occur to me that I didn't notice whether Mr. Derby, the womanizer, got off the bus, too. I figure he must live in Brantwood, since he was on that bus.

After the lesson, Inez suggests we go to a pub. Catherine and I check our watches; the evening buses run once per hour, so we still have some time. We end up in a quaint restaurant on a nearby street. As with any pub in the British Isles, the place is packed by eight o'clock. Luckily, there's still a table in a back corner that we can squeeze into. Inez offers to get the first round. The ale warms me up, and we chat animatedly with each other. The second round is on me. I work my way through the guests, and, in passing, I see a particularly cheerful group of very young adolescents sitting at a table. I can't help thinking they should be home and even in bed by now. They undoubtedly have school tomorrow.

At the bar, I order two ales and a crème de menthe—Catherine is crazy about this drink for some reason.

The bartender looks at me darkly. "This is alcohol," he says.

I nod in agreement. *Yes*, I think to myself, *it is*.

"I'm not going to serve you," the stern bartender says. "And I don't believe your friends can drink, either." He points to the table with the teenagers. "I don't think any of you are older than fourteen!"

It takes me a second to understand what he means. "I don't belong to that group! My friends are sitting over there." I point at Catherine and Inez. "And I'm much older than fourteen—I'm actually twenty-three."

The bartender knits his brow and scrutinizes me skeptically. "You can't seriously expect me to believe that, can you? Can I see your ID?"

I cooperatively pull out my card, then hold it out over the counter. The bartender looks as though he's got egg on his face.

A colleague polishing glasses next to him grins broadly. "See! I told you!"

Funny, I think. Apparently, the men had made a bet as to whether I am an adult or not.

The bartender sheepishly hands me back my ID. "I'm sorry," he says in a friendlier tone. "I see you're from Germany. You have to understand; we have very strict laws here. If I get caught selling alcohol to minors, I'm as good as behind bars."

I smile at him warmly. "It's okay," I say. "I think it's good that you're so diligent." I take the tray with our drinks and return to my girlfriends.

They find the story insanely funny, and I laugh a little, too. Secretly, however, I find it annoying that I look so much younger than I actually am. The fact that people think I'm a student rather than a teacher is darned inconvenient.

"It's no big deal," Inez says. "When you're older, you'll be glad that you look younger than your age."

"Perhaps," I say, "but it's a pain to be over twenty and have people treat you as though you're some teenybopper who doesn't know what she wants."

"Hmm," Catherine says thoughtfully. "Do you really think there's such a big difference? Twenty-year-olds aren't all that wise and mature. Sometimes I feel very much like a teenager myself."

I look at her resolutely. "I don't. I really feel like we're adults now. I don't like when people treat me condescendingly."

"I admire that you feel that way," Catherine says. "But at our age, we don't really have that much experience. It's only through experience that a person can become wise. I mean, when I look at myself critically, I realize I have a lot to learn."

"I feel the same way," Inez says. "That's the main reason why I'm happy for the opportunity to live abroad."

I stay silent. If I tell them what I experienced that made me grow up so quickly, they either wouldn't believe me, or they would ask too many questions. And that is something I'm not ready to share yet. Also, I don't announce what I really think because I don't want my new girlfriends to think I'm arrogant. But I know I'm an adult, I know what I want, and I know I'm confident and self-assured.

Inez sets down her glass of beer and tilts her head to the side, gazing at me questioningly. "What do you wish to achieve here, Lea, if it isn't to grow up and become wiser?"

I don't even need to think about it; I respond immediately. "I'm incredibly curious about life. I love being in a new country—meeting new people and experiencing different cultures. It's tremendously fascinating to me. Sometimes I want to seize life greedily as though it's a prized possession, the same way other people collect rare coins or stamps."

My friends gaze at me with fascination. What is it? Is my hair messed up? Do I suddenly have a pimple on my nose? I can see my reflection in a long mirror hanging on the opposite wall. My cheeks are bright red, and my eyes are lit up. My face is aglow with passion. Embarrassed, I take a drink from my large glass of beer so I can hide my face.

Catherine says gently, "There is something about you, Lea, that I just can't describe. I noticed it immediately when we met for the first time earlier today. You have an inner glow. Sounds stupid, I know, but that's how it seems."

Inez nods. "I think the same thing. It seems like you're happier than most people. Are you in love?"

I put down my glass and laugh. "In love? No way. I would be the first to know, believe me." But I think, *It's true. I am in love. But not with a man—with life.*

To steer the subject away from me, I ask, "And what about you? Are either of you in love? Do you have boyfriends back home?"

The diversion works. Inez tells us about an ill-fated love, which made it easier for her to leave Spain. Catherine has a boyfriend in France, who she sadly hasn't seen during the year she's been studying abroad.

She takes out her phone and shows us a photo of him. "Actually, I think it's good that we're spending time apart. I'm pretty sure that we'll end up getting married and staying together for the rest of our lives. I want to experience life on my own before that, though. I think it will make him respect me more."

"Do you doubt that he does?" I ask. "He looks like he's the same age as you."

"We are the same age. We went to the same school."

I shake my head. "Then why do you think he doesn't respect you enough?"

"Well, because I'm just a woman. But that's the way of the world, isn't it? Men always think that they're stronger, more reasonable, and wiser than women. My boyfriend always treats me as if he has to protect me from the world." Catherine's face darkens slightly. "As if I'm too helpless to survive without him."

I look at Catherine. I know I look younger than I am—the bartender reminded me of that earlier—but Catherine really looks like a little girl, although she's only about two years younger than I am. She's petite with a peaches-and-cream complexion, big black eyes, and ridiculously long lashes. She naturally triggers a protective instinct in me. Sitting next to her, I feel much bigger, stronger, and older.

Inez says bluntly, "Well, I wouldn't worry about his finding a new girlfriend while you're gone. You're way prettier than any other girl on the planet."

Catherine turns red at the compliment. It's nice when someone so beautiful is so modest. It's as though she doesn't realize that what Inez so graciously asserted is true.

"In any case, he didn't want me to go to England," Catherine says. "He was convinced that I would be helpless and fail miserably, and I want to show him that's not going to happen." She seems stubbornly resolute.

"I understand why you would feel that way," I say. "I couldn't stand being with someone who looked down on me and treated me like a child. Did you read that novel about the girl who falls in love with a rich, handsome man? He convinces her to prove her love to him by engaging in strange sexual practices. I found the author's portrayal of women really disturbing."

"I know exactly what book you mean," Catherine says. "I was really disturbed that she let him push her around like that, like she's a complete airhead. I definitely don't want somebody like that in my life."

Inez shrugs. "It's nice to have a strong shoulder to lean on every once in a while. It was exactly the opposite with my ex-boyfriend in Spain. He was hopeless. I felt like his mother. He wanted me to take care of him and everything that concerned him, but if I had a problem, he didn't lift a finger to help me. It was the main reason I broke up with him."

She seems angry and sad, but I giggle involuntarily. "Don't take it to heart, Inez," I say apologetically. "Men are complicated! That's why I want to be single for a while. No one has yet to discover the perfect man."

Inez sighs, then says bitterly, "But that doesn't prevent us from falling in love with losers. I suppose it comes with the territory."

Catherine says dreamily, "My Christian's not a loser; I just need to prove to him that I'm not."

Inez gives her a cynical look. "Well, then, good luck!"

I say softly, "I'm sure you'll succeed, Catherine. You're going about it the right way."

A few minutes later, we get up, put on our jackets, and stroll out into the night toward the bus stop.

Chapter 3

My first week in Gatingstone flies by like an arrow. I get used to the routine of school quickly, and find that working with the students is a lot of fun. I have it easy. I'm the first German many of them have ever met, so I'm a novelty to them. Even though my clothes are not significantly different from theirs, they think of me as an exotic being from another planet. The language teachers are grateful when I initiate discussions about German culture with the upperclassmen. The students sit openmouthed and listen in amazement. It's a strange feeling to be admired for the ability to speak my own language, something that comes so naturally to me. Of course, the students' English is so excellent, even the most diligent German student studying English could never compete.

I'm touched by the younger students' intensity and seriousness as they struggle with the German language. It's becoming clear to me just how difficult it is to learn German. For example, they are eternally mystified why nouns in German are masculine, feminine, or neuter.

"Why," they ask me again and again, "is the German word for table, *Tisch*, masculine, but another word for table, *Tafel*, is feminine?

Why is the word for window, *Fenster*, neither feminine nor masculine but neuter?"

Yes, why? Good question, I think.

I feel sorry for them. These poor kids have to study laboriously and memorize what I learned so easily since I was weaned. I have to fight the urge to laugh when a student misuses a German article—it sounds so funny! For example, they say *der Huhn* instead of *das Huhn*, for "the chicken," or *das Bauer* instead of *der Bauer* for "the farmer." I bite my lip and correct them quickly. If I were in their shoes, I wouldn't appreciate it if the teacher giggled hysterically every time I made a mistake.

That said, they laugh when something sounds like a naughty English word. In an advanced class, I asked the students to summarize the facts (*Fakten*) they read about in a chapter of their book. The German word *Fakten* apparently sounds like "fucked him" in English! The class couldn't stop laughing the whole hour. The next time I spoke about facts, I used a less obscene-sounding German phrase.

In the simpler family narratives used for the lowerclassmen, the word for father, *Vater*, occurs frequently. *Vater* sounds similar to the English word "farter," so there, too, the lessons often go off the rails. Unfortunately, there's no substitute for *Vater* in German, so I have no choice but to be strict and call the class to order.

I'd already gotten used to this as a student back in Germany. I knew what to expect when I had to use the important and irreplaceable English word "fiction," which to Germans sounds like the word *ficken*, meaning "to fuck." In this regard, I'm probably like many young teachers around the world. I can easily empathize with my students. Under any other circumstances, I would be only too willing to laugh along. But here it would demean my authority. Sometimes I have to turn toward the window and hope that no one sees me struggling to suppress my laughter.

When I tell the Seafields these stories, they find them hilarious. Edwin has taken a brotherly responsibility for me and is often very insistent on explaining which gestures or expressions are absolute no-no's in English culture. For example, you can indicate the number two with the index finger and middle finger, but only with your palm facing out. If you do it showing the back of your hand, it's insanely indecent.

In the afternoons, Edwin, Linda, and I often go on bicycle trips in the surrounding area. Essex County is gorgeous. It reminds me of Jutland, the northernmost part of the Danish peninsula, with its similarly sweeping panoramic views of the rolling countryside and the occasional small stands of trees. As a child, my family often visited Denmark during the summer holidays.

English country roads are narrow, long, and winding. They wind and curve endlessly, hugging the contours of the houses and farms that they connect. The roads are carved deep into the hills and valleys after centuries of use. They were never straightened out as they were in the German state of North Rhine-Westphalia, which was ruled by Napoleon's brother, Jérôme.

An English teacher once explained to my class why people drive on the left side of the road in England. Supposedly, the lanes at the time were very narrow, and knights and other horsemen could barely pass each other. Since they never knew who they'd meet on the road in those days, they kept to the left so they could easily reach for their lances or swords with their right hands, ready to fend off the enemy. I wonder if the theory is true. Traveling on the narrow roads, I figure it makes sense, even if cycling on the left takes some getting used to.

One afternoon, we go a bit farther than before and come to a small white church standing all alone on a hill. We lean the bikes on the cemetery wall and look at the old gravestones, many of which have fallen askew with barely legible ancient inscriptions.

"What kind of strange church is this?" I ask Edwin. "Where is the village?"

Edwin told me that there had been an entire village here in the Middle Ages. Most of the residents died in the plague, and eventually other people scavenged building materials from the abandoned houses. But they respected the church and the cemetery too much to tear them down, so that's why they are still intact centuries later.

On other days, Catherine and I meet up to go shopping in the village. Sometimes we buy things; other times we just window-shop. Most days we meet for lunch in the cafeteria or in the teachers' lounge.

"You know, it's a pity we have almost no contact with the other teachers because of the separate teachers' lounges," Catherine says one morning.

Anne, a small, wiry Scottish teacher with freckles, overhears her remark. "That's true, Catherine," she says. "I hadn't even thought about it, but it would be nice if colleagues from other departments socialized more. Would you two like to visit my flat in Brantwood sometime? I could invite some of our younger colleagues."

Catherine and I nod at the same time. So far, we've only seen our hosts' homes. We're curious to see how young teachers here live.

"May I make a suggestion?" asks Catherine.

"Of course," says Anne.

"I'd love to make crêpes for you and the other teachers. They're a Breton specialty."

Anne smiles. "Oh, that would be wonderful. I love crêpes! Are you sure it won't be too much work? I'm thinking I'll invite about eight people."

"Lea will help me," says Catherine. "Won't you, Lea?"

"Of course," I say. "I'd be delighted to help."

"Good," replies Anne. "I'll check to see if Saturday night works for everybody."

• • •

On Saturday morning Catherine and I go to Tesco, the supermarket in Gatingstone, and buy ingredients for the crêpes. We can hardly wait for the party.

Of course, it happens again, but this time to both of us. When the cashier sees the bottle of cognac on the conveyor, she pauses and eyes us critically. "Are you girls eighteen?"

"Of course I'm eighteen," I say, and hastily add, "Actually, I'm twenty-three."

Now the cashier looks even more doubtful. "Then show me your ID, please."

A bit unnerved, I pull the card out. The cashier looks at it without comment, then gives it back to me and taps the price for the cognac on the cash register.

Afterward on the sidewalk, Catherine and I stare at each other incredulously.

"'Actually, I'm twenty-three,'" Catherine says, mimicking me. "That doesn't sound suspicious at all!" She almost falls down, she's laughing so hard.

I force a smile. I'm starting to feel like Oskar in Günter Grass's *The Tin Drum*, who still looks like a child or a dwarf as an adult.

"Luckily, you're with me," I say pointedly. "I look a couple years older than you."

Catherine is so amiable that this comment only leads to more laughter.

In the evening, we meet on the bus to Brantwood. Catherine is carrying the grocery bags from Tesco.

"Oh boy," she says. "I haven't made crêpes since I was a kid; I'm a little nervous. What if they don't turn out well?"

"Oh, then we'll just say it's a special recipe from your village."

"Funny," Catherine says, but her voice sounds strained.

Neither of us has dressed up. Instinctively, we're both wearing jeans, sneakers, and a sweater. As always, Catherine looks insanely beautiful. Just in case, I'm wearing mascara and a touch of lipstick. With makeup, I look more twenty-three than fourteen.

When we finally reach Anne's, I'm a bit surprised to find that a certified teacher has to share an apartment, although I know an English teacher's salary is well below what a German teacher earns.

We ring the doorbell, and Anne opens the door for us.

"Hello, my dears," she says warmly. She gives each of us a kiss on the cheek. "Come in and put your things down, then you can meet the others."

We bring our shopping bags into the kitchen, which is small and a bit cluttered, but functional.

"Excellent," Catherine says, "a gas stove—it'll be much easier to make the crêpes."

Anne leads us into the living room. Our fellow teachers have taken their places on the few seats available.

"Everyone at least recognizes each other," Anne says. "But, just in case, I'll introduce everybody again. Here are our assistant teachers, Lea from Germany and Catherine from France. Lea and Catherine, that's Gill, who you know already from the teachers' lounge. Daniel teaches math; then there's John, Phil, Amy, and Ethan."

I look at each face one by one, nodding amiably. Then my heart stops. The athletic heartbreaker. The so-called womanizer.

He looks quickly in my direction, then turns away to talk to Amy, a blonde who, to the best of my knowledge, is a physical education teacher, too.

"Are you hungry?" Anne asks.

Everyone gives an enthusiastic "Yes!" so Catherine and I rush into the kitchen and immediately begin to whip up the crêpe batter. Like a pro, Catherine stirs it up quickly.

"Hey!" I say. "I see you have some experience with this."

Catherine stirs even faster and says, "Yes. My sisters and I operated a booth at Fest Noz in our village. We had to crank out these things in a hurry." She tells me, somewhat nostalgically, about the Breton folk festival, where villagers hold hands and dance to the nasal sound of the district's bagpipes.

Anne peers into the kitchen. "Do you two need help? Is there anything I can do?"

But we send her back into the living room. A fat gray cat sneaks around our legs. She starts to follow Anne out, but then rests near the kitchen door.

Catherine places two pans on the stove and melts a little butter in each. Then she drips a small dollop of batter into the hot fat. She skillfully manipulates the pans at lightning speed until the dough is just a white film on the bottom of each pan. It smells delectable.

Catherine concentrates on the edges of the crêpes. "Almost done." She takes a pan firmly by the handle, steps back, and says, "Watch out!"

She jerks the pan upward. The crêpe swirls once on its axis, then lands perfectly, the crispy brown side facing up.

"Wow," I say, deeply impressed. "Up till now, I've only seen television chefs do that. I never thought I would see that live."

In amazement, I watch Catherine toss the next crêpe in the same way. "Oh, it's nothing," she says. "Anyone can do it."

"I'd never be able to do that," I say, but I'm suddenly tempted to try.

"Of course you can," Catherine says. "Would you like to try?"

Of course! I wait until after Catherine prepares two more crêpes. Then I take the pan firmly by the handle.

"Jerk it up quickly," Catherine explains. "Here, let me show you again." It looks like magic.

"Okay," I say. "Let me try. One, two, three . . ."

I jerk the pan up, but I miscalculate and use too much force. My crêpe shoots up into the air, briefly sticks to the ceiling, then falls to the ground. How did the cat reappear so suddenly? She's right where she needs to be. She attacks the crêpe, and it disappears into her stomach. Catherine and I look at the cat, then each other, in amazement. Her eyes are dancing with delight, and we burst out laughing. *Oh man*, I think, *I never thought that making crêpes would be so much fun.*

"Excellent!" Catherine giggles. "At this rate, everyone will starve, but the cat will roll around on the floor, fat as a tick."

Again, we laugh uncontrollably.

I notice someone at the kitchen door and look over quickly. It's Ethan Derby, leaning on the door frame. He's watching us carry on with our nonsense.

"Hi," I say, suddenly feeling uncharacteristically shy. "We're almost ready to deliver the first batch."

"Beautiful," he says. Then he turns around and disappears.

Catherine spoons some more batter into the pans. "Huh," she says. "That's one beautiful man. If my Christian knew that such a handsome Englishman was hanging around us, he wouldn't sleep at night."

"Hmm," I answer, but I feel my cheeks burning. I hope Catherine thinks it's from the heat in the kitchen. I must admit that Catherine is totally right. Ethan is really attractive. I wonder if he's dating the Amy girl?

"He's probably already taken," I say despondently as I vigorously stir the batter.

"No, he's not," says Anne. She's peeking through the door into the kitchen. Darn! She obviously overheard our conversation.

"He claims that he still hasn't found 'Miss Right,'" Anne sighs. I get the impression that she'd like to be the one. "Can I steal those crêpes?" she asks.

"Yes," says Catherine, "and take this jam, too. Make sure everybody gets some." She presses the jar into Anne's hand.

"The crêpe idea was actually pretty silly," I say to Catherine after Anne leaves.

"Why?"

"Because we don't have time to socialize with the other teachers. We're in the kitchen, reeking of fried fat, while everybody else hangs out in the living room."

Catherine pushes her hair away from her forehead with the back of her hand. "True. Come on. Let's finish up so that we can sit with the others."

We work silently. I don't toss any more crêpes into the air. The cat watches us longingly but in vain. Anne goes back and forth between the kitchen and living room to pick up and serve crêpes.

"They're fantastic," she says. "Our compliments to the chefs."

After half an hour, we've used up all the batter. Catherine and I prepare the last few crêpes for ourselves and go into the living room.

The diners greet us with applause. "They were delicious, tasty, so good," everyone says.

"Thank you," Catherine says politely.

"Unfortunately, we're one short," a voice pipes up from the sofa. "The cat ate it."

Irritated, I look in that direction and see Ethan. I begin a witty retort by saying something like, "Wrong! We made it for him, of course," but I realize that Ethan's not smiling. He looks almost stern. *Hello*, I think, *is he serious? What's up with that?* I consider apologizing, but I bite my tongue. The hell with that! The whole episode was hilarious, and I find myself fighting the urge to giggle—especially when I think of the cat!

I cheerfully plop myself down on the narrow couch next to Catherine. We savor the crêpes while all around us everybody's laughing and chatting. I concentrate on my food. Anne is right. These really are the best crêpes I've ever eaten. The warm, sugary dough practically melts in my mouth. I close my eyes and taste a hint of cognac. The floral note is very subtle and delicate. The cherry jam goes well with the buttery taste of the crêpes. Mmm. I'm almost delirious.

I open my eyes. Everyone is happily chatting, but only one person is silent—Ethan. His eyes rest on my face, questioning and pensive. I quickly lower my gaze and stare at my plate. Crap! He's been watching me devour my crêpes. How embarrassing! He probably thinks that I'm some kind of bulimic with a crêpe fetish. My first impulse is to quickly finish up my crêpes. But something inside me rebels. Why should I spoil my own enjoyment for him? What do I care what this guy thinks? So I continue to savor my crêpes. I refuse to look in his direction but focus on my plate instead.

Catherine whispers to me, "Ethan's been staring at you this whole time, Lea."

"Probably because he thinks I'm crazy," I say. "*Mysterium tremendum et fascinans*."

Catherine thinks the comment is hysterical and laughs. I laugh along with her, but my heart's not in it. I don't want to admit it, but I feel myself falling for Ethan. He really is my dream guy, tall and broad shouldered with dark hair and eyes. This dream guy is the reason poor Jens from Hohensyburg didn't have a chance with me from the outset. Ethan curls his lips in a way that makes him look so serious, and he doesn't laugh when others do. He's mysterious, a bit secretive, and irresistible. Just a few days ago I loudly proclaimed how much I liked being single—and now this! Crap, crap, crap!

Let it go, Lea, a warning voice in my head tells me. *Falling in love will just make your life more complicated and exhausting—that's not what you want.* But I feel like an invisible vortex is dragging my soul in the direction of the elegant, quiet guy sitting at the end of the sofa. I try not to look at him so I won't get carried away altogether, but it's useless. It feels like there are only two people in the entire room: Ethan and me.

The evening marches on. The red wine is not very good, but I still drink more than I should. I'll definitely end up with a hangover tomorrow. My cheeks redden, and I feel wild and free. I'm naturally outgoing, but when I drink too much, I become even more extroverted and exuberant. I've been told I'm the life of the party. I do look at life in a quirky way, and my vivaciousness tends to thaw others out. I can feel that happening now, and it would be an even better party if quiet, elusive Ethan wasn't there, sitting at the end of the couch. Ethan. He reminds me of the cat waiting for more crêpes to fall down from the ceiling. Although I'm in a good mood, he vexes me.

A little later, I find myself getting tired and leap to my feet. "It's late. I need to go home," I say to Catherine. I have no idea whether it's really late or not. I've lost all sense of time.

But Catherine agrees. She looks at her watch and nods. "Oh, yes. You're right. It's time to head out."

"Are you going to take the bus?" Anne asks us. "I don't like that idea. It's too late, someone might harass you."

Ha, I think, *if you only knew, Anne! I'm already feeling immensely harassed here in your living room.* Ethan's presence makes me think incessantly about him and nothing else.

"I'll drive you home," Anne says, but Ethan interrupts her in a calm, authoritative voice.

"That's out of the question, Anne," he says. "You've had too much to drink. I've only had water all evening. If someone's going to take the girls home, it definitely should be me."

Oh great! He doesn't even ask us. And he called us "the girls" as if we are still babies. *How old is he, anyway?* I think with irritation. Did someone say twenty-seven? He's only four years older than I am. And, although he appears to be rather sophisticated, he doesn't look particularly old. On the contrary, he looks lanky and youthful. This guy is kind of driving me crazy.

Ethan stands up and holds out his hand to Catherine, helping her to her feet. I feel a hot attack of jealousy. I have the urge to sit down again so that Ethan can help me up, too. That, however, would definitely be beneath my dignity. Instead, I hold my head high and say my good-byes. Although I drank a little too much, I don't think anybody notices.

In the hallway, I find my coat and swing it over my shoulders. It suddenly feels very light—somebody is holding it.

"Allow me," Ethan says. "It's too cold out there for you to not put it on properly."

I hold my arms out like a doll, and Ethan helps me put on my coat. His hands rest on my shoulders for a second, and I feel electric shocks shooting through my body. *Crap*, I think for the hundredth time this evening. *You are in trouble, Lea! You've fallen head over heels for this guy.* My knees tremble as I follow Ethan and Catherine to a car parked in front of the townhouse. Anne and the other guests wave from the doorway. "Good night!" they say. "Thank you for the crêpes!"

Catherine and I sit down in the backseat, and Ethan revs up the motor and drives off. After the lively chatter at the party, it seems too quiet in the car.

Catherine asks me softly, "When do you have to be at school Monday morning?"

I whisper back, "Ten o'clock."

"You're lucky!" she replies. "You can sleep in."

"Yes, but I have a longer trip to school than you do," I say. "I have to leave the house at least half an hour before class starts."

"But that'll change soon; your new landlords are coming back from their vacation. They live in the village, which is closer."

"Yes, I move there next week," I say.

We fall silent again. I think about my upcoming change in accommodations. I really like staying with the Seafields, and I would prefer to spend the whole year there, but it's not an option. The house only has one bathroom, and there always seems to be a bottleneck there. And their relatives can't visit with me in the guest room. Besides, there's always some petty, or occasionally significant, dispute between mother and daughter. Linda is enormously stubborn, and puberty seems to have made it worse. I find it embarrassing to witness their arguments over makeup, clothes, and boys. I think it makes Melissa uncomfortable, too.

The silence in the car is almost oppressive. Catherine is too shy to make conversation with our charming driver. But it feels rude not to at least try.

I clear my throat and say, "What a nice evening. I think it was so great that Anne invited everybody."

Ethan says, "Do you?"

"Of course! It'd be a shame to pass by your fellow teachers on a daily basis and never get to know them."

"Mmm," Ethan says. "How can anyone really get to know somebody well in just one evening? I think such gatherings are rather pointless."

Well, that's pretty revealing. Apparently, he isn't even a tiny bit curious about us—or me. Catherine gathers her courage and says, "But it's so nice when people cook and eat something delicious together."

Ethan doesn't say anything. I think he's being pretty darned rude for not at least complimenting us on our delicious crêpes. Evidently, Ethan's not big on social niceties. We fall into silence once again. I mull over the events of the evening. When I think about the crêpe landing right in front of the cat's nose and her stunned face, I can't help it—I start to giggle uncontrollably.

Catherine glances at me and smiles.

I say, "Kitty!"

Then Catherine starts to laugh, too.

Ethan doesn't laugh with us. His dark eyes are watching us in the rearview mirror. Maybe he's worried that we're so tipsy, he'll have to carry us out of the car. Maybe he thinks we're going to vomit in the backseat. Who knows?

We reach Catherine's place first. She thanks him politely and wishes us both good night, then disappears into the house.

Being alone with Ethan makes me nervous. It's oppressively silent in the car. I'd like to learn more about him. I'd like to ask a thousand questions. Who are you, really? Why are you suddenly so important to me? Why is it that my heart beats so loudly in your presence that I'm sure you must be able to hear it? And—most importantly—do you feel it, too? Do you notice the electricity between us?

Instead, I stay mute and look out the window. He pulls in front of Powlands Farm and waits a moment. I do, too. Who's going to say something first? Surprisingly, he does.

"It seems to me that you have a very joyful spirit," Ethan says.

I'm stunned. Of all the things that I expected him to say, that was the least likely of all. My mind is spinning. Why did he say that? What's he implying—that I'm some sort of ridiculous silly goose? Does he find me repulsive? Is he criticizing me? Do I have to be somebody else to please him? I think, *Yes, I'm a joyful spirit, and I'm not ashamed of it.*

"That's right," I say.

Ethan frowns. "Unusual."

Then he gets out, opens the door for me, sits back behind the wheel, and drives off.

"Unusual." What does he mean by that? Criticism? Admiration? What does this imply? I enter the house and sneak on tiptoes to my room. It's very late, and everyone is asleep.

I lie in bed and think, *Lea, why are you losing sleep over this? You're attracted to someone who thinks you're "unusual." The comment was perfectly straightforward. Who would be attracted to someone who's unusual? It was clearly a put-down. Forget about this guy, relax, and go to sleep.*

I fall asleep, but I can't stop thinking about Ethan.

Chapter 4

In the days after the party, my thoughts continue to revolve around Ethan even though I barely see him at all. During breaks, I casually stroll in the direction of the main teachers' lounge, hoping to run into him. One time before class starts, he runs past me, a stack of books under his arm. He nods at me coolly and hurries by. It makes me introspective. Apparently, Ethan's not crazy about unusual girls. Next time I see him, I'll have to be careful not to come off as so unusual. What's the alternative? Usual? Despite my frustration, I smile.

My stay at the Seafields' is coming to an end. I'm moving to my new hosts' house over the weekend. The Lanes live just a stone's throw away from the school. I've checked out my new home a few times after school. It's a small, old stone house located directly on the main road that runs through Gatingstone. A tiny front yard is overshadowed by a huge walnut tree, and a sign next to the front door proudly announces that the little house is called Walnut Cottage. As I gaze at the simple structure, I wonder what it's like inside, beyond the windows. It's just the type of house that I liked to draw as a child: a door in the middle of the façade; three floors, each with a window to the right and left of the door, with two more windows on the top floor. Nothing more, nothing less.

On Sunday morning, I say good-bye to the Seafields, and Melissa drives my suitcases and me to Walnut Cottage. Because I'll still be in the area, there are no tearful farewells. Melissa assures me that I can drop by anytime, and they would love to have me over for Sunday dinner. It's comforting to know that this family has become so close to my heart. I think they feel the same way; otherwise Melissa wouldn't have been so insistent on inviting me back.

I ring the doorbell, and the door opens. An elderly couple greets me warmly and invites me into the living room. Mrs. Lane is tall and stout with dyed dark hair, a deep voice, and large glasses that give her an owl-like appearance. She has big white teeth (also false, I think!), which she flashes amiably at me. Mr. Lane is humpbacked and at least a head shorter than his wife. His hair is thinning, and he has a mustache, which was undoubtedly very dashing back in the day. He is not wearing dentures, and his mouth is small and wrinkled. They introduce themselves as Abby and Glen. Glen hastens to drag my bags upstairs to my room, while Abby settles me down onto the sofa. She scurries away in her plush fur slippers to make me "a nice cup of tea."

Ah yes, "a nice cup of tea." To the English, a cup of tea is sacred. When arriving at someone's home, a visitor is immediately—and I mean immediately—offered a cup of tea. To refuse is unthinkable and the biggest gaffe you can make. It's as if you declined to shake hands in Germany. I'm no big fan of tea, but I've poured so much of it down my throat since my arrival in England that I've had to forgo my habit of sweetening it with sugar. Otherwise, I'm sure I'd have put on weight.

Abby seems to have no problem with that. She throws three sugar cubes in her cup while she examines me with friendly curiosity. She asks me about everything: my family, my studies, the journey here, school, my boyfriends and female friends, and so on and so forth. Glen comes back downstairs and, sighing, settles deeply into a plush armchair. He stretches his legs onto an ottoman and picks up his cup of tea. While we talk, my eyes glide across the room. The wallpaper clashes loudly with the carpet—sunflowers on the wall and a paisley pattern on the floor. Ouch. A gas fireplace dominates the room, its blue flames dancing merrily. It's hot as hell in here.

Glen and Abby talk extensively about their vacation in Holiday Village in Bournemouth, from which they've recovered very nicely. They shared a house with a friendly couple, Ada and Oz, and Oz had a terrible cough. They are very happy to be away from Oz's constant and extremely irritating hacking. Abby demonstrates how his cough sounded. Pretty bad. Oddly enough, Abby tells me, "Oz didn't cough when his wife left the room, only when she was present." Isn't that weird? What was that all about? Speaking of coughing, Glen cheerfully lights a cigarette and begins to smoke like a chimney. *Wait*, I want to scream, *I'm definitely a nonsmoker. I can't stand tobacco smoke*! But I don't say anything. I can hardly forbid people from smoking in their own living room. Abby reaches for the pack and slips out a cigarette, too.

There's only one thing I can do: escape to my room. I drink my tea quickly and ask Abby where I'll be sleeping.

"I'll take you up, love," Abby says. Love. She's only known me for half an hour. I have a lot to get used to.

Huffing and puffing, Abby leads me upstairs. "Here's our bedroom," she says, pointing to the door on the right. "And here's the bathroom."

I look inside. The bathroom has carpet. Carpet in the bathroom—I never would have believed it if I hadn't seen it myself. There's a toilet, a small sink, and a bathtub.

I ask timidly, "You don't have a shower?"

Abby stares at me as though I'm a Martian. She frowns. "A shower? No. We only bathe once a week." Then she remembers something. "If you want to take a shower, you can use this."

She bends over in front of the cabinet underneath the sink and pulls out a hose with a rubber cap, which fits over the bathtub faucet. At the other end is a nozzle that looks like the arm of a watering can. *Oh dear*! I sigh. I can see some interesting, and possibly tough, times are coming my way.

Then Abby tells me the house has no central heating. "In winter, we stay in the living room and the kitchen. Glen turns on the oil here in the morning." She knocks on a device that's faintly reminiscent of a radiator. "Then it gets good and hot here in the bathroom."

With a quivering heart, I follow her into my bedroom. In the middle of the room is a high double bed, covered with a bedspread made of 100 percent polyester. It has ruffled edges with a hideous print of pink roses. There are nightstands on either side of the bed, a chair, and a chest of drawers.

I think back longingly to the Seafields' spacious and tastefully decorated guest room. But I don't want to offend the large, good-natured woman. "Nice. I think I'll be very comfortable here," I say listlessly.

Abby gives me a big, grateful smile and tells me that supper is at six o'clock. She disappears back downstairs.

I sit on the polyester bedding and look around desperately. How did I end up here? What do I do now? Should I look for a new room tomorrow? Suddenly, for the first time since my arrival in Gatingstone, a profound homesickness assails me.

Although I don't like my accommodations at all, I keep busy unpacking my suitcases until supper time. I stow my clothes away in the dresser and stack all my reading for the exam on it. On one of the bedside tables, I place my small electronic travel alarm clock. At night it lulls me to sleep with its regular, soft ticking. I really don't want to hurt the old couple's feelings, so I'll have to act as if I want to stay here. I wrap myself up in my warmest sweater because it's icy cold in the room. I can see my breath when I exhale. By the time Abby calls out that supper's ready, I'm already deeply engrossed in one of my books.

I set aside my book and hurry down the creaky stairs. I push open the doors to the dining room on the left, but the room is deserted, with only a bare, dark wooden table with four chairs and a small cupboard. The chairs are pushed under the table, and the table is empty. The electric fireplace is cold, as is the entire room. Did I hear her correctly? Did I come down too soon? Was it someone calling from the street?

I tap gently on the living room door.

Abby opens it, beaming at me. "Come on in! And for God's sake, you better take that warm sweater off. You're going to burn up in here."

It's true. The room is stifling hot. Positioned in front of the TV is a small camping table with three folding chairs. Glen is sitting in one of the chairs, carving a chicken.

Abby says apologetically, "You see, we try to make the living room nice and cozy during the cold season. Come, sit here." She pulls a folding chair out, inviting me to sit. "I'll just get the salad from the kitchen."

I plop down and think for the thousandth time today, *Help! How in the world did I end up here?*

Glen adds to his wife's explanation. "In the summer, we use the dining room. But the electric fireplace in the dining room eats up so much electricity it's like watching money burn. It's damned expensive, dear."

Aha, I think. So that's how it is. I'm the guest of a couple of misers. I've never seen anything like it. Fortunately, the food isn't so miserly. I'm amazed at how delicious everything tastes. Apparently, Abby is very passionate about her cooking.

After dinner, I help Abby clean off the table, and in a flash, Glen folds up the camping furniture and pushes it against the wall behind the sofa. Then he sits down happily in his chair, a pack of cigarettes in one hand and the remote control in the other.

While Abby rattles around in the kitchen, Glen turns on the TV full blast and lights up another smoke. I sit down in the other chair, wondering how long I'll be able to endure the noise and the smoke. Upstairs, my icy, lonely room awaits me.

Abby pokes her head in from the kitchen and yells, "I hope it's not too loud, love, but Glen's a bit hard of hearing! Used to be too loud for me, too, but eventually I got used to it!"

It's earsplitting, but I shake my head. *I can't move in as a paying guest and completely disrupt their household routines*, I think.

Abby soon joins us. They are deeply involved in a daily soap opera called *Crossroads* or something like that. Apparently this is the season premiere after the summer break.

Abby is completely entranced. She greets the appearance of each actor as if he's a long-lost, much-beloved relative.

"Look!" she says to Glen. "That's Benny. Oh, he's my absolute favorite. And look, he hasn't changed a bit. Or do you think he's gained a little weight? And there's Mary—cute as ever. What do you think? Will she marry Jake? Hopefully not. He's really not right for her. They'll be divorced within a year, just you wait and see!"

Although my eyes are tearing up from the tobacco smoke and my ears are ringing from the loud television volume, I find the elderly couple quite amusing, so I hang out with them until the program ends. Then I stretch and tell them that I need to go to bed.

Abby is appalled. "You can't just go to sleep," she says. "You have to have a nice hot drink!" A hot drink before bed is another one of their customs at Walnut Cottage. She springs to her feet. "I'll make some coffee for all of us."

"Oh no, please, not for me," I beg. "If I drink coffee at this hour, I'll be awake all night." It seems normal enough, but Abby looks at me as if I'm crazy.

"Did you hear that, Glen? She can't sleep when she drinks coffee. Isn't that something? I've never heard of that." She's completely oblivious. "What are we going to do with you? You absolutely must have your hot drink."

I surrender, saying, "Maybe some hot cocoa?"

Abby radiates happiness. "Of course! Cocoa! Why didn't I think of that myself? Sit down, love, and I'll make you a nice cup of hot cocoa."

And so I sit back on the sofa again, sipping my good night cocoa. Abby offers me homemade cookies, so I try one. They're delicious—crunchy and buttery, with a hint of ginger.

Glen dunks his cookie into his coffee and glances at me somewhat sheepishly, as if he's done something naughty.

Instantly, Abby says sternly, "You can't dunk your cookies. What will Lea think?"

"That they're dunking cookies," he says mischievously. "You have to dunk them."

I smile. Aha. Without his dentures, he can't eat these cookies. "It's okay," I say, dipping my cookie in the cocoa, too, which makes it taste even better. Glen winks at me conspiratorially. Abby continues to protest, but it's only for show, as evidenced by her indulgent smile. By the end of the night, I'm no longer homesick. I have a feeling that I'll stick with this old couple till the end.

But what about my bed? Oh my! I'm no princess from "The Princess and the Pea," but this monstrosity they call a bed is another thing entirely. It's soft and squishy like a ripe plum, with hard, unyielding bedsprings that poke up between the soft spots. Half asleep, I figure I must decide between sleeping on the soft spots or the bedsprings. But most of the time I land somewhere in between, and each time I roll over onto a bedspring, I feel as if I've been punched.

In the morning, I limp downstairs like an old rheumatic woman. Nothing escapes Abby's sharp eyes. She asks if I'm in pain, and I consider telling her the truth. I don't want to offend her, but sometimes honesty is the best policy. I confess that the problem is the mattress. Glen and Abby exchange knowing glances but say nothing. Two days later, I have a new mattress. Apparently, they were already aware of the problem. I'm really touched that they remedied the situation so quickly, especially since their finances are so obviously tight.

Although I don't want to keep griping about the bedroom situation, I have good reason to. The room is unheated—there's no radiator—and winters here in Essex County are just as cold as they are in Germany.

One afternoon, Glen knocks on my bedroom door. "I have to seal the window, dear," he says. In one hand, he is holding a roll of paper towels, and in the other a small knife. While I watch him in fascination, he begins to plug the gaps between the panes of glass and the metal frame with the paper towels. Apparently, he's done this before.

"Glen," I say, "does this means that I can't air out the room the whole winter?"

He scratches his head and looks at me thoughtfully. "You don't need to. It's cold enough already."

That's quite revealing. The fact is, my room gets colder and colder every day. The bed is made English style, which means there are two sheets, one covering the mattress and one underneath a wool blanket. Then everything is completely tucked under the mattress. When I was still back home in Bielefeld, I had a hunch about all this. I decided to bring my own down sleeping bag, but my mother vetoed the idea, saying, "You can't do that, Lea. It will offend your hosts." I can't believe I was stupid enough to listen to her. While my mother is at home, snuggled under her down comforter with the central heating on, I'm freezing to death as I try to fall asleep.

Each morning, Abby awakens me with a cup of tea, which she brings to my bedside. The first morning, I was scared out of my wits to see someone entering my room at dawn. The shadow moved to the window and pulled the curtain back, so that the first rays of sunlight hit me right in the eyes. "Good morning, love, I've got your tea," she said.

I've tried to dissuade her from this habit, especially since she makes no exception for days off when I can sleep in over the days that I have to go to school. Abby is relentless. A good English hostess brings a cup of tea to her guest's bedside every morning, and that's final!

At this point, I've found I'm no longer completely against it. I shove my pillow under my head, grab the cup, and pull the blanket under my chin to keep warm. Then I bring the cup to my mouth with numb fingers. The warm, strong drink gives me the courage to push back the bedcovers and face the room's frigid air.

One afternoon I visit the Seafields and complain to Melissa about my cold bed.

"How do the English endure such strange bedding?" I ask. I can speak frankly with Melissa. It's fun for her to hear my comments on English lifestyle.

"How many pillows do you have on your bed?" she asks.

"Only one, of course," I say. "At first I had four—heaven only knows why—but I gave Abby three of them back. Now I only have one."

"Oh," says Melissa, "that was a big mistake."

"Why?"

"Because you need the pillows to keep you warm. Here in England, you stuff them on the right and left side of your body under the bedcovers. That's how we stay warm."

Help! Why didn't anybody tell me this before? Now the pillows are gone. I suppose I can tell Abby that I want the pillows back, but instead I buy a hot-water bottle. Every evening I fill it with boiling water in Abby's kitchen and take it to my icy bedroom. Then I curl up under the cold sheets with it, hoping I can fall asleep before it gets cold. Abby notices this undeniable I-am-cold signal, and very soon I'm lying underneath three heavy wool blankets, pressed flat like a fly between the pages of a book. Not good. Making the bed each morning is now an especially tedious task, because I have to sort out the sheets and three blankets, smooth them on the bed, then tuck everything under the mattress. Then I drape the pink bedspread on top of it. It's maddening.

But I hadn't counted on the exuberant graciousness of the old couple. One day at lunch, they wink meaningfully at each other. The whole afternoon and evening, the air crackles with excitement, but I don't know why. As the evening in front of the TV begins, Glen disappears, then returns. What are these two up to? Later, as I lie in bed, the penny drops. My bed is comfortably preheated. From beneath the sheets, a cord leads to an electric socket. I'm now equipped with an electric blanket. What other wonders are in store for me in this bizarre little house?

Just as I'm snuggling under my mountain of blankets, Abby discreetly knocks at the door, then looks in.

"Well, is that better now?" she asks, beaming at me.

"Absolutely," I say truthfully. "Many, many thanks!"

"The only thing is, the store said that you can't fall asleep with the blanket switched on. You'll have to pull the plug now."

I obediently hop out of bed and unplug it, then quickly dive back under the covers. Abby wishes me good night and disappears. After about ten minutes, though, the miracle blanket and the entire bed cool off again. In frustration, I bite into my one and only pillow.

I try the electric blanket for a couple of nights. I even plug it in three hours before going to bed. Again, it becomes cold ten minutes after I unplug it. As I'm preparing the hot-water bottle, Glen and Abby make dubious faces.

"Dear," Glen says, "if you use the hot-water bottle, then the electric blanket could be destroyed."

Argh! What now? With a heavy heart, I remove the electric blanket, fold it neatly, and give it back to my hosts. Abby frowns, obviously disappointed. Two days later, their bedroom door is cracked open and

I recognize the telltale cord peeking out from under their bedding. The electric blanket has found a new home.

The next morning, Mr. Henley asks how I like my accommodations. I confess that I don't know where I can study in the little house.

"I discussed it with your hosts," he replies. "You can study in the dining room. You can use the dining table as a desk, and there's also heating in there."

Oh, so it's already been planned. Of course, I don't tell him that Abby and Glen eat their meals on a camping table in the living room to save on heating costs. I don't want to embarrass them. So, in the evenings, I curl up on the armchair in the living room, trying to understand D. H. Lawrence novels through dense clouds of tobacco smoke and the earsplitting racket of television soap operas. I gradually get quite good at blocking out everything around me.

Sometimes Abby falls asleep while watching TV. When she wakes up, she's racked by a terrible cough.

"Abby," I say, "you smoke too much. You need to quit."

"Oh no," she replies. "That has nothing to do with it. I inherited sensitive lungs from my mother."

Why don't I just search for new accommodations? Mainly because it's extremely difficult to find something here in the village. I could search in neighboring towns, but then I would have to take a long bus ride to school every morning. The Lanes' house borders school property; I'm at work in two minutes. And something else—I've become quite fond of the old couple. They are so touchingly concerned with my well-being. For example, I mention one day how nice it would be to have a bicycle. The next day, Glen comes home with an old beat-up bike that he borrowed from a sister. The bike is black, heavy, and at least fifty years old, but Glen greases up the chain, inflates the tires, and shows me where to park the old wreck in the shed.

Now I can explore the area with my new bike. I cycle on country roads, over stubbly fields, and into villages. I discover old churches and dreamy parsonages. The sunny, mild autumn weather is perfect for bicycling. However, nights are bitterly cold.

Catherine also borrows a bicycle, and we take bike tours together. We constantly stop to take pictures so that we can impress our loved ones back home with the beauty of the landscape. Neither of us has Internet where we live, so we often visit the local library, where we can use the Wi-Fi and upload our photos onto Facebook.

When I log on to Facebook, I discover a friend request: *Jens Heller would like to be your friend*. Who? I don't know him. My first inclination is to click "Reject," but I inspect the profile photo more closely. Oh, now I know who it is. It's my savior from the night at the casino, sweet Jens, who invited me to the Italian restaurant. I hesitate a moment, then click "Accept." He was so nice to me; it would be rude to reject his request.

Now that I have access to his Facebook page, I poke around a bit. There are some cuddly childhood photos, along with pictures of the adult Jens at his sister's wedding. He is wearing a dark suit and looks quite dashing, as he had as a chauffeur. There's a photo of Jens with a small dog sitting on his lap, and one where the dog is bigger. Then I watch a video of the dog doing elaborate tricks, some of them quite impressive. Training this dog must have been quite an undertaking. There are a few pictures from the Mediterranean Sea, at some sort of hot springs resort. Jens doesn't look bad in his bathing suit.

I look for a Facebook profile for Ethan, but I turn up an error message that says, *Sorry, we couldn't find any results for this search*. It figures. I didn't expect anything else from my mysterious, handsome heartthrob.

There are some advantages to living in a closed-off, stuffy house like Walnut Cottage. I'm practically forced to get out of the house and find something to do. I register for a French course; I've always regretted not having studied the language in school. Catherine and I join the local tennis club, too, although neither one of us knows how to play. We sign up for lessons, and as soon as we have a couple of hours under our belts, we get the keys to the village tennis court and play until our wrists ache and our arms are heavy.

One day at lunch, Anne asks us, "How would you two like to meet me and a few other colleagues at the pub? We go to the Bell quite often—it's on the main road. We'd love to have you there."

Anything is better than watching *Crossroads* through a thick blanket of tobacco smoke. Catherine's sentiments must mirror mine exactly. She immediately asks, "When will you be there next?"

"How about tonight at eight o'clock?"

"Great, we'll be there," I say.

That evening, we push open the pub's door and find the place is already packed. Catherine and I stand at the door, looking around the room for quite some time until we finally find our colleagues seated in a rear corner. As we approach the group, Anne shouts a cheerful greeting. At her behest, everyone moves closer together to make room for us. We sit on a bench by the window. Catherine is on my left, and Ethan is pressed firmly against my right side.

I'm madly in love with him, but his direct proximity feels a little too intense at this delicate stage of infatuation. Ethan's body feels solid and muscular. He smells like good aftershave. His presence has such a strong physical impact on me that the entire right half of my body glows, as if I have a massive sunburn. To make matters worse, Ethan and I are so tightly crushed together that he has to put his arm around the back of my bench so he doesn't fall out of his seat altogether. I try to relax, but my body trembles all over. If he's really as much of a ladies' man as people say, he must notice. I'm torn. Half of me wants to jump up and flee the pub, the other wants to stay here forever.

"What do you want to drink?" Anne asks us. "Since I'm the one who lured you out, the first round is on me."

Catherine opts for her beloved crème de menthe, but I vacillate. I could drink a beer, but English beer is so different from German. I still haven't gotten used to it.

"I'd like a malt whiskey—neat," I finally say.

I swear I feel Ethan's body shudder next to me. But why?

Anne looks at me in amusement. "Are you sure?"

"Yes, very," I say.

She goes to the bar to get our drinks.

Ethan shakes his head. "Do you even know what a malt whiskey is?"

"Yes," I say. "It's made with malted barley roasted over a peat fire. That's why it tastes so wonderfully round and smoky."

"Hmm," Ethan says. "I'm surprised you have experience in the matter, considering your tender, young age."

Annoyed, I sit up as straight as I possibly can and unsuccessfully try to scoot away from him. "How young do you think I am?" I ask.

"Nineteen," he says.

"Ha!" I reply. "I'm twenty-three."

"Even if you were thirty, malt whiskey would be the wrong drink for you. Only old men drink it here in England," Ethan says.

"That's ridiculous," I say hotly. "Why should old men be the only ones to treat themselves to a good whiskey?"

"Because it's unusual for sweet, young things to drink whiskey," Ethan replies.

Here we go again. Unusual. It's no surprise I'm at the end of my rope. I look askance at him. My goodness, he's so handsome! He has very long lashes for a man. His hair is relatively long, and his enviable curls wreathe his face. He often pushes his hair away from his forehead. I would love to run my hands through those curls just to see how they feel.

Anne comes back with a tray and sets our drinks in front of us.

"Cheers," she says. "It's so great that you're both here, too!"

We raise our glasses, and I sip my whiskey. Mmm. It tastes just like the whiskey I had during my semester in Lancaster. I'm not a big drinker; I'll nurse this one glass the whole evening. But I do know how to appreciate a fine drink. I close my eyes and try to imagine myself in a low, thatched cottage in the Highlands. The malted, smoky taste makes me think of the wide-open, mountainous countryside with sheep grazing on a distant green hill. But as soon as the sharp alcohol hits my stomach, I realize I should have chosen an ale. I become very warm, then my cheeks get ruddy. This always happens when I indulge in a stiff drink.

I suddenly realize that Ethan's arm, which was on the back of the bench, is now casually resting on my shoulder, as if it belongs there.

I'm getting so warm that I feel as though I'm going to spontaneously combust. I look around the table. My colleagues are laughing and chatting comfortably. No one seems to notice my turmoil. Good thing. What about Ethan? He engages in conversation occasionally but is conspicuously silent most of the time. His arm remains on my shoulders, and I don't shake it off. It feels so good where it is. My heart's beating so hard I'm positive Ethan can feel it.

When Ethan says something, his deep voice buzzes in my ear. His breath smells a little like beer, but it's not at all unpleasant. The whiskey makes me talkative. I chat about my semester abroad in Turkey. I experienced so many fascinating things there the stories just bubble out of me. The others find my descriptions and anecdotes amusing, and I realize I've become the center of attention. And the whole time, like the hum of a rotating gyroscope, the closeness of my dream man envelops me. I feel every twitch of his muscular arm. Every once in a while, I feel his arm press ever so slightly on my shoulder.

A little voice in the back of my head asks, *Is his arm there because it has no other place to go, or is it a caress? Is Ethan trying to give me some sort of sign? If so, does it mean he has feelings for me?* Then I think of Linda's warnings. Maybe I should gently but firmly duck out from under his arm and move away a bit. But I can't bring myself to do that. Every fiber of my being is screaming for me to stay right where I am.

Eventually, Ethan shifts his weight and removes his arm. I hold my breath and wait, hoping to feel it again. Sure enough, he places it back around my shoulders. This time, it's even heavier and warmer.

He whispers something very softly in my ear, so that only I can hear it, "You're ridiculously beautiful, you know that?"

My heart almost throbs out of my chest. For days—weeks—I've dreamed of Ethan saying something like that. Now it's actually happening. I'm totally embarrassed. Just to be on the safe side, I don't say a thing.

Ethan sweeps a strand of my hair off my shoulder and examines it closely. "Your hair is a very strange color, a bit reddish in this low light."

I swallow. "I inherited the reddish tone from my father."

"You should take better care of it. You have very dry split ends," he observes.

He's right. I should have let the hairdresser cut off the split ends a long time ago, but I always end up postponing it. I curse myself that I didn't take care of it sooner. I'm sitting next to my heartthrob, and he notices that I neglect myself. I need to do something about it for sure. I vow to go to the hairdresser the very next day.

At some point, Catherine stands up and says she's tired and needs to go home. She says good-bye to everybody. Then someone else says the same thing. I lose track of time completely. Only when the Bell's owner rings the bell and announces, "Last orders, please!" do I realize that it's time for me to go, too.

The bench is less crowded now, so I lean away from Ethan to grab my bag. I feel his arm firmly pull me closer to him.

"Do you really have to leave?" he asks.

"I do," I say, desperately trying to act relaxed. "We have to go to class tomorrow."

"A shame," he says. He lets go of me and stands up abruptly. Once he's removed his arm from my shoulders, I feel very cold and exposed. His physical proximity was very pleasant.

I say hastily, "But we could meet again soon. That would be nice."

"Yes," Ethan says, "maybe." He makes no further comment. We walk into the cold night air. Everyone says their good-byes. Ethan and the rest of our colleagues go their own ways. I slide my hands deep into my jacket pockets and walk the few hundred yards to Walnut Cottage alone.

When I arrive, I unlock the door and rush upstairs on tiptoes. The house is dark and quiet except for the sound of snoring from Abby and Glen's room. I am under my mountain of sheets and blankets within ten minutes. Just before falling asleep, I remember I completely forgot to fill up my hot-water bottle. But I don't need it tonight. I'm as warm as if I had a fever.

Chapter 5

Over the next few days, I hear and see nothing of Ethan, but my thoughts continue to constantly revolve around him. I can't stop thinking about how wonderful it was to feel him close to me at the pub. I wonder whether I should take the initiative to ask him out on a date, but then I think how embarrassing it would be for him to reject me. I'd rather spare myself the heartache.

Instead, I go to the hairdresser. There's one here in the village, located on the main street. The shop is tiny and has room for only two clients at a time. The hairdresser is a young, plump blonde woman named Mandy. She seats me in front of a mirror, explaining what she wants to do. She has the high-pitched, squeaky voice I'd expect from an English hairdresser. Englishwomen, as a whole, speak in much higher registers than German women. I wonder why that is.

Mandy interrupts my thoughts. "You're new here in the village, aren't you? I haven't seen you around."

I tell her that I'm teaching for a year at the comprehensive school.

"And do you like it?"

"Yes, it's very nice," I reply.

"Autumn break is coming soon," she says. "Are you going back to Germany?"

Good question. Autumn break means I get a week off next week. I'd been wondering whether I should go back to Germany. Catherine is going back home to Brittany. It might be lonely for me here. On the other hand, going home isn't particularly tempting. My dorm room is occupied, and although it's nice to be with my parents, when I'm around them for more than two days, they tend to forget I'm already a grown-up. It gets to the point that my mom won't let me out of the house without a hat, and my father tries to engage me in deep conversations about my future.

"No, I'd rather use this time to see more of England," I answer. "I was thinking about going to Cambridge."

"Oh, yes," she squeaks enthusiastically. "Cambridge is really beautiful! You absolutely must go there. My sister lives there, and I visit every once in a while. Cambridge in autumn is a dream!"

But visiting Cambridge isn't so easy. "Unfortunately, it's very expensive there," I say. "I don't know whether I can afford to go on my meager budget."

The hairdresser furrows her brow. "You're right. The prices are inflated because of all the tourists." She silently continues cutting my hair. Suddenly she stops and says, "Unless . . ."

"Unless what?" I ask.

"Unless you're not that picky about accommodations."

"I'm not," I say immediately.

"In that case, I could ask my sister if she has a little corner you could stay in. I know there's a storeroom with a bed in her shared apartment. I've slept there a couple of times."

A storeroom doesn't sound too good, but I just nod and say, "That would be great."

"Okay," Mandy says. "We shouldn't dawdle. I'll ask her now."

She puts the scissors and comb down in front of the mirror, fishes a cell phone out of the pocket of her smock, then finds a number. While she squeaks into the phone, my thoughts drift. Do I want to do this? Cambridge may not be such a wonderful autumn dream if you have nowhere to stay but a storage closet. It also gets dark earlier in autumn—and cold. I can see myself freezing on the university town's streets because I don't have anywhere else to go. Perhaps it would be smarter to stick with the Lanes and go to London, or explore the surrounding area.

Mandy claps her phone shut and says, "Okay, it's a done deal. Emmy says you can come. You'll need to bring your own sheets, but you can get a blanket and a pillow from her."

I ask warily, "How much?"

Mandy waves her hand dismissively. "Oh, nothing. You can stay for free. She can't charge somebody in good conscience for staying in that hole."

Oh great. That inspires confidence. On the other hand, I would have a roof over my head and a bed—for free. With that kind of deal, I could afford to warm myself up in a nice café or restaurant. If it becomes unbearable, I'll just come back to Gatingstone.

"Wonderful!" I say. "It's so nice of you to hook me up with your sister. How do I get there?"

"I'll write down her number and address as soon as we're done," Mandy says, reaching for the scissors and continuing to snip. With all the travel planning, I haven't paid much attention until I realize my hair is much shorter than I've ever had it.

"Do you like it?" Mandy asks.

"I don't know. It seems a bit short to me," I reply nervously.

"The split ends were quite long. I had to take quite a bit off to get to the healthy hair. Look, you can do whatever you want with it." Mandy pulls my hair back into a ponytail. Then she discovers something.

"Oh, you have a scar here." She touches the area behind my ear with her cool fingertips. "A pretty long one. An accident?"

I don't answer; instead, I say brusquely, "Well, now I'm presentable again. Thanks for the haircut. How much do I owe you?"

Mandy's a little stunned by my tone but says nothing. She unties the cape from around my neck, shaking the hair onto the floor, and rushes over to the cash register. I pay her, then take the piece of paper on which she scribbled her sister's information.

"Thank you," I say. "I'll tell your sister you say hi."

"Oh, yes, please. Have a lovely holiday in Cambridge."

I smile at her kindly. I'm a bit ashamed of my gruffness. "I'll let you know how it goes," I promise, then leave the salon.

Over the next week, the conversation in the teachers' lounge turns increasingly to the short holiday. Anne is traveling to Scotland to visit her mother, Gill is staying home, and Mr. Henley is going to Paris.

"What are you doing?" Anne asks me during a break.

"I'm going sightseeing in Cambridge."

Everybody congratulates me.

"That's a good plan," Mr. Henley says. "You'll like Cambridge. It really is a very lovely city, with all the beautiful, old university buildings and wonderful churches and museums. It's just unfortunate it's so difficult to access by train."

I look at him questioningly.

"Well," he says, "the whole English rail system is very impractical. All trains go to London. Driving from Gatingstone to Cambridge by car takes an hour, but by train it takes twice as long."

An idea occurs to Anne. "Ethan is driving to Cambridge next week. His brother's getting his doctorate at Trinity College, and he wants to visit him. I'm sure he would be happy to take you. I'll ask him for you."

Immediately, my heart skips a beat. Ethan. I've tried really hard to banish thoughts of him from my mind. I haven't seen him since the pub. If he were attracted to me, he would have already sought me out. I've replayed the evening at the pub in my mind many times, and the bottom line is that he was only flirting with me, nothing more. So later, when Anne tells me that Ethan is willing to give me a ride, I decide not to make a big deal about it. *It's just a practical arrangement*, I tell myself. But I'm really not being honest with myself. Leading up to my vacation, I catch myself thinking more about the car ride than about my actual stay in Cambridge.

Abby and Glen are concerned about my plans. "I'm worried, love," Abby says. "It definitely will be terribly cold. The storage room won't be heated." As if it's any warmer in my bedroom! She finds some bed linens and brings them upstairs. "You should at least take one of the wool blankets from your bed."

Glen also peeks into my room. "Especially since you get cold so easily," he says, winking at me.

I smile. "Go ahead and tease me! I know where the electric blanket went. No, don't worry. I can cuddle up with my hot-water bottle."

"And what are you going to eat there, you poor thing?" Abby asks. "You'll be completely emaciated when you come back."

They're worse than my own parents, I think. I secretly hope I come back a little emaciated. Abby's home cooking is taking a toll on my girlish figure. I intend to live on bread and yogurt in Cambridge. Of course, I don't tell them that.

Deep worry lines crease Abby's forehead. "You could catch a very bad cold, perhaps even pneumonia. You eat so little, you wouldn't have the strength to fight it off. What would your poor parents say if you were to die?"

I laugh and throw my arms around Abby's rounded shoulders. "Don't be silly, Abby. Everything's going to be just fine. I'm looking forward to the trip. You'll see, I'll still be my old self when I get back."

Secretly I think, *Is that true?* Ethan's also going to be in Cambridge for a whole week. Will he deliberately stay out of my way, or will we meet up occasionally? I'm falling back into the habit of constantly thinking about him.

On Saturday morning, Ethan parks his MG in front of Walnut Cottage. Abby squints through her sheer curtains.

"You didn't tell us that you're going to Cambridge with a young man," she says accusingly. "I don't know if that's right. He even has a sports car. He'll drive too fast, that's for sure. What would your parents say?"

I roll my eyes. Glen catches my eye and grins. Unlike Abby, he isn't worried about my ride. "Let's leave Lea alone now," he says to his wife. "I assume she's perfectly capable of taking care of herself." He reaches for my travel bag. "Come on, dear, I'll take you to the car."

Well, this is a little embarrassing. I wanted to walk out to the car looking cool, composed, and sophisticated. Instead, poor toothless Glen accompanies me to the street while Abby shuffles alongside him in her frayed fur slippers.

Ethan waits behind the wheel while Glen puts my bag in the trunk. Ethan's suitcase is in the back, and next to it is a long bag, perhaps for golf clubs. I also see a pair of rubber boots. He looks as though he's packed for an adventure.

Abby appraises Ethan thoroughly. When she sees how attractive he is, she wrings her hands. "Oh, I don't feel good about this whole thing, Glen," she says so loudly that Ethan must hear her. "Don't you want to think it over a little more, love?" she asks me.

"No, Abby, I don't," I say quite emphatically as I rush to the car. I open the passenger door and fall into the seat.

"Hi, Ethan," I say simply, then, "Can we get out of here quickly, please?" I slam the door shut.

Ethan grins in amusement as he zips down the road. "I didn't know that you brought your parents with you to England," he says.

I force a smile. "The two treat me as if I were their own daughter. Recently someone did mistake me for their daughter. Abby was overjoyed."

"Of course she was. Nobody would ever believe that old crow could have such a beautiful daughter."

I turn to stone. What a weird compliment. I don't know what to think of it. I'm delighted to be called beautiful, but to say something so mean about Abby hurts me, too. I study Ethan's face uncertainly. He can feel it and smiles at me. I instantly melt. He has long, deep dimples when he smiles. He's unbelievably handsome. Insulting Abby was probably just a slipup. What he said might make sense if a person only saw her and wasn't familiar with her dear, sweet spirit.

As Ethan drives, I occasionally wince and push myself deep down into my seat.

"What's the matter?" he asks.

I cover my face with my hands and squint through my fingers. "I can't get used to driving on the wrong side of the road. I constantly have this feeling that someone is going to hit us head-on."

He laughs. "You don't have to worry. I'll get you safely to your destination."

I look at his large, strong hands calmly gripping the steering wheel. I put my hands in my lap and try to relax. We're lucky—the weather for our trip is perfect. A radiant blue sky arches over us. The sky is so clear that I can see far off into the horizon. In the distance, I see white spots, which are sheep grazing in the green meadows. The leaves of the trees shimmer in various shades of gold. I sigh happily and try to take in all the beauty surrounding us.

"You really like being here in England," Ethan observes.

"Definitely. I spent a year abroad in Lancaster two years ago. It's very nice there, too, but I didn't expect such beauty in this corner of England."

"It depends on the weather," Ethan says. "Sometimes it can be just terrible."

He focuses on the road. We've left the main highway and are now winding our way along the narrow country roads. I take the opportunity to stare at him openly. Once again, it occurs to me that Ethan completely matches the mental picture I've had of my dream man. It's as if I created him from a dream-man kit. He has wonderfully mysterious eyes and a great body. He rolls the windows halfway down, and his gorgeous curls dance in the wind. Every now and then, he pushes them away from his face. Any girl would be happy to spend the rest of her life with a man like this by her side. Maybe, maybe, I have a teeny-tiny chance to be the one. I have to make a good impression on him.

"Satisfied?" Ethan asks.

I blush. "With what?"

"With me. Don't think that I can't see you looking at me."

I quickly look out the window. I'm embarrassed. "I'm sorry. I don't know you well yet, and I'm just curious."

"I like to hear you say 'yet,'" he says. "It sounds as though you'd like to get to know me better."

Oh yeah, I think. *You have no idea.*

After a while, Ethan breaks the short silence. "I feel the same way about you. I like you. You're not only very beautiful, but you also have a very special spirit, which is appealing."

Wow! The compliment knocks my socks off, especially since I've been wondering what Ethan really thinks about me. I was worried that he thought I was silly, and now this. I feel like I've just won the lottery. Nevertheless, I hear a little warning voice inside me say, *Maybe he's just flirting with you, Lea.* He's definitely done that with a lot of women. He doesn't have the reputation of being a heartbreaker for nothing.

Ethan continues, "English girls are all so desperate to find a man. They put so much effort into it and pursue men so doggedly that sometimes I feel as though I'm being torn apart by a pack of hyenas. It's different with you. You seem so easygoing. It seems like you really don't care what men think about you."

I want to confirm this, but I bite my tongue. It's not true in regard to Ethan, so that would be a bald-faced lie. I'm also a bit irritated by the comment that I don't care what men think. Is he criticizing what I'm wearing? In fact, I was superconscientious about the outfit I selected for this trip. I'm wearing my best-fitting jeans, which make me look skinnier than I am, and a pale-pink blouse that complements my complexion. I've left the top two buttons undone, so he can see some cleavage. I'm also wearing a tweed blazer I bought especially for this trip.

Ethan seems to be able to read my mind. To my relief, he adds, "I'm referring to your behavior, of course, not your looks."

I remain silent and look out the window as happiness surges through me. Ethan likes me. He wants to get to know me better. How great is that?

We drive through one picturesque village after another. Many of them have a pond in the middle of town where ducks swim around peacefully. Almost every town also has an old church that presides solemnly over its residents. The houses are made of wood or covered in stucco. Some are pink, like the Seafields' house. Others have blue-gray or bright-yellow façades.

Just when I think I've had enough excitement before breakfast, Ethan says, "Would you like to take a break in Saffron Walden? We could grab a bite to eat at a pub."

Of course I would! I've been squinting at the clock on the dashboard the whole trip, aching inside because the time is going by so quickly. I would love nothing better than to travel with Ethan around England for all eternity.

He stops in front of a beautiful Tudor building with a white plaster façade framed with black timber. There are bay windows of crown glass on either side of the entrance. A sign over the door says "The Coach and Horses." It's an old-fashioned inn, probably one where people rested their horses on a long journey. I feel like I'm in a movie. Here I am in England, in one of the sweetest little towns in the region. I'm about to enter a fantastically picturesque restaurant, and a stunningly handsome man is opening my car door. Ethan reaches out his hand to help me out.

I stand up, breathlessly happy. "It's so beautiful here!"

Ethan looks at me in amusement. "You're doing it again."

"What?" I ask.

"Enjoying life. When you say, 'It's so beautiful here,' you really mean it, don't you?"

"Of course," I say.

"That's kind of unusual," Ethan says, "but also quite pleasant."

"I'm relieved to hear that," I say. "I had the impression that you thought my being 'unusual' was a negative trait."

Ethan shakes his head and walks into the pub. Hurray, Ethan won't hate me if I'm unusual!

The host takes us to a table near the bay window. There are a few other guests, but the restaurant isn't very full yet. I order a baked potato with cheese, and Ethan steak and kidney pie.

"It's good that I get to eat before entering the wilds of Cambridge," I joke.

Ethan looks at me questioningly. "Wilds?"

I tell him how worried Abby is that I'll starve to death within the week.

Ethan frowns. "That doesn't sound good. How did you end up with this family?"

"Through Mr. Henley. He arranged everything in advance."

"Yes, but surely he thought of it as a temporary measure," Ethan says, "until you find something else."

"Maybe, but I feel comfortable there now. They've practically adopted me, and it's touching how they take care of me."

Ethan looks very serious. "I disagree. These people interfere in your life way too much. You're their tenant. Nothing more. It shouldn't matter who you travel with or what you do in your spare time. Personally, I wouldn't tolerate it."

I consider this. There might be something to it. They really do treat me too much like a child.

Ethan leans forward and looks at me sternly. "If I can give you some advice, Lea, you should find other accommodations as soon as possible. You're not doing yourself any favors by living with this old couple. They're forcing you into the role of a little girl, which isn't good for you."

On the one hand, I am flattered that Ethan seems to be concerned about me. On the other hand, the Lanes have grown on me, despite all their quirks. They're even trying to quit smoking. I suggested that instead of buying cigarettes, they should put that money into a piggy bank and, after two months, buy something they couldn't otherwise afford. This proposal seemed to be a big hit with them—not surprising, considering that they always seem to be strapped for cash. When Glen complained that he lacked a satisfactory substitute, I bought him licorice toffees. Every evening I put them in a little bowl on his side table. Could I really give these two notice? I'd rather not. I know that I would miss them, and they'd miss me.

It's too complicated to explain, so I just say, "Yes, maybe you're right. Let's see how it goes."

When our food arrives, we grab our cutlery and dig in. Ethan looks up from his plate and studies me thoughtfully. *I hope he likes what he sees*, I suddenly think.

"You listened to me," he says with satisfaction.

I don't understand. "Excuse me?"

"I mean, your hair."

"Oh yeah." I laugh in relief. "Now I get it. You noticed I went to the hairdresser."

"You can laugh about it if you want," Ethan says, "but I have an eye for such things. I think it's horrible when women don't properly care for their long hair. It looks a thousand times better and healthier."

I appreciate the compliment and say, "Well, then, the visit to the hairdresser was definitely worthwhile." It occurs to me that it was worthwhile for another reason, too. "Thanks to your advice, I was able to get accommodations in Cambridge," I add.

"Oh, really?"

I tell him about Mandy and her sister, who I'll be staying with.

Ethan furrows his brow. "Well, I hope you won't be disappointed. It sounds kind of strange to me."

"Oh," I say, "it's only for a week. If I don't like it, I'll just go back right away."

But Ethan isn't satisfied. "You've simply got to plan things out better, Lea. Life is too short, and lack of planning could spoil everything. Unsuitable accommodations could end up ruining the whole week for you."

I shrug. "Perhaps. But things like that aren't very important to me. In the worst-case scenario, by the end of the week I'll know what not to do and I will have learned something."

"Yes, you'll know that you shouldn't plan things last minute," Ethan says. "I've never heard of someone arranging accommodations through their hairdresser. No way is that going to work."

I tilt my head to the side and say, "It's sweet that you worry so much about me. You're almost as bad as Abby and Glen."

"I'm not as worried about the actual accommodations, Lea, but I am worried about you. The way you waltz through life is worrisome. One of these days, you're going to fall flat on your face."

I shrug again. "And if that happens, it won't matter. I'll just pick myself back up and keep on dancing."

Ethan looks at me very thoughtfully for a moment, as if he is trying to solve a very tough puzzle. Then he shakes his head and focuses on his meal again.

We talk about this and that, even about things that have nothing to do with school or our colleagues. I laugh as I relate several funny anecdotes. The guests at the other tables seem to be looking at us in amusement. Ethan acts rather restrained, only occasionally smiling a little. I try my best to make his wonderful dimples appear but fail. Oh well. That's to be expected from my dream guy. I like his somber mood, and I particularly adore a hint of brooding mystery about him. In my favorite novel, *Pride and Prejudice*, the hero, Mr. Darcy, is just like that, and so is Mr. Rochester in *Jane Eyre*. His deep, dark secrets make him seem unapproachable and mysterious. This could work out wonderfully. I could be the funny, bright, and cheery one, and gradually I would soften his scowl. He would compensate for my frivolousness and liveliness with his seriousness. We would be the perfect couple. I hope he thinks so, too.

I have to pull myself together! I'm dreaming about something that will probably never happen. I don't have the slightest idea if Ethan is thinking along those same lines at all. So many women are crazy about him—and probably have a better chance with him than I do. It doesn't make sense that he would choose me. *Remember, Lea,* my inner voice says, *the fact that you two are riding together is completely accidental. He didn't invite you. After this car trip, it's all over.* At the same time, a small glimmer of hope begins to grow inside me. Didn't Ethan tell me that he finds me extremely attractive and that I'm different from the women he's met? Maybe this is the beginning of something new and wonderful.

Back inside the car again, we continue our ride to Cambridge. Ethan is taciturn, and I feel nervous. Maybe I make him nervous, too. How great would that be?

At some point, he clears his throat and says, "You shouldn't do that."

I'm startled. What does he mean? Can he read my thoughts? Has he guessed what hopeful, dreamy ideas are whirling through my head? Carefully, I ask, "What?"

He nods in the direction of my hands. "Bite your fingernails. You're tearing your cuticles. It's ugly and self-destructive."

This warms my heart. He's so lovingly concerned about me! A man would only say something like that to a woman who is important to him. The remark was so stern and intimate, as if we've known each other for a long time. I like the quiet authority that he radiates. I stop biting my nails and sit on my hands.

We soon reach the outskirts of Cambridge. In the distance, the battlements and towers of the old town rise above the university buildings.

Ethan asks me for the address, and I read aloud, "Somerset Close."

"Oh my goodness," he says, "that's way too far out of town. It's at least a twenty-minute bus ride downtown."

Oh dear. I didn't think Emmy's shared apartment would be so inconveniently located. If this were a cheesy romance novel, Ethan would say, "You know what? You don't have to stay there. Come and stay in my room with me." Wow! Would I really want to, though? Maybe . . . It would be a bit bold of him. I don't want to be a one-night stand. I want to be his wife, but he must first court me for a considerable length of time. Okay, maybe not *so* long, but at least a little while.

When I don't say anything, he types the address into his GPS device and says, "Okay, I'll just drop you off at your door."

We drive north from the city, but it's not quite as far away as Ethan had so gloomily predicted. After about ten minutes, we are driving along residential streets and passing small two-story brick homes, all of which look exactly the same down to the smallest details. We find the correct house number, and Ethan pulls up in front of it. Now my heart really sinks. I have to say thank you and good-bye to him now, but I really want to spend more time with him.

Ethan turns to me and says, "So, what are your plans this week?"

My heart skips a beat. "Well, I'll check out the city. I don't really have any specific plans yet."

He smirks. "It figures. You just waltz through life without a plan."

I smile back. "Yes, that's me. It works pretty well. You should try it sometime."

He scrutinizes me with his mysterious brown eyes. Then he says, "Just in case you have time for a real plan in the middle of your haphazard drifting, I'd like to suggest something."

I'm all ears. Maybe he wants me to meet up with him.

Instead he says, "There's a wonderful little museum in the city. You've never seen anything like it. It's a glorious hodgepodge of the craziest things under the sun. It's located on Castle Street and is called the Cambridge and County Folk Museum. Worth a visit."

Oh, so that's all it is, I think, heart sinking. He just wanted to give me some sightseeing tips. I swallow my disappointment and say, "Oh, that sounds terrific. I'll go there first thing tomorrow morning. Thanks for the tip."

I find the door handle and get out. Ethan also gets out, opens the trunk, and lifts my bag out. My bag and his suitcase were lying next to each other. *So nice and cozy*, I think wistfully. But it's all over now. Ethan accompanies me to the door. He looks at the scruffy garden and the house's simple façade and wrinkles his nose. *When Ethan wrinkles his nose, he makes it look very classy,* I think.

"Well, you've landed in less than genteel quarters," he says, "but you can't expect too much when it's arranged by your hairdresser."

I laugh. "That sounds a bit snooty. I thought it was rather generous of Mandy. Anyway, I'm just a poor student. A luxury hotel would be rather unaffordable."

A worried expression darkens his face. If these shabby accommodations evoke such tender concern from him, it would be worth having even shabbier quarters. "Well, hopefully you won't have to leave tomorrow," he says.

"We'll see," I say. "Let's just see how everything pans out."

"In Lea fashion," he says.

"Exactly."

He turns to go, then something occurs to him. "I just had an idea . . ." he says.

I hold my breath. An idea? Oh, yes, please!

"As a PhD student, my brother is allowed to invite guests to dinner at the Master's Lodge at Trinity College. Does that sound interesting to you?"

I'm too stunned to speak, so I just nod. A dinner at Trinity's venerable dining hall! That would be the most amazing thing that could happen to me here.

"Well, then, you can come with me," Ethan says quite casually, as if we were only going to see a movie. Not that going to the movies with Ethan wouldn't have also been fabulous, but this . . . !

I beam at him. "I think that's unbelievably nice of you. When should I be ready?"

"I'll pick you up here tomorrow night around six. I believe one of his tutors will be serving sherry at his apartment. We're invited, too, of course."

Oh man! I can't believe my luck. As his car rolls away toward the city center, I practically float to Emmy's door. There is no doorbell, only a rustic door knocker. I knock a couple of times before a short guy with tangled hair opens the door. He looks as though he just got out of bed, although it's already afternoon.

He yawns right in my face, then says, "Hello. What can I do for you?"

"I'm Lea König. Emmy's sister, Mandy, made arrangements for me to stay here for a few days."

He scratches his uncombed head and looks at me dubiously. "As usual, nobody tells me anything."

I stand there and try to look as friendly as possible.

"Okay," he says, "come on in." He goes back inside and up a staircase. I hesitate. Should I follow him? What now?

He calls over his shoulder, "My name is Bob. Emmy is at work—she's a waitress at a café in the city. I believe Nancy is at the university." He stops on the upper landing, pushes open a door, and smirks. "Your suite is located here."

Very funny. The room is ghastly, worse than anything Abby could have dreamed up. Thank God Ethan can't see this. This isn't a storage room; it's a broom closet. It contains a strange contraption that looks like a prison bed with a suspiciously thin, sagging, gray mattress. There's no room to walk. The whole place is filled with junk: an ironing board, overflowing moving boxes, boots and shoes, cleaning supplies, a pair of skis, a broken chair, and on and on. It smells moldy, and a thick layer of dust covers everything.

"This is nice," I say ironically, but no one hears me. Bob has disappeared, probably back to his bed.

There is a tiny window high up on the wall. *Well, at least I have that*, I think. I don't have any other choice, so, sighing, I open my overnight bag and find the bedding. With Abby's fresh-smelling sheets, I manage to prepare the cot so it's not quite as crappy. The door to the bathroom is open, so I peek inside. I want to check out the bathroom now so I don't end up rousing the irresistible Bob from his beauty sleep later.

The bathroom looks as though a tornado hit it. Over the course of all my shared housing as a student, I've never seen anything like it. Every square inch of space is crammed full of plastic bottles, old rusty razors, and empty and half-empty cosmetic bottles and jars. It looks as though it hasn't been cleaned for at least half a century—including the sink and the bathtub. If it weren't for the fact that I so desperately need to use the toilet, I would refuse to go in.

I return to the storage room, sit down on the bed, and mope. What am I doing here? How should I spend the rest of the day? Resolutely, I get up, grab my coat and purse, and leave the house.

I decide to take the bus into Cambridge. I can go out to dinner and take a little stroll around the city. I saw the bus stop on the ride in. It's located on the main road, which branches off from Somerset Close. Surely, the next bus will come sooner or later.

I stand and wait. And wait. And wait. Finally a little old lady with a cane waddles by.

"Excuse me," I ask. "When does the next bus to Cambridge come?"

"Never, from where you're standing, love," she says, grinning as she continues on her way.

I trot up behind her and tug on her sleeve. "What do you mean?"

She smiles even wider. Her mouth is missing some teeth. "You're on the wrong side of the street. Go to the bus stop on the other side."

Darn it! Now I understand. I forgot that the bus would be driving on the left side of the street. How stupid can I be? I cross the street and wait barely two minutes before a bus comes and I hop on.

The bus zips toward downtown. The towers and battlements that Cambridge is so famous for loom larger. The autumn sun falls at an oblique angle and lights up the buildings in red and gold. The contrast between the long shadows and the rays of sunlight beaming down from the clear sky is beautiful. The bus crosses the River Cam, where pedestrians stroll along its bank. I decide to get off at a circular courtyard that I assume connects several old, beautiful buildings.

I end up in the historic center of Cambridge, where the beautiful colleges are located. Regular traffic isn't allowed in this part of town, but hundreds of bikes whiz around everywhere. I have to remember to pay attention and not look in the wrong direction when I cross the road. An impressive building looms ahead of me. It looks like something out of a movie set. Scrolls and pillars decorate the stone façade where the turrets and parapets meet.

A girl is leafing through a travel brochure, so I ask her, "Which building is this?"

She nods amiably and explains, "This is Trinity College. King's College is farther down the road. You must visit the chapel there, it's quite stunning. If you look carefully, most of the colleges have signs telling you which building is what."

I thank her and look around. There are tons of people here, mostly tourists. I feel thankful for my free accommodations. With these crowds, an overnight stay in Cambridge must be exorbitant. Students in their final semester are wearing black flowing capes and black caps. I didn't realize they actually wear their graduation gowns on the street. They look so quaint. I take photos like crazy.

I approach Trinity College and walk under an arched gateway into the courtyard. There's a small, flawlessly green lawn you can only find in England or at a monastery. It looks like a green velvet carpet intersected by wide stone walkways, and old, stately buildings border each side of the square. The windows are made of crown glass. What lies beyond them? I wonder if Ethan's brother lives in one of these buildings.

My heart beats quickly at the thought of eating dinner in the Gothic dining hall tomorrow. I'm sure the girl who told me about the chapel would die to have the opportunity. It's outrageously exciting. Then it hits me like a lightning bolt out of the blue. I brought absolutely nothing in my modest travel bag that I could wear to such an event. Heavens! What does a person wear to the Master's Lodge, anyway? I'm completely stumped. I bet the tourist girl would be at her wit's end, too. I could just go in my good jeans and pink blouse, but I would surely be underdressed. I wish I had Ethan's cell phone number so I could ask him.

I turn around and walk away from the colleges. Being here doesn't help me at all with my urgent wardrobe issue. I cross the road to where dozens of colorful shops are located. Since they all look so expensive, my heart sinks. I doubt I'll be able to afford anything they have to offer.

A sign for Laura Ashley catches my eye. Laura Ashley dresses are so distinctly British; surely I'll be able to find something there that befits the occasion—if I can afford it. I push the door open, and a saleswoman promptly greets me. "Can I help you?"

Normally I hate when salespeople impose themselves on me, but today I'm thrilled to have her help. "I've been invited to the Master's Lodge at Trinity College, and I have no idea what I should wear," I tell her.

"I think you can wear something casual. It hasn't been a formal venue for a long time. You could even wear jeans," she suggests.

I look at her dubiously. "Even if you want to impress your companion?"

She smiles. "Well, in that case I would advise that you wear something a little more sophisticated." She leads me to a rack with a wide variety of dresses. She pulls out one after the other, holding each up for my consideration. I steal a glance at the price tag. Uh-oh. This is definitely not the store for me. I can't afford this place at all.

I clear my throat and say, "And if a person would like to impress her companion, but unfortunately doesn't have much money?"

I would have bet that she'd shrug and show me the door, but she laughs heartily and puts her arm around my shoulder. "Come with me," she says and leads me to the back of the store where folded items are neatly stacked together on a shelf.

"These pieces were returned because they have tiny imperfections. I think some of them might fit you, though. Why don't you try them on?" She points to the fitting room.

I try on a very dignified-looking dress. It's slate gray and falls just below the knee, and has slim three-quarter-length sleeves and a large floral print. The hem has a slight defect in it. I step out, and the saleslady clasps her hands together and beams. "It looks perfect! Just between us, it looks a lot better on you than it did on the lady who originally bought it, especially with your strawberry-blonde hair. Wonderful!"

She conjures up a pair of ballerina flats similar to the color of the dress. "Try these on for size!" She guessed my size right off the bat—the shoes are a perfect fit. Though the dress is affordable, the shoes, unfortunately, are not. I remove them, sighing and sadly shaking my head. My fairy godmother mourns with me when I say that I can only afford the dress, but she gives me some advice. "You can definitely buy similar shoes at one of the larger department stores in the newer part of the city."

I spend at least an hour finding similar shoes as well as matching gray tights. Ravenous, I look for a quick snack and end up at McDonald's. At least I have enough money for that. Now what? I went shopping instead of exploring the beautiful old town. It will be dark and uncomfortably cold soon. It's time to head back to my room. Tomorrow I'll do what I missed out on today.

Then the church bells begin to ring. I love English church bells—they're not the boring, booming tones like back home. Instead, they play beautiful, rippling musical scales. Even the village church in Gatingstone has an impressive repertoire of sounds. I follow the peal of the bells. They are coming from King's College. People rush toward the chapel, which is more like a huge church. It's a spectacular Gothic marvel, with delicate stone fan vaulting and luminous stained-glass windows. At the entrance is a sign with an invitation to the Evensong. How beautiful! I join the people rushing in and enter the church. It is filling up fast. I'm lucky enough to snag a place relatively close to the altar and wait for whatever comes next.

A choir of only men and boys steps up to the choir stalls, which are backlit with large white candles. They are wearing red and white choral robes and have crisp Tudor-style white collars. Though I have an overwhelming desire to do so, I'm not allowed to whip out my camera. The bells fall silent, and the choir begins to sing. The song is unearthly beautiful—so pure and clear. I've never heard such a wonderful choir in person. I close my eyes so I can fully appreciate the glorious music.

It's inevitable that in moments like these, the memory of what happened to me a few years ago comes back. It's only then that I can freely think about it instead of pushing it back into the far recesses of my mind. I send a silent prayer of thanks to Heaven that the gift of life wasn't taken from me. I love life. Only people who have experienced something similar can understand how precious life becomes after you've almost lost it.

I'm so moved that I get all misty-eyed. My goodness. I had no idea I would get to experience such a moving evening. I'm deeply grateful and happy. Furtively, I dab my tears away with my handkerchief, although I don't need to be embarrassed. I see other guests pulling out their handkerchiefs, too. The heavenly perfection of the choir's voices pierces me right in the heart.

After the service ends, the crowd pushes its way outside. It's nighttime now, and the cold air hits me in the face. There is significantly less traffic on the road. I walk to the same bus stop where I had disembarked earlier in the afternoon. This time, I make sure to wait on the correct side of the road. On the bus schedule, I see that the next bus leaves in an hour. Great. I'm freezing. Impulsively, I firmly grip my shopping bags and hike down the road, passing houses set behind small front yards, their illuminated windows warm and inviting. The autumn wind swirls, and dry leaves rustle.

It takes me forty minutes to arrive at Somerset Close, but I tell myself that the exercise was good for me. Plus I saved the cost of the bus fare and avoided staying in the broom closet as long as possible.

What more could I want? I knock on Emmy's front door, and after a long while, I hear steps approaching. A bearded man with a ponytail peeks out.

"Yes?" he asks, visibly annoyed, as if I'm a door-to-door salesperson or something.

"Hi, I'm Lea. I'm staying here for a few days."

"Okay, then just come in." The guy turns around and disappears again. I don't see him the rest of the evening—or anyone else who lives here, for that matter. An hour later, I'm in bed, which is just as cold, stiff, and uncomfortable as it looks. I curl up with my hot-water bottle and try to ignore the squealing, giggling, and hooting that accompanies the running of the bathwater from the adjoining bathroom. It's probably Emmy and the bearded guy. Later, I hear bedsprings creaking rhythmically and satisfied groans. I fall asleep exhausted.

Chapter 6

When I wake up in the morning, I realize that I'm all alone in the house. It's eerie—the building feels haunted. I imagine I see ghostly figures, then in an instant they're gone. It's kind of fitting that everything is empty and abandoned at the crack of dawn.

The bathroom is even more chaotic than it was yesterday with puddles still drying on the floor from last night's pool party. Wet towels lie on the tiles where they were dropped. I take a little birdbath in the sink, then go down to the kitchen. I see a piece of paper among the dirty dishes on the table. On it someone has scrawled:

Hi Lea. Help yourself. Key is under doormat if u r late. Em

Okay, a little welcome at last. I'm glad they at least know I'm here.

Help yourself . . . Does that include food in the kitchen? My stomach growls. There's a box of Weetabix by the note. I search for a clean cereal bowl—no easy feat—and fill it up. I find a container of instant coffee and some milk. After a meager breakfast, I put on a pair of rubber gloves and attack the dirty dishes. After about half an hour, the kitchen looks halfway decent. If I'm staying here for free, the least I can do is return the favor and help clean up the mess.

I decide to go first to the museum that Ethan told me about yesterday. It sounds like fun, and I want to tell him that I took him up on his advice when I see him tonight. The walk back yesterday wasn't all that bad, so to save on bus fare, I trek into town. Soon I'm walking along the main street, my coat collar up and my purse under my arm. The cars whiz past me. I envy the drivers. It takes me more than half an hour to go where they can be in five minutes. But it doesn't matter; the weather is still nice, if a little nippy. I slide my hands deep into my coat pockets and bury my chin into my coat collar.

A car stops right next to me, and I look in the window. It's probably someone asking for directions. I see a vaguely familiar face beaming cheerfully at me.

"Lea!" he shouts. "Hooray! I've found you at last. Come on, get in the car. I'm taking you into town."

I am completely floored, but I tear open the passenger door and jump in. Jens is sitting behind the wheel of a VW Golf.

"What are you doing here?" I ask, shocked.

"I came to England for semester break. I wanted to see what you've been up to." Jens laughs, obviously overjoyed to see me.

And me? I'm rather irritated. I can't help but think that he's stalking me.

"How in the world did you know where to find me?" I ask suspiciously.

He sees the tension in my face. "Oh, Lea, please don't be angry with me. I didn't want to shock you, but I've been reading your posts on Facebook. You didn't exactly keep your trip to Cambridge a secret."

"Yes, but Cambridge is pretty big. How did you know where I was?"

"We have a mutual Facebook friend, Anja Winter. She gave me your address."

Anja is one of my roommates. I gave her my address so she could forward any mail that arrived for me in Münster.

Jens continues, "First, I went to Gatingstone and checked with your hosts—charming people, by the way—and they gave me your address in Cambridge. It was easy."

Way too easy. I wouldn't have added him as a friend if I'd known this was going to happen. This is a real problem. Jens is a nice guy, and I appreciate that he saved me from starving and freezing to death in Hohensyburg, but his appearance here doesn't quite fit my plans.

I say frostily, "Well, fine, now that you've found me, would you be so kind as to take me into the city so we can go our separate ways?"

His face drops. He looks so pathetic that my annoyance melts away instantly. It is rather flattering that he traveled so far just to see me.

"Are you really going to be so cruel to me?" he asks sheepishly. "Look, I didn't mean anything by it. I thought you might be a teeny-tiny bit happy to see a familiar face from home."

I smile weakly. "You're not all that familiar to me, Jens. I only met you once."

"Well, that's why we should spend more time together," Jens says unflappably, "so we can get to know each other better."

"Oh great!" I shake my head and stare out the windshield.

Jens shifts into gear.

"So, dear Lea," he says, "let me play chauffeur for you. Where do you want to go?"

"For me, into town. For you, back to Germany," I say stubbornly.

Jens's expression is pensive. Then he says, "Okay, but before I leave you again, allow me to grant a single wish of yours, to make amends for pouncing on you like this."

"Ha! A wish? What kind of a wish would that be?"

"I don't know. Think about it, and when we get to town, tell me what it is. A great meal at a restaurant . . . a visit to a nice café . . . no matter what you choose, your wish is my command."

Jens drives in silence, and I look at him out of the corner of my eye. I can see the disappointment in his face. He was so good-natured in Hohensyburg; now he stares straight ahead at the street, his face tense. I sigh inwardly. He's such a nice guy. How do I make it perfectly clear that his efforts are in vain? I'd wanted to avoid hurting him when we were in Münster. That's exactly why I'd been so relieved that I was heading off to England. Damn Facebook!

I wrack my brain. What should I wish for? That he accompany me to the museum? That would be too easy. A nice meal at a restaurant would mean we'd have to sit across from each other, with him gazing deeply into my eyes. That wouldn't be smart. As we drive over the bridge leading into Cambridge, I come up with a genius, albeit slightly devilish, idea. A little revenge wouldn't be so horrible.

"Okay, Jens," I say. "As a matter of fact, something did just occur to me. I would absolutely love to explore Cambridge in a punt. Can you imagine how nice it would be to view the city from the water?"

"What, if you don't mind my asking, is a punt?" Jens asks.

"A flat-bottomed boat which you propel with a pole to glide along the River Cam. I've seen them in lots of photos, and I've always wanted to ride in one of those things. I think you can rent one."

Jens's face brightens. "That's a brilliant idea! Sounds like fun. Okay, Lea, let's do it."

Instantly, he pulls to the side of the road and asks a pedestrian where the nearest punt rental station is. We park on the outskirts of the city and walk into Cambridge. I chuckle a bit when I see how happy Jens is once again. He whistles cheerfully as he strolls along. I happen to know that this so-called punting is an art in itself. He won't be whistling for long; that's for sure.

We find a pier where an entire fleet of punts awaits eager tourists. The owner is just setting up his kiosk and has set out a price list.

"Well, you're here rather early," he says. "Most of the time we don't start until around noon. It's still pretty cool on the water now."

Jens looks at me dubiously. "What do you think, Lea? Should we come back later when it's warmer?"

I can be pretty stubborn. "No, my friend," I say. "You can't chicken out now. You're hoping that you'll be able to worm your way out of this. We're riding on the boat now, as promised."

We select one of the long, flat boats. I get in first and carefully lower myself onto the bench. The owner hands me a cushion to sit on and explains to Jens where he needs to stand in order to navigate the punt. It's somewhat like maneuvering a Venetian gondola. He hands Jens the long pole, wishes us a good trip, and shoves the boat gently into the river.

I'm very comfortable. The sunlight is warming the back of my dark coat, so it's really not that cold. Jens looks rather clueless, his legs wobbly. The boat floats directly across the river over to the dense reeds on the opposite bank. I can see it coming already—he's going to lose his balance and fall into the water. That'll teach him to follow me all the way to England. As the boat rams into the embankment, Jens does a little dance, and I can't help myself—I just have to laugh. It says something about Jens that he doesn't even blink. Instead, deep in concentration, he adroitly begins to push the boat back toward the middle of the river. He has the same look on his face as he did when he was fixing my earrings at the Italian restaurant. He manages to push the boat a bit farther. He's actually surprisingly adept at this. We almost crash into the reeds a couple more times, but Jens eventually gets the hang of it, and it goes much more smoothly. After a while, I relax. I begin to enjoy the boat trip. Who would have thought? Occasionally Jens catches my eye and winks at me. I try to ignore him, but I can't. He exudes a kind of contagious joyfulness.

The river is not much wider than a creek. The water is calm, and small waves lap at the boat's hull. The morning light catches the water, making it sparkle. Occasionally a few quacking ducks swim past us. Some sit on the bank, preening their feathers. We approach the colleges, surrounded by their manicured lawns. They look majestic in the morning mist. Here and there, groups of students wearing their quaint gowns rush to various events. I take some photos, then sit back down and gaze dreamily around me. Weeping willows, their long branches hanging in the water and moving with the gentle current, line the river. Colorful autumn foliage sweeps past us. Occasionally, leaves fall down upon us like confetti.

"So," Jens says suddenly. "Now it's your turn, Lea."

I'm startled out of my daydream. "My turn? What's that supposed to mean?"

"You want me to believe that you have no desire whatsoever to even try it?" he says.

Good point, actually. Why not? It can't be that hard. If Jens can do it, I suppose I can do it, too. Just push against the riverbed with the pole, guide your hands back up the pole, lift it out of the water, and repeat.

"Okay," I say. "Relief crew. Sit down, and I'll take over navigation."

We carefully step around each other. Jens sinks onto the cushion while I get cracking. Oh dear, I didn't think that standing on a floating surface could be so tricky. I do a little dance, similar to the one Jens did earlier. But this time he's the one who's laughing heartily. I furrow my brow and concentrate. I don't want to make a fool of myself, especially after Jens so skillfully mastered the task. We are in the college district now, and people are strolling along the riverbank. I definitely don't want to make a scene.

For a while, everything is coming along quite well. I've found my rhythm, and we glide along smoothly. I give Jens a triumphant look, and he nods approvingly. But then it happens. Somehow my pole snags in the soft, silty riverbed while the boat continues to glide forward. What do I do now? I yank at the stubborn thing and lose my balance. There's no use trying to fight it. I squeal and stumble about in a most undignified way. With lightning speed, Jens jumps to his feet to rescue me. I reel straight into his arms, which he wraps around me firmly. We fall onto the bench at the same time—luckily not into the water.

The whole situation was so precarious I giggle in relief. Jens laughs along, his arms still wrapped tightly around me—a bit too tightly. I'm not so crazy about that. *Going out to eat would have been harmless in comparison*, I think. I delicately remove myself from his embrace and look around. Crap. What I feared has actually happened. We are directly under one of the picturesque bridges spanning the river. Leaning over the railing is a whole row of smiling faces. Apparently, we've entertained everyone brilliantly. Someone turns away, and I see dark curls and broad shoulders disappear down the bridge. *Crap! Crap!* I think again. *Was that Ethan? He apparently saw the whole show. What does he think of me now?* I smooth out my clothes and sit back down on the bench.

"Your turn to operate the pole," I say sternly. "I think it would be best if we turn around and go straight back to the dock. I've had enough of this adventure."

He seems a bit downcast but does what I tell him to do. "It's a shame," he says. "I was just starting to have fun."

"Yes, I can imagine," I say grumpily, thinking more about his embrace than about the actual boating.

He smiles guiltily. "I really enjoyed that. Don't you want to lose your balance again?"

"Absolutely not," I say curtly and angrily look away.

After a while I look over at him again. I have to be careful that I don't lose my resolve. Jens looks heartbreakingly sad. Oh my goodness, he really does seem to like me a lot. I sigh. The whole thing strikes me like something out of Shakespeare's *A Midsummer Night's Dream*—unrequited love, which leads to many trials and tribulations and a lot of grief. *On the other hand*, I think, *I'm glad it's not that way for me.* After all, I'm on my way to falling for a man who also loves me. All signs point to my relationship with Ethan working out—he so much as said so. With great anticipation, I think about the beautiful meal I'll have with Ethan this evening at Trinity College, and I'm instantly in a good mood again.

Jens notices and says, "I like you so much better like this, Lea. You're back to your old self. I love it when you look happy—like in Hohensyburg. It doesn't seem like you to let a little mishap throw you off course."

It's true. I think about how we tumbled around the boat, and the situation suddenly strikes me as really quite amusing. I start to giggle, and soon we are both laughing heartily.

"At least we didn't fall into the water," I say. "How embarrassing that would have been!"

Jens nods happily, then says, "Actually, I did another good deed for you and rescued you from an unexpected bath."

"That's what you think!" I cry. "I'll show you." I lean back and forth, rocking the boat, but Jens has amazing balance. Although he can't stop laughing, he doesn't fall into the water.

We cheerfully agree to return the boat to the rental kiosk. I tell Jens, "Thank you. It was really nice of you to take me on a boat ride." We're both rather confused as to what we should do next. I feel bad just saying good-bye, although that's exactly what I had in mind.

"Can you spend the rest of the day with me?" Jens asks. "I promise I'll leave Cambridge and never bother you again. But it seems kind of stupid for us to sightsee alone, doesn't it?"

Of course, he's right. I suggest that we go to the museum Ethan told me about. As it turns out, it is well worth seeing. Jens and I spend almost two hours admiring the many exhibits and learning about the city and the surrounding area's history.

"This is so exciting," I say. "So much that I've read about in English literature makes sense to me now thanks to this museum. For example, I read a book by Thomas Hardy, who lived at the end of the nineteenth century. He was concerned that industrialization threatened the customs and traditions of the era. He wrote his book to preserve those traditions, which I now understand."

Jens looks at me. "You're very smart, Lea," he says. "I really admire how you immerse yourself in your work. Unfortunately, I'm not well acquainted with English literature. My English was never good enough."

It's good to hear his sincere admiration. I've sometimes wondered if my love of English literature isn't somewhat antiquated. Jens's response makes it feel like a noble pursuit again. I point out pictures hanging on the walls and objects in the display cases that are mentioned in some old books I've read. He listens attentively and seems to be really interested. If he's not, he's doing a very convincing job of pretending to be.

On the way from the museum back to the center of town, we come across a small church on a hill.

"Look, what kind of odd, little church is that?" I say. "Come on. Let's check if it's open."

The tiny church has enough room for only three pews. A sign on the wall explains that the church, dedicated to St. Peter, is a historic site and no longer used for church services. It also says that in exchange for a small donation, visitors can tug on the bell rope and make a wish.

"Oh, that's great, we've got to do that," I say immediately. I dig around for a coin, but Jens beats me to it.

"One ring is on me," he says.

I toss the coin into the offertory box and go to the church bell's small bay area. I hold the rope tightly in both hands, close my eyes, and pull, silently making a wish: *Dear God, please help me find the right man to spend my life with. Someone who can make me happy, and who'll be happy with me, too.* The sound of the bell is louder and deeper than I would have expected. It's beautiful.

Jens asks, "Well? What did you wish for?"

"I can't tell you, otherwise the wish won't come true," I say.

Jens then wishes for something and pulls the rope. As he rings the bell, he looks quite thoughtful, almost overly serious. I don't ask what he wished for, because I can already imagine what it is. Too bad for him. *Our desires simply clash*, I think stubbornly.

We step back outside and blink in the sunlight. "Shouldn't we grab a bite to eat?" Jens asks.

Uh-oh. This means we'll have to sit at a table together, looking into each other's eyes. But my stomach growls, so I nod and say, "Yes." We discover a cute café in the city center where we can get a light lunch. We sit at a round table covered with a white tablecloth, and through the crown glass, we watch pedestrians hurry down the street. Jens and I are too busy people watching to gaze into one another's eyes. We both enjoy thinking about what people are doing and imagining where they're going. We also participate in a little good-natured teasing about our little misadventure on the punt. We both eat a bowl of soup, then have a cup of coffee. We feel so comfortable we end up ordering another cup of coffee and, later, scones with strawberry jam and clotted cream.

Finally I look at my watch and say, "I need to head home soon."

Jens asks sadly, "Really? Why? What do you have to do there?"

To tell you the truth, nothing. There's still plenty of time before my date this evening. I'm not really that crazy about going back to that messy, little broom closet, anyway. So I say, "Let's take a little stroll through the town."

We pay—that is, Jens pays. It's quite touching how he's making every effort to ensure that his presence isn't a burden to me. After we leave the restaurant, we stroll past the colleges along the River Cam and admire their magnificent façades. They are especially exquisite with their images reflected in the water. Narrow medieval streets run between the buildings, and the sound of students from the music college practicing their instruments spills out from the open windows. I hear the sparkling notes of a harp and the cool tones of a clarinet. We wander through the courtyards of the colleges, cross a bridge, and find ourselves back on the banks of the River Cam. We walk along the river and enjoy the views of the old buildings from a distance. Finally, we reach Jens's car.

"We could round off the day with a nice dinner," Jens says hopefully.

"No, I can't," I say. "I have a date tonight, Jens."

"A date?" Jens looks disappointed. "Oh." Then he says coolly, "Well, I don't want to get in your way. It seems I'm a bit superfluous here, but I'll drive you back to your place, anyway."

It would have shown more character on my behalf to refuse his kind offer of a ride, but I have no burning desire to walk forty minutes on a concrete sidewalk back to Somerset Close. So I get in the car.

As Jens starts the engine, I say softly, "Please, Jens, don't be mad. Your visit caught me off guard. How could you expect me to jump up and down with excitement? Today was a lot of fun, but nothing more. To suggest anything else would be dishonest."

Jens is morose and silent all the way back to the house, and I decide to let the matter rest. I know that I've hurt him, but what else could I do? He's not the first admirer I've had to reject. He pulls up to the curb in front of my place, and I glance at him. He really is a nice guy. I would like to be friends with him. On impulse, I say, "We don't have to say good-bye forever. Maybe we can get together again as friends."

Jens turns away and says sharply, "No, Lea, I'd rather not. I admit, I fell for you. But it means nothing if it's one-sided. Let's just say good-bye. I hope you find someone who you feel as strongly about as I do for you." He hastily rubs his hand over his face. I climb out of the car, and he pulls the passenger door closed from the inside, restarts the engine, and drives away.

I watch his car as it disappears down the road and think about what he said. What poor Jens doesn't know, but might suspect, is that I've already found the man I desire the way Jens desires me. My heart skips a beat as a thought occurs to me: I'm almost sure that the man of my dreams feels the same way about me.

I decide to suppress all thoughts of Jens and his broken heart. I don't want to spoil my evening with Ethan. I glance at my watch—he's coming in about an hour to pick me up, and I want to look stunning. I still have a lot to do.

At six sharp, I'm standing in the entrance hall of the house, waiting for Ethan. The front door opens, and I meet a dark-haired version of my hairdresser.

"Oh, hi, you must be Lea," she says, greeting me amiably. "Wow, you look very chic. Are you going somewhere this evening?"

"Hi, Emmy, thank you so much for letting me stay here," I say.

"It's okay," she says, waving me off. "We always have guests in that little chamber. I'm sorry to have to say this, though, but you'll have to leave the day after tomorrow."

I look at her incredulously. What! Why? Did I do something wrong?

Emmy sees my confused expression and quickly explains, "All my roommates are gone, and I'm going to stay with my boyfriend's family. I'm sorry, but I can't let you stay without anyone here."

Great! This is definitely a dreadful turn of events. I've been looking forward to a beautiful week in Cambridge, and now I'm getting kicked out. I wrack my brain for a solution, but I'm interrupted by a car pulling up out front. Emmy curiously pokes her head outside and says, "*Ooo!* What a fabulous car and an even more fabulous man! I won't stop you, love."

Love? At the moment I'm not feeling any love at all.

"Have a nice evening," Emmy says, then disappears upstairs.

I hurry outside, pulling the door closed behind me. Ethan is waiting in the car. I get in quickly and buckle myself up.

"Hello, Ethan," I say.

"Hello." He looks me over carefully from the top of my carefully coiffed head—I pinned my hair up—to my new ballerina flats. Of course, he can't see the dress because I have my coat on. His gaze gives me goose bumps. Ethan is wearing black jeans, a white T-shirt, and a dark blazer. His casually elegant look is quite attractive, and my clothes go very nicely with his style.

Ethan is silent and acting mysterious again, so as we drive I ask, "Have you had a nice day? Did you have a nice time with your brother?"

He responds, "I'd rather hear about your day."

"Cambridge is a beautiful city—and I've seen a whole lot of them," I say. "I even visited the museum you told me about. It was really worth it. Thanks for the tip."

Now surely Ethan will tell me something about his day, but instead he's silent. After a while, he says, "You're doing it again."

"What?"

"You're biting your fingernails."

Damn, he's right. I immediately stop. "Sorry," I say. "I'm a little nervous. I've never dined at a fancy dining hall before."

A slight smile flits across his face. "It's nothing special. Actually, it's not unlike any other university dining hall, except the people wear funny clothes and behave strangely."

"What do you mean by 'strangely'?" I ask.

"Oh, let's just let it be a surprise." Ethan falls silent again.

We park outside the old city center, get out, and walk to Trinity College. I'd like to hold Ethan's arm so everybody knows that we're together, but he doesn't seem to share the same sentiments. I shove my hands into my coat pockets, which feels good. It's very cold. Maybe I should have worn jeans.

We enter the college, and I follow Ethan upstairs. I look at his strong back and broad shoulders and think for the thousandth time tonight what a lucky girl I am to be on a date with this beautiful man. Ethan knocks on a door, and we find ourselves in a very English-looking living room. A warm, lively fire burns in a stone fireplace. Ethan helps me out of my coat, and I turn around. Only men are present, some wearing long black robes. They're facing the fireplace and holding sherry glasses. Someone offers me a full glass from a tray, and I gratefully accept it. Another man shakes my hand and tells me he's the host. He's older and has graying temples and bushy eyebrows. Ethan introduces him as Mr. Binsby, his brother's tutor. His brother's also here and resembles Ethan, but he's smaller and slight. He has the same curly hair, but it's cut shorter. He's wearing a dark gown.

"My brother Theo," Ethan introduces him.

"Hi, Lea," Theo says. "Nice to meet you. My brother told me you wanted to look beyond the walls of our college. I hope you like it."

I look around enthusiastically and say, "Oh, yes, it's wonderful. I'm so happy to have been invited." Secretly, I feel a little pang. As far as Theo knows, this is just a little sojourn for a curious student from abroad; it's definitely not a date. I sip my sherry to hide my disappointment. It's delicious and warms me up quite pleasantly.

Theo looks at me with amusement and says, "I think I've seen you before."

"Oh, really?" I say. "I can't imagine where. I've only been in Cambridge for two days."

"This morning," Theo says mischievously. Suddenly, I get a sinking feeling. "From the bridge behind the college. You and your companion had quite the tussle."

Oh dear! My face turns crimson. I had hoped and prayed that those weren't Ethan's dark curls I had seen on the bridge. That the episode has come up at all is absolutely the worst-case scenario. Mortified, I have no idea what to say. Theo good-naturedly describes what he saw from the bridge to everybody within earshot, including his brother. All the gentlemen enjoy the story immensely, which is hardly surprising since I would, too, if I were in their place. I curse myself for suggesting the stupid boat ride. Jens would be so delighted to know that my little revenge plot backfired. Only as the general merriment fades, and someone thankfully raises another topic of conversation, do I dare look at Ethan. He looks very pensive and definitely not amused.

Damn! That's the end of us, I think, my heart sinking. He must think I have a secret boyfriend or that I'm a silly little floozy who will take up with any guy. I feel miserable. I'd like to say good-bye right now and go straight home—maybe even on foot—and mope. I'm desperate for Ethan to think well of me.

It's time to head to the dining hall. We empty our sherry glasses and put them on a low side table in front of the tufted Chesterfield sofa. Ethan wordlessly brings me my coat, and I drape it over my arm. We're not going outside; we return downstairs and go through a large engraved door. I wish Ethan would whisper something comforting, like, *Don't let it bother you, Lea, we've all been through an embarrassing situation on a punt,* but I wish in vain. He seems quite irritated. *Maybe, just maybe,* I think in my usual optimistic way, *that's a good sign.* He's so in love with me that he's jealous. That wouldn't be so bad, would it? But what will happen next remains to be seen.

The dining hall is beautiful. Oil paintings, all portraits, hang on the dark-paneled walls. Large votive candleholders, emitting a soft, elegant light, are set out on the long, dark tables. The tables match the simple long benches. At the front of the dining hall is a raised platform where the college's professors and selected lecturers sit on ornate chairs at a separate table. I later learn that this table is called, appropriately, the "high table." The original of Hans Holbein's famous painting of Henry VIII hangs above it. I feel as though I am Harry Potter in the Hogwarts dining hall—except the food doesn't fly through the air.

I take a seat next to Ethan. We're almost as close as we were that time at the pub in Gatingstone. "I wonder what they're serving," I whisper to him.

He pushes a piece of thick paper that was already on the table toward me:

>Spicy Red Lentil Soup
>Cod with Basil
>New Potatoes
>*Petit Pois à la Francaise*
>Sun-Dried Tomatoes & Courgette in a Walnut Crust
>Swiss Roll with Jam and Custard

I'm impressed. It sounds delicious. But before the meal can begin, everyone must stand. The rector solemnly welcomes us, raises his wineglass, and makes a toast to Her Majesty the Queen. Everyone courteously murmurs "The Queen" and nods to each other; then the delicious food is served.

I manage to forget my earlier awkwardness. I'm excited to be here in this incredible place, sitting next to my dream man and eating this wonderful food. Conversation is lively and witty—not surprising, as all the people here are quite learned. They talk about science, politics, and art. I hold back but occasionally involve myself in a conversation with someone, trying to respond as skillfully as I can. Ethan barely speaks, but it doesn't bother me. I've already figured out that he's the strong, silent type. It's quite charming. I enjoy his calm presence at my side. He's so steady and dependable. When he does speak, it's always an interesting contribution, and I feel proud. My dream man is so smart.

As the meal comes to an end, Theo asks me, "What do you think? Do you want to go to the kitchen?"

I have no idea how to respond to this question. Is it like at a youth hostel, where guests help clean up? "What, to wash the dishes?" I ask.

I've hardly said the words when I realize how stupid I sound. Everyone is stunned, then starts laughing. Even Ethan laughs along, and I can see his dimples, which I love. I would say something stupid again just to see them.

Theo shakes his head and says, "No, Lea. Tonight's a party night. After dinner, there's a disco in the old college kitchen. We can go dancing, if you'd like."

Dancing is my life, so I say, "I'm totally there!"

Theo exchanges a glance with Ethan, who grimaces. Of course! Ethan doesn't like to dance. But he agrees to go, and we leave the dining hall. We walk down a hallway to a large room with huge, empty fireplaces. Oxen were undoubtedly grilled there in the Middle Ages. There's a disco set up in the corner with a student DJ selecting the music.

I tug Ethan's sleeve, shouting, "Why are there giant tortoises hanging on the wall?"

Ethan responds, "They're the remains of feasts from centuries past. You've surely heard of turtle soup?"

I look at the shells and think about their original inhabitants that were used to make hundreds of gallons of soup. I'd like to talk about this more, but the beat of the music makes further conversation virtually impossible. I try to pull Ethan onto the dance floor, but he makes a dismissive gesture and moves back against the wall, his arms crossed. He casually watches the commotion. Luckily, I quickly find a wiry student who dances really well. We immediately cut a rug, so to speak, on the stone tiles and have a ton of fun. I glance over at Ethan occasionally, who apparently has no desire to dance whatsoever. When one girl after another asks him to dance, he sullenly declines by shaking his head. I'm more than just relieved—I'm maliciously gleeful, to the point that I almost feel guilty. When there's a break in the music, I weave my way over to him. My heart is throbbing like crazy—this time from dancing. Gasping for air, I ask, "Wouldn't you like to dance a little? It's so much fun."

But Ethan resolutely shakes his head. "We can go whenever you've had enough of your little fling."

Aha! So that's the deal. He's only here because of me. He really seems to find the whole thing quite silly. I can't go back onto the dance floor without feeling guilty. What a pity.

I shrug and reply, "Okay, then let's go." I think to myself, *Now what? He's probably just going to take me back to my dreadful accommodations.* I'm back to thinking that I really don't mean anything to him. Clearly I've let my imagination run away with me and am way off the mark.

Then Ethan gives me one of his rare, special smiles and says, "Thank you for being so understanding. That's very sweet of you." He gazes at me openly and tenderly. Now my heart is racing again—this time because of Ethan. He conjures up my coat from somewhere and helps me into it. I can feel his hands on my shoulders like I did at Anne's.

"Are you going? We're leaving, too," Theo says, who is suddenly standing next to us with a petite, sexy blonde on his arm. "This is Kathleen. We want to take a walk. It's getting unbearably hot and stuffy in here."

Kathleen tosses her long hair over her shoulder and looks lovingly at Theo, who's grinning like a Cheshire cat. Apparently, he's made a conquest. I bet these two will end up in the same bed tonight.

The four of us leave the building. The cool autumn night welcomes us. It smells of dry leaves and the nearby river. Muffled music and the laughter of guests emanate from the old kitchen. Rectangles of light shine from the windows and illuminate the courtyard's manicured lawn. Kathleen and Theo walk ahead of us on the footpath toward the River Cam and its grassy riverbank. We stroll behind them. Ethan takes my arm in his, and I can feel how tense he is.

"I hope you're not mad at me," I say uncertainly.

"Why would I be?"

"Because I made a scene on the river today."

"It doesn't bother me," Ethan says nonchalantly. "You can do whatever you like while you're in Cambridge." He sounds so somber that I once again wonder whether he's interested in me at all. We walk silently side by side for a while; then Ethan says abruptly, "I was just wondering who your companion was."

I dare to hope again and say hastily, "Nobody special, just an acquaintance from Germany. We bumped into each other quite by chance here in Cambridge."

"Ah," Ethan says. Nothing more. Am I mistaken, or does his arm relax? I would like to believe so.

We come to a high wrought iron gate at the entrance to the college grounds. Theo and Kathleen are already on the other side. As we approach, Theo mischievously slams the gate. When I reach for the handle, Theo says, "It's no use. The gate is locked. You'll need to climb over." He takes Kathleen by the hand, and they disappear into the darkness, laughing.

I look at Ethan. "Is this true?"

"Yes," he says. "I'll show you how."

He places one foot on a hinge, throws a leg over the gate, and pushes himself effortlessly over it. It barely took a second for a fit physical education teacher, but I stand there uncertainly. Does he really expect me to do that wearing a dress? I suddenly feel determined. Let me have at it! After all, I've always been pretty good at sports.

So I hike my dress up, grab the gate's frame firmly with both hands, and pull myself up, just like Ethan showed me. But as I stand on the hinge and look over at Ethan, I lose my nerve. My goodness, it's a long fall to the ground from here! My knees wobble. I just need to swing my leg over the gate. I hold my breath and . . .

Riiiip! My new dress is not up to the task. I'm stuck up here, and something is torn. Crap! I could cry. But I grit my teeth, swing my other leg over, and let myself drop to the ground—right into Ethan's waiting arms. He presses me against his chest, kisses me on the lips, and releases me. Whoops. Now I'm pretty dizzy. I hold on to the gate tightly and breathe deeply. I look down and see that my dress is torn from the hem almost up to my waist. I'm showing quite a bit of leg.

Ethan seems amused. "Oh, what a pity."

Between the fiery kiss and involuntarily showing off so much skin, I feel bewildered. "That was a brand-new dress," I say plaintively, wrapping my coat around myself. "Now it's ruined."

"Don't take this the wrong way," Ethan says, "but I didn't like it, anyway. You looked like a Catholic schoolgirl in it. And those ballerina flats . . ." He reaches for my hair and unpins my updo, and my hair falls to my shoulders. Normally I wouldn't appreciate being manhandled like this, but when Ethan does it, I feel special and fraught with excitement.

"You should always wear your hair down and have the courage to dress a bit more provocatively," Ethan says. "You're much too pretty for such a frumpy outfit."

I make a mental note of everything he says. If I want to please him, I'll need to dress differently. I vow to adjust to his tastes immediately. If I had known, I would have worn something a little more daring, like the dress I wore to Hohensyburg.

"I'm sorry," I say sheepishly. "I thought something dignified would be more appropriate for the occasion."

"Dignified? What rubbish," he says firmly. "You're young and beautiful. You can flaunt it to the world. Personally, I don't want to be seen with a Catholic schoolgirl. It's not my style at all." He glances appreciatively at my bare leg. "A little sexy is okay." He notices that I'm shivering. "Here I am droning on while you're freezing to death in your torn dress. Come on, let's go back to the car, and I'll take you home."

His sudden thoughtfulness melts my heart. He's not only my dream man but a gentleman, too. Ethan turns and pushes down on the gate's latch. The gate swings open easily.

"Hold on a minute," I say. "The gate was unlocked this whole time?"

"Of course," Ethan says quietly.

I am outraged. "Does this mean that I didn't really have to climb over the gate?"

"It does," Ethan says impassively. He laughs at the bitter expression on my face. "It's an old student prank, Lea. At some point, every student at Cambridge falls for it. Today it was you."

"Well, that's just great," I say angrily. "And here I thought you were a gentleman."

"I'm not—not one bit. I'm even going to kiss you without asking permission," Ethan says. He lifts my chin and kisses me far longer and more passionately than he did just moments ago. His kiss is sweet, and I feel like putty in his hands. I'm no longer cold; instead, I feel warm and fuzzy inside and out.

Ethan ends the kiss abruptly and says brusquely, "Now, true to my word, I'll take you home."

I'm deeply disappointed. I was hoping that this romantic evening would last even longer. Stupid dress! I can't go anywhere looking like this. I have no alternative but to return to my room. We trek through the Trinity College courtyard and walk past the old kitchen's illuminated windows. The music is still blaring. If I had insisted on staying longer to dance, my dress wouldn't be torn and I'd still be having a lot of fun. On the other hand, Ethan wouldn't have kissed me. *It was worth it*, I tell myself in consolation. Even better, he has now wrapped his arm around my waist. It feels wonderful. Silently, we walk to the car. A thousand thoughts swirl around my mind. What does the future hold for us now? Is this just a flirtation or the beginning of something more? What do I mean to Ethan? Do I mean as much to him as he does to me? Of course, I don't dare ask these questions aloud. I'm afraid I might not like the answer. I tell myself I'd rather wait and see how it goes, although I'm dreadfully anxious. I've never been with anyone so perfect before. I don't want to say or do anything that will scare Ethan away. I would never forgive myself.

Ethan unlocks the car and opens the passenger door for me. He waits until I'm in, then sits behind the wheel and takes off. Ethan doesn't say a word. I'm sure he's just as preoccupied as I am. I wonder if similar thoughts are going through his mind. I consider breaking the ice with some small talk, something like, "What a nice evening." I decide against it. *Sometimes silence is more significant than a lot of useless chitchat*, I think. Ethan is the strong, silent type, and, of course, silence is golden. When he speaks, he always has something important to say.

Ethan finally does say something: "You're doing it again."

Crap! I immediately stop chewing my nails and sit on my hands.

He pulls up in front of the house and cuts the motor. Now what? Should I ask him in? Suddenly, I picture us in the horrible broom closet, surrounded by dust. No, that wouldn't do at all. Besides, it wouldn't be appropriate to bring someone else when I'm a guest myself.

"I'm surprised," Ethan says. I'm all ears. What is he talking about? "Since your dress tore, you've been acting very differently than usual."

I don't understand what he's getting at and say warily, "Oh yeah?"

Ethan nods. "When I first met you, you seemed so free and easygoing. If you had a mishap, you just laughed it off. I almost found your lightheartedness a bit irritating."

Now I feel even more uptight than before. What is he saying? Does he dislike something about me? I concentrate intensely on his words and pray that I can tell him what he wants to hear. I have a hunch that this has something to do with my being "unusual."

I ask carefully, "What mishaps are you talking about?"

Ethan grins. "Every time I see you, there are mishaps, Lea. First there was our encounter at the train station, when you couldn't find the door handle. Then there was the episode where the cat ate a crêpe. From what I understand, your scene on the river was particularly entertaining. Oh, and there was the time you lost your umbrella on the bus."

Oh yeah, I remember everything exactly and blush. At the time, I thought it was hilarious when my umbrella flew away. But not so much right now. Strange.

Ethan continues, "The thing with the dress was just a stupid accident. I would have thought you'd take it in stride like you take everything else."

I think it over. Yes, Ethan is right. I'm starting to doubt myself now.

Ethan smiles at my concern. "Don't worry about it too much, Lea. It was just something I noticed, nothing more. In principle, it's okay. To be honest, I actually believe it's better not to laugh about everything. A ripped dress is annoying, especially when it's brand new. I'm sorry, it was my fault. I'd like to make things up to you by buying you a new dress."

I protest vigorously. "That's out of the question! I was the one who was stupid enough to climb over the gate. It was bound to go wrong."

"Did you pack another dress with you?" he asks.

"Why?"

"One of Theo's classmates is celebrating his birthday tomorrow. His parents live in a converted barn near Cambridge. We can go if you'd like."

Hurray! Boy, do I ever! I think, but I say, "I would love to."

"Okay," Ethan says. "I'll pick you up here tomorrow, same time as today."

I screw up my courage and ask, "What about tomorrow morning? Can we do something together in Cambridge?"

"No, that won't work," Ethan says. "Theo and I are going hunting very early in the morning. Actually, that's the main reason I came up here to begin with."

A lightbulb goes off in my mind. The long piece of luggage in the trunk was a rifle! I now hold Ethan in even higher esteem. He's a hunter! How cool is that? It goes perfectly with my image of him—the quiet, elegant English gentleman who passes the time by going hunting. *Mr. Darcy sends his regards*, I think to myself.

Oh well, I'll have to go to Cambridge by myself tomorrow. I hope Ethan's a little sorry that he has a previous engagement, too. It suddenly occurs to me that the day after tomorrow, I'll have to head home. Of course, I could find a bed-and-breakfast, but that would be prohibitively expensive. Should I tell Ethan? Maybe he'll change his plans if he knows I have to leave. No, it would seem a bit undignified, as if I were begging for his attention. I say nothing.

"Well, then, Lea," Ethan says, "see you tomorrow. Have a good night." He leans over and kisses me lightly on the cheek. It could mean anything: we belong together now, you and I, or it was a nice kiss earlier, but as it turns out, there was nothing to it, or I often kiss girls on impulse. I hope it means the first one.

I say good night and walk toward the house. I search for and find the key that Emmy hid for me and step inside the cold, dark house. As soon as I close the front door, I hear Ethan's car zoom off in the distance. How happy I would be sitting next to him in that car! But, no, I lie down on my stiff, cold bed in the dark broom closet, huddling with my hot-water bottle. What did Ethan mean about my lightheartedness and my laughter? Does he like it when I laugh or not? Should I try to be more grown-up and serious to be a better match for him? Are the wives of English gentlemen the type who spend their leisure time hunting? Do they laugh a lot or not so much? How do they act in the English novels I love so much? Does Elizabeth Bennet laugh much? Yes, she does. Hmm.

I stay awake for a long time.

Chapter 7

The next morning I wake up with a headache. The pillow on this dreadful bed is too flat and hurts my neck. I rub my neck, wondering what the day will bring. One thing is clear: I've got no time to lose. I've got to accomplish an important task: I must find a new outfit. Because Ethan doesn't like it, repairing the Laura Ashley dress would make no sense, even if I could find a sewing kit in this chaotic house.

My head pounding, I drag myself into the empty kitchen. Are my roommates asleep, or are they already out? I prepare some breakfast and a cup of instant coffee. As I spoon my Weetabix, I consider whether the state of my finances will allow me to buy a new dress and some new shoes. After those purchases, the chances of extending my stay in Cambridge are nil. Well, it would definitely be a worthwhile investment. I intend to transform myself into a seductive-looking woman. Ethan's jaw will drop when he sees me tonight. What did he say? Fragments of what he said buzz around in my head. Didn't he say something like "No Catholic schoolgirl clothes . . . something sexy . . . not so buttoned-up . . . flats are stupid . . . let your hair down"? I can make myself look sexy. I've done it many times in the past. Ethan should remember that yesterday I dressed conservatively to fit in with the distinguished style of the colleges. *And I did*, I think rebelliously. If I had gone with the look I'm planning for tonight, the venerable professors would have toppled from the high table by the dozens.

I wander into the city on foot, my purse under my arm. The weather is wonderful again, with the type of deep-blue sky only seen in northern Europe in the spring or fall. It spans the distant towers of the medieval city. Bright leaves fall gently, whirling in the quiet morning air and rustling beneath my feet. This must be perfect hunting weather, and I'm happy for Ethan. Although my head still hurts, when I think of Ethan and last night's passionate kisses, I practically float above the sidewalk.

When I reach the city center, I look wistfully at the beautiful old buildings reflected in the River Cam. I'd intended to see more of them and the old town. I hear there's a fantastic collection of ancient Roman sculptures at one of the colleges . . . Well, if my life goes the way I dream it will, this won't be the last time I'm in Cambridge. Then I can make up for lost time. I head, with determination, to the modern part of the city, which is filled with appropriately trendy clothing stores.

After three hours, my feet as well as my head hurt. It took a long time to find what I was looking for: a superchic red dress with a plunging neckline—so low cut that I had to buy a new lacy black bra, and so short that I also had to purchase matching panties. After a long search, I also found a pair of high heels in the same shade of red. Then I treated myself to a break at a salon. Although I didn't need a hair cut, I wanted a deep-conditioning treatment so my hair shimmers and shines.

When I'm finally done with everything, I look for a place to grab a quick bite to eat, my stomach growling mercilessly. The nice café where I went with Jens comes to mind. If I remember correctly, they have a nice selection of magazines lying around, so I could rest there, have something to eat, and read. After all, I'm going to have to stuff my weary feet into some very uncomfortable high heels again tonight.

I'm happy to see that the same table where Jens and I ate yesterday morning is vacant. I sigh as I settle into a chair and stretch out my legs. Heavenly! The waitress recognizes me and greets me amiably, almost as if I were a regular. She brings me a cup of coffee and a large piece of freshly baked quiche, hot from the oven. Like yesterday, I enjoy watching the passersby while I eat. *All that's missing is someone I can chat with*, I think. It was fun sitting here with Jens and talking. I make a mental note to come here with Ethan sometime.

How is Ethan doing on his hunting expedition, anyway? Has he bagged a few prey, maybe a few pheasants or partridges? What does he do with them? Would a good wife need to pluck and grill them? More importantly, has he thought of me this morning? Is he looking forward to tonight? I'm so excited. Now that I have a great outfit, I can hardly wait for the hours to pass until he picks me up for the party.

I order a piece of apple pie and a pot of tea, and after some time, I've perused nearly all the magazines. As the shadows gradually lengthen, I pay, gather my many bags, and start my long walk toward Somerset Close. I plan to take a little beauty nap on the narrow bed, then lock myself up in the bathroom and shower in the tub, crouched under the handheld showerhead while trying my best to avoid the gray ring of dirt that has accumulated over a thousand sloppy baths. If Ethan and I ever get married, I swear I'll install a really nice shower in our house—the same one that everyone in Germany has. I smile as I think of my friend Marga. We shared a dorm room for a semester in Lancaster. After her first shower there, she marched into our common room, wet towel wrapped around her, and said sullenly, "Now I know why the English prefer baths rather than showers!" Never more than a thin trickle—either freezing or scalding hot—came out of that showerhead.

I get dressed in my tiny broom closet. Unfortunately, there's no mirror, so I go downstairs to do my makeup in front of the cloudy hallway mirror. I hear the bathroom door suddenly slam shut. Is it a ghost? I thought I was alone. I just finish applying my makeup when the front door bursts open, practically giving me a stroke. Bob stomps in. When he sees me, he stops and lets out a loud wolf whistle.

"Hello, beautiful, do we know each other?" he says.

"Not really," I say coolly. I collect my makeup and rush upstairs.

From the bottom of the stairs, he calls up to me, "Any chance for a date with you, beautiful stranger?"

I pretend not to hear him and go back to my room. Some men! After spending time in the filth-encrusted and chaotic clutter of the bathroom and the kitchen, I'm 100 percent certain there is no way I could ever be even slightly attracted to a man who lives in this house. On the other hand, his admiration makes me feel good. Although I'm quite satisfied with my reflection, Bob was a welcome guinea pig. Now I know my outfit will have the desired effect.

Right at six, I hear the loud rapping of the house's rustic door knocker. My heart is beating with excitement, and my headache is finally starting to go away thanks to an aspirin.

I hear Emmy's bright English falsetto. Then she calls upstairs, "Lea, your handsome admirer is here!"

I slip into my new high heels. I have deliberately postponed the moment. They are barely more comfortable than the torture-shoes I wore to Hohensyburg. Man, I swore to never wear those shoes again, much less buy a new pair! What a person won't do for love! I grab my purse and tread daintily down the stairs. Ethan looks up. Judging from the admiration reflected in his face, the hard day of shopping was definitely worth it.

"Wow," he says. "You look great, Lea."

Emmy stands next to him, staring at me, her eyes glazed. "I definitely agree. You two are perfect together. Looks like it'll be a great night." When I take my coat from the closet, she adds, "I'm really sorry that we have to throw you out so soon, Lea. I hope it doesn't upset your plans too much."

"It's okay," I say. "Don't worry about it." I slip into my coat and follow Ethan out to the car.

He opens the passenger door for me, then sits down behind the wheel. As he pulls away from the curb, he asks, "Why are they kicking you out? Did you misbehave?"

I laugh. "No, of course not. Everyone is leaving tomorrow, so I can't stay there alone."

Ethan sniffs. "As though anyone who lives there has anything worth taking. So, now what?"

"I'm going back to Gatingstone. What else?"

Ethan silently watches the road. After a while, he says, "What a shame."

"Yes," I say, "I'm sorry, too, but I can't afford a hotel. It's just that simple."

Ethan frowns. "Unfortunately, I don't know what to tell you. I'm staying in Theo's cramped quarters."

"It's fine," I say. "I can use my remaining vacation days to study for my exam. I need to do that, anyway."

Am I mistaken, or does Ethan look disappointed? I change the subject. "How was hunting?"

"Good," Ethan says.

"Did you bag a good haul, or however you say it?"

"It was all right."

I notice that Ethan is quiet again this evening, but it doesn't matter. It's one of the things I find so sexy about him. I gaze out the window and watch the landscape whiz past. Occasionally I look over at Ethan. He looks insanely handsome. Today he's wearing a light-blue polo shirt with jeans. He's loosely knotted a gray cashmere sweater over his shoulders. With one hand he brushes his curly hair away from his face. My eyes are drawn like a magnet to his lips. They look so tempting. For a moment I close my eyes and think about last night's kisses. I hope he kisses me again tonight.

Eventually, Ethan breaks the silence. His eyes roam up my legs, which are very much exposed. "Well, today you've gone in the other direction," he says.

I freeze. What does he mean? Did I do something wrong again? Oh no! I try to act cool, my heart pounding. "Oh yeah? In what way?"

"Now don't get upset," he says calmly, "but the party we're going to is rather informal. You'll be quite conspicuous in your sexy outfit."

I could scream in frustration. Oh great! After I've gone through so much trouble to please Ethan, my outfit is wrong again. On top of it all, I had to burn through a ton of money to buy it. I'm no longer looking forward to the party. My first thought is to ask Ethan to turn around and drive me back, but that would mean giving up my evening with him. I'm so attracted to him I don't want to lose even a moment with him.

"How annoying," I say. "Then I completely misunderstood you. I thought you had something against Catholic schoolgirls."

Something sparkles in Ethan's eyes. "Not against Catholic schoolgirls—just their clothes."

The insinuation gives me goose bumps. I remind myself that he's a womanizer. He looks at me again, and this time his eyes wander over to my cleavage. "As I said, don't get upset, Lea. You're a student from Germany, so everybody there will understand that you're unfamiliar with the usual dress code."

His remark unsettles me even more. *Oh great*, I think. *Everybody will think that I'm a freak who doesn't know what she's doing.* I'd give my right arm to suddenly be in my jeans and a T-shirt. If only I could do something to make my clothes look a little less sexy. I glance down. My plunging neckline is so low you can see the edge of my black lace bra. Great! There's not even enough excess fabric to cover the spot with a discreet safety pin. No wonder—that was exactly the intended effect.

Ethan tries to make me feel better. "But don't be nervous. I think it's really nice that you went to so much trouble. All the men will definitely envy me this evening."

He probably meant to console me, but why don't I feel any better? Instead it sounds more like he's saying, "Oh boy, Lea, you look pretty slutty. Did you have to dress like that? It would have been much better if you'd dressed a little more modestly. The only good thing about your outfit is that everyone is going to think I'm the type of guy who can easily score a date with a sexy girl." These thoughts don't exactly calm me down. My headache is back.

"You're doing it again," Ethan says.

I stare at my fingers. No, definitely not. I haven't been biting my fingernails. "What do you mean?"

"You're so tense. When I first met you, you were so unflappable. You would have laughed this off."

I search my heart. Is this true? Yes, he's right. What's wrong with me?

As if he can read my thoughts, Ethan asks, "What is it? Where's your more relaxed self?"

Yeah, where is it? I can hardly explain it to myself. I just know I'm a different person around Ethan. With him, I'm not the old self-confident Lea. I'm tense. My head throbs.

Ethan smiles at me as he gazes at me from top to bottom. "Do I make you nervous?"

Whew. Yes, it's true. He put his finger on the problem exactly. But I'll be damned if I tell him that. Instead I violently shake my head. "Oh rubbish, not even a little," I say. *Lie, lie, lie!* hammers inside my head. I look angrily out the window. I'm furious with myself. I quickly give Ethan a once-over, and he immediately catches my eye. He winks at me. He's very satisfied with himself—anyone can see that clearly. To make matters worse, he starts to whistle to himself. It makes him seem even more confident and attractive. If he were to pull the car over to the curb and take me on the spot, I would be utterly powerless in his arms. He can do what he wants with me. He is just so amazing.

We drive up a tree-lined driveway and stop in front of a large, square building that vaguely resembles a barn. The rather bold architect designed huge windows for the wooden façade. The light emanating from them is warm and inviting. Ethan parks the car in between the other cars on the mowed lawn. We walk up a gravel path to a glass door framed by the large wooden barn door. From inside, we can hear music playing.

We ring the doorbell, and a slender older woman opens the door. I want to greet her as the lady of the house, then realize her clothing looks suspiciously like a servant's uniform. She takes our coats into the reception area and disappears. Through a door left wide open, I see a bright room with a high ceiling. The party's in full swing there. There is a buffet and many young people dancing. The men are all casually dressed like Ethan, but some of the girls are almost as dressed up as I am. Theo rushes up to us. Beside him is a slender, sophisticated-looking guy with a very narrow, straight nose. Theo introduces him as James, the birthday boy.

James pats Ethan amicably on his shoulder, and Ethan presents him with a bottle of champagne. Then James turns to me.

"Lea! I guess you're Ethan's latest conquest. I'm so glad he brought you; his women get more and more beautiful each time." James gazes at me appreciatively. "At some point, there will be a woman so beautiful, it will be impossible to top her. Then that will be the end of your running around, Ethan. Maybe it's already happened?"

I think to myself, *Gosh, I hope so*. But I'm also a little embarrassed. I don't feel comfortable when men lay the compliments on so thick.

James grabs my hand and says, "I'm going to kidnap this beauty, Ethan. It's my right as the birthday boy." Hmm. I resent being treated like I'm some sort of commodity, but I follow him obediently, anyway.

James pulls me onto the dance floor, then spins me once in a circle before he holds me close and sways with me. He's an excellent, talented dancer and also probably spent a small fortune on dance lessons. As we dance, he manages to make lively conversation—a real charmer. The dancing, along with his witty repartee, helps me relax. My headache vanishes. James chats, laughs, and boldly jokes that after our second dance, he probably knows more about me than Ethan does. He makes me laugh almost constantly. While we swirl among the other couples, I catch a glimpse of Ethan and Theo, who are drinking and chatting with other guests. Ethan occasionally seems lost in thought, then turns to another guest.

"I like your supersexy dress," James whispers in my ear. "You girls on the Continent are so sophisticated; you understand how to look your best. English girls run around half naked, wearing dresses that look like underwear, as if that were chic."

I laugh again. "You do English girls a disservice," I say. "There are lots of very nicely dressed girls here." And it's true. I notice with a sense of liberation that I'm not overdressed one bit. The girls wearing only jeans and T-shirts eye me enviously. I've been seized by the guest of honor, and he seems to have no desire to let me go. We dance to every song until we're both out of breath.

James pulls me over to the buffet and asks, "What would you like to drink? Champagne? Beer?"

"Just water, thank you. Alcohol makes me terribly silly."

"I imagine that would be very nice," James says, and hands me a glass of champagne.

"All right, but only one glass in honor of the birthday boy," I say. "Then I must check in on where Ethan's gone."

"Oh bullshit. Ethan," James says. "The old bore. What do you girls see in him? He can barely talk."

He's right about that, but that's precisely what makes Ethan so dreamy. James is a really nice guy, and fun to chat and dance with, but Ethan is way more mysterious. I scan the room but can't find him.

James follows my eyes. "He's probably in the billiards room with his brother. They always disappear in there when there's dancing, along with all the others who hate to dance." He hands me a large glass of water and says, "Come on, we'll sit over there on the stairs and rest a bit, then you can tell me more about your lovely students from Gatingstone School."

Two girls are making a beeline toward James. "I think you should take care of your other guests," I say quickly.

"All in due time," he says. He turns his back on both of them, then leads me upstairs to an airy, wooden stairway that connects the lower floor with the mezzanine. We sit side by side on one of the steps and look down at the dance floor. From here, I can see the billiards room where Ethan is leaning over the green pool table. His curly hair shines under the ceiling light fixture. He's removed his jacket and rolled up his shirtsleeves, revealing his tan, muscular arms. A group of giggling girls joins him on the pretense of watching the game, but they're probably watching the player much more. I'm relieved that Ethan completely ignores them.

"I find it quite lovely that you're here," James says. "You're like a breath of fresh air. Tell me, how do you like it in England?"

So I tell him. Then I ask him what he's studying. It turns out he's a biologist working on his doctorate. He vividly describes his experiments on the mating habits of locusts. His eyes sparkle so mischievously the entire time I have to laugh. I'm enjoying myself immensely, although I'm a little irritated. Didn't I come with Ethan? He could put a little more effort into paying attention to me. Is he ashamed of me because of my dress? Have I said or done something to displease him? Hopefully not. In any case, James finds me adorable. He showers me with admiration, and I feel like a rose that hasn't been watered in a while. James is as sweet as Jens. The more I tell him about my studies, the more he looks at me with respect.

"I had no idea that English literature is so exciting," he says. "I slept through my lit classes. But your eyes flash with excitement when you talk about it. It makes me want to go home immediately, bury myself deep into an armchair, sip on a good whiskey, and read a Thomas Hardy or a George Eliot novel."

I laugh. "I hope I can inspire my students like that one of these days."

James grows serious. "Tell me, how are things going with you and Ethan?"

I hesitate. "What do you mean?"

"Aren't you worried that your relationship will fall apart when you go back to Germany?"

I blush. "I don't know whether I'd really say we have a relationship. We haven't known each other for very long."

"Then there's hope for me yet," James says. He tries to put his arm around my waist, but just then the two girls pop back into view. They are walking very quickly in our direction.

I jump to my feet and say, "Your friends are coming. I can't hog the guest of honor the whole evening." I flit downstairs as fast as my high heels will carry me, then head for the billiards room. Once there, I hold Ethan's arm tightly and start trembling immediately; his touch always does that to me.

He looks down at me. "Well, at least you're able to amuse yourself," he says with a reproachful undertone.

"I'm sorry," I say. "I didn't know you had a problem with it. You seem quite entertained by your billiards game."

"Only because you seem to prefer another guy's company," he says sullenly. His jealousy makes me feel good, I must admit. "Come on, let's go. The loud music is annoying me."

"Okay," I say. "Let's just say good-bye to James real quick."

Ethan squeezes my arm tightly. "Nonsense. He'll eventually realize that we left. Come on."

He directs me to the exit, and the servant appears out of nowhere and holds out our coats for us. Outside, the refreshing, cold night air washes over me. I had a really great time at the party, but I'm excited to be alone with Ethan. I've seen far too little of him over the course of the evening.

Apparently, he feels the same way. As he buckles up, he mutters, "I find it a bit strange that a person goes to a party with someone but they apparently prefer to have fun with someone else."

I prick up my ears. Oh joy! That actually sounds like jealousy to me. "Ah, James is quite nice," I say. "He's a great dancer, and he made me laugh the whole time. I had a delightful conversation with him."

Then something happens that I don't quite understand. Ethan turns to me, and I see that he's quite furious. "Lea, I didn't like how you flirted with him, giggling loudly and sitting on the stairs so everyone could see up your skirt." His gaze is intense. "I really like you, but there's something about you that really bothers me."

I'm terrified. Oh dear! I never intended to provoke such a rage in him. Although I have to admit, when Ethan is feeling passionate—even angry—he looks more irresistible than ever. I rejoice a tiny bit that I mean so much to him.

"Go on," I say.

"Even though you're almost an adult"—I think, *Hello! I'm already an adult!*—"in many ways, you're still a little girl. You don't take life seriously enough. Everything's just a big joke."

I look at him, perplexed. What is the matter with him?

Ethan presses further. "When you make a stupid mistake, you have to take it seriously and acknowledge it. You have to think about how you can avoid it in the future. Frankly, I'm really frightened for you. You're completely naïve. You need to grow up and act like an adult."

Oops! He's sounding very shrill. I gasp for air. How do I respond to that? Best not to say anything. I swallow. Maybe what Ethan's saying is true. I admire him so much; there has to be something to it. Ethan presses his lips together, as if forcing himself not to say anything else. He starts the engine, and we drive into the night over the winding roads.

"Do you understand what I'm saying, Lea? Think about it! Do you really think that James likes you as a person? He doesn't. I can't believe you're so naïve. James was glued to you because you look so sexy. I'm sure he was hoping to sleep with you as some sort of birthday present."

I listen carefully and come to the following conclusions: Ethan is definitely jealous. Hooray! He also thinks I'm sexy. Not bad. But he thinks I'm naïve and reckless. Not so good. I rebel against this last conclusion. How well does Ethan really know me, anyway? Not enough for him to judge me like this. On the other hand, I'm a little confused. What if he's right? I need to watch myself in the future. Maybe Ethan does see something in me that needs work. Maybe I went overboard with the whole zest-for-life thing. Could it be that some people find me rather annoying? I never considered the possibility. I sigh. *Lea*, I tell myself, *it looks as though you have to work on yourself more*. It's a pity if Ethan actually turns out to be right. My whole life plan will fall through. He's supposed to be the calm, serious one while I'm the fun-loving, lively one—like Mr. Darcy and Elizabeth Bennet. Does Elizabeth become quieter and settle down more later in life? Unfortunately, Jane Austen doesn't say anything about that.

But I must object for the sheer sake of fairness. "I must have misunderstood you," I tell him. "If so, I'm sorry. I was under the impression that you like it when I dress up."

Ethan frowns. "It's okay." He briefly gives me a once-over, giving me goose bumps. "But if someone's wearing seductive clothes, it's even more important that she acts like a lady. Otherwise, people will immediately draw the wrong conclusions. It would be good if you acted a little less like a giggling teenager."

I see. That makes sense. I nod thoughtfully. I'm definitely learning a lot from him. I like that he seems to think about me so much. Jens does the same thing. I suddenly remember how Jens said such nice things about me when we sat together in the small Italian restaurant. It was different than it is with Ethan. He probably only wanted to flatter me because he thought I was pretty. It's better that Ethan isn't so sugary sweet. He detects and addresses my weaknesses, which gives me a strange sense of security. I'm important enough to him that he risks losing me by being so honest with me. It's a very protective, masculine trait. Kind of amazing, really.

I sneak a sideways glance at him. He looks back and smiles his charming smile, which always makes my knees weak. "It doesn't upset you when I talk so openly with you?"

I shake my head vigorously. "No, I think it's good that you're telling me these things. People can float through life, making terrible mistakes and doing stupid things, and no one dares to say anything from indifference, maybe, or out of a false sense of respect. It's quite possible that people dislike me without my knowing it. I think it's good that you're so honest, Ethan."

Again, he smiles at me in a way that totally warms my heart. "I have such a soft spot for you, Lea. I fell for you the moment you looked so helpless on the train. Where do we go from here? Do you still want to spend more time with me, even if I'm such a creep?"

I look at him, dumbfounded. "You? A creep? That never crossed my mind. I would never call you that; you only have my best interests in mind."

He places a hand on the back of my neck and steers with the other. The gesture is wonderful and tender, and I love him for it. When we arrive at Somerset Close in the wee hours of the morning, Ethan leans over and gives me a gentle kiss. I look deep into his eyes and melt. I hear myself saying, "Do you want to come in?"

Ethan looks at me long and hard, then says, "I would really like that, Lea, but I don't think it's a good idea. I don't want our first night together to be on a cot in a dusty storage room. It should be somewhere romantic and unforgettable, don't you think?"

Once again, I've got to give him credit, even though my body is misleadingly sending completely different signals to my brain. I nod and say, "Yes, that makes sense."

"I'll see you in Gatingstone, then," Ethan says.

"Yes, I'm going back tomorrow."

"I look forward to it."

"Me, too."

After another long kiss, I get out of the car. As Ethan speeds away, I'm so dizzy I need to hold on to the door frame a moment. Then I find the key and unlock the door. Once again it takes me forever to fall asleep.

Chapter 8

The next morning, I grab my bag and make my way to the bus stop. The railway station is located south of town, and as the bus drives through the city, we roll past the old town with its beautiful buildings and colleges. I feel sad that I didn't see or do as much as I thought I would. I definitely need to come back again.

Later, on the train to London, I mull over the experiences of the last few days. I think about Jens, and our boat ride and trip to the museum. I wonder if he's back in Germany. I shake my head. What a crazy guy! I can't believe he traveled hundreds of miles across Europe to see someone who wants nothing to do with him. What would Ethan say about such unseemly behavior? Jens is even more naïve than I am!

I think about the wonderful evening at Trinity College and how I jumped over the gate. I threw away the ripped dress—I won't need it anymore, since Ethan doesn't like it. Of course, I packed the red dress. I'll definitely wear it again; only next time, I'll be on my best behavior. Ethan will be amazed! He is staying in Cambridge with his brother until the end of the week, but once autumn break is over, we'll see each other almost every day at school and in the evening, of course. I'm looking forward to all the good times we'll share.

The lady sitting across from me smiles warmly at me, probably because I'm beaming without even realizing it.

"A nice day, isn't it?" she says in her best British manner. According to British custom, talking about the weather is the best way to start a conversation.

I smile back and say, "Oh, yes. The last few days were quite beautiful. Cambridge showed me its very best side."

"Oh, so you're a tourist?"

"Yes and no," I say. "I'm working for a year as an assistant teacher and visited Cambridge during autumn break."

"How nice! It's one of the loveliest cities in the region," she replies. "You're from Germany, aren't you?"

I blush a bit. "Oh, so you can hear my accent, then? I was hoping I'd lose it while living here."

"Oh, you should keep it," she responds generously. "It's quite charming."

"It's not so great for someone who wants to be a language teacher," I say.

The lady, who is making a very good impression on me, asks me where I live.

"In Gatingstone," I answer. "I'm working at the comprehensive school there."

"Oh," she says, "what a nice coincidence! I live in Gatingstone, too. I was just visiting my brother and his family in Cambridge. We can travel home together."

In London, we'll need to get off the subway at King's Cross station and catch a train at Liverpool Street station. From there, the train will take us to Brantwood, where we'll catch a bus to Gatingstone. I'm glad to meet this woman; she'll know exactly where to go in London, which will make things much easier for me. The woman, whose name is Alice, tells me about her brother's large family and her visit with them. She had a nice time, but she's also happy to be going home.

"I'm single," Alice says. "It's hard for them to understand, but I've learned to appreciate my peace and quiet. They can call me an old maid if they want."

"I love my peace and quiet, too," I say. "It's not so easy where I'm staying." I tell her about Abby and Glen, and how the loud TV, lack of central heating, and cigarette smoke make it difficult to study.

"Is that the old couple with the small cottage on the main street?" Alice asks. "He regularly wins top prize at the annual garden show. His tomatoes are legendary."

"Yes, that's them."

"Their cottage is really too small for three people."

"Oh, yes," I agree.

Alice pauses and seems to think. She looks at me, then back out the window, once or twice. Finally, she says, "I'd like to propose something to you." I'm curious. What could it be? "I live in one of the cottages at Weaver's Mews. My house is too big for me alone, so I have a roommate. Maura works at Marks and Spencer in Chelmsford, but she's returning home to Ireland in two weeks, and her room will be vacant. Would you be interested in being my new tenant?"

The offer sounds very tempting, and I inquire about the price. I'm pleasantly surprised by Alice's answer. It's significantly less than what I pay the Lanes. If I could move in with her, I'd save more money and have a better place to study.

Alice sees that I am pleased and adds, "There are a few caveats that explain the price. I work in London during the week, which means you must be very independent. I can't go shopping or cook for you, and you'll need to take care of your own laundry. I'd also be very grateful if you would take over some of the housework."

I'm not put off by these caveats at all. On the contrary, I think about Ethan's admonition in Saffron Walden. He's right; Abby and Glen do spoil and mother me too much. It's time to free myself from the clutches of the good-natured couple and win back my independence.

I would have liked to just say yes right away, but Alice says, "Come over one evening, and I'll show you the room and the attached bathroom, as well as the rest of the house. Then you can decide."

The attached bathroom sounds too good to be true. In my mind, I'm as good as moved in. "I have a question," I say.

"Sure, anything," she replies.

"Does your cottage have central heating?"

At that, Alice throws back her head and laughs uproariously. "Yes," she sputters. "You poor child! Yes, the house has central heating."

My decision is final. I'll go tomorrow to take a look at it.

When we reach London, we change stations and travel on to Gatingstone. Alice tells me a bit more about herself. When she was younger, she was a police officer. Later, she worked for Scotland Yard in the United Arab Emirates. A rich sheikh proposed to her, and they got engaged.

"God, how naïve I was! I thought that he wanted to live a Western lifestyle. But I soon realized that although I would be his legal wife, he would have lots of other women, too. It was only a short engagement. No matter, I still have the engagement ring. That alone was worth the trouble."

I look at her furtively. She must have been very pretty to have such an exciting past. She's not unattractive, and she's very well-groomed. Her makeup is professionally applied, and her clothing is elegant. Unfortunately, she's grossly overweight. Not even her elegant green coat can hide that fact.

"Yes, yes." Alice sighs. "I know exactly what you're thinking. Believe me, I was considerably slimmer in those days. When you come to my house, I'll show you a few old photos. I don't know exactly how I've put on so much weight. I actually eat very little. I peck at my food like a bird."

We reach Gatingstone and say good-bye. I promise to come by tomorrow.

"Isn't it great that we met?" Alice says. "I find you to be quite delightful. I believe we'd have a very nice time living together."

With a heavy heart, I lug my travel bag back to the Lanes'. How can I tell the amiable, old couple that I'm giving my notice? I decide not to say anything until I've seen the house and I'm sure.

Gatingstone greets me like a mother whose daughter has returned home. The cricket lawns seem greener than usual. The sinking sun casts long shadows over the village, and I can hear children playing. Lawn mowers purr, and everything smells of fresh grass and outdoor grilling. When I approach Walnut Cottage, the door opens immediately, as if Abby were lying in wait for me. The Lanes couldn't have known I was coming back from Cambridge so soon.

"Hi, love!" Abby shouts in greeting. "You're back home already. How lovely! You must have missed us." She is beaming.

"Unfortunately, I had to move out of my accommodations in Cambridge," I explain.

Abby clicks her tongue sympathetically. "Oh, you poor thing. How in the world did that happen? You need to tell us everything. Run in and freshen up a bit. I'll call Glen in from the garden and make us a nice cup of tea. Then we'll talk." She shuffles eagerly to the kitchen in her fur slippers.

My heart sinks at the thought that, sooner or later, I'll have to tell them about my moving plans. I wonder how they'll react? I think about Ethan's words of wisdom again. He's quite right. The pair hovers over me way too much, and Abby's mothering is almost too much to bear. It will do me good to be independent again. I didn't move here for a year to live with substitute parents. What a very lucky coincidence that I ran into Alice on the train. I enter my cold bedroom with the window insulated with paper towels and the ridiculous bedspread, and I think anyone who saw my living conditions here would agree with my decision.

Soon I'm sitting with the Lanes at their camping table, eating a piece of Abby's unrivaled angel food cake and sipping a hot cup of tea. The two hang on my every word; they want to know everything. It's all a bit too much. I'm tired from all the traveling, and my head starts to hurt again.

"Your accommodations were actually as bad as we feared?" Abby asks.

I nod. "Even worse. I've never seen so much dirt and disorder in my entire life."

Abby looks around her perfectly cleaned living room and says happily, "How awful."

Glen clears his throat awkwardly and asks, "And how did it go with the young man?"

Abby chimes in, "Did he make any advances?"

They await my answer with bated breath. They're both sweet and mean well but have no restraint. They want to know whether I crawled into bed with Ethan! I am reminded of his advice, and it's gradually beginning to dawn on me that he is right.

I set my cup down on the camping table and say, "Excuse me, but I believe it's time for me to go to bed."

"You should do that, love," Abby says. "You're looking quite pale. It seems to me that Cambridge wasn't good for you. I'm certain there was mold in your room there. It's a good thing you're back with us."

Back with us. Earlier I wouldn't have thought anything about this comment, but now I feel as though Abby's throwing an invisible net over me, pulling the rope tighter and tighter. Walking upstairs to my room, I feel like a preteen who's rebelling against her parents, except I already went through all that a long time ago.

The Lanes turn up the TV volume full blast the minute I leave the room, and the sound of it follows me upstairs. The now very familiar melody of *Crossroads* blares through the house. The cold air hits me as soon as I enter my room, and I can see my breath when I exhale. I lie down in bed, pull the pile of wool blankets over me, and reach for my book to read a little. It's quite strange. Until recently, this cottage felt like a real home away from home for me—a pleasant and cozy substitute home. Now I'm seized by restlessness. I can't wait to move out of here and on to something new.

The next morning I'm fast asleep when the door to my room flies open and Abby marches in, sets down the compulsory tea on the bedside table, spoon clinking against the cup, then goes to the window and pulls the curtain back.

"Good morning, dear," she chirps. "I think you'll feel a lot better today than you did in Cambridge. Here you even get your tea served to you in bed. Good, isn't it?"

I don't tell her that in reality I think it's dreadful. I would have loved to sleep in an extra hour! I look out the window and see that it's a terrible, rainy day.

"Glen will be happy it's raining," Abby says. "His garden was bone-dry." She winks at me, then leaves the room.

I pull the blankets over my head, cursing under my breath. Once I'm awake, I can't fall back asleep. Resigned, I sit up and reach for the cup. As the warm English tea hits my stomach, though, my thoughts about Abby and her quirks become more conciliatory.

What do you do on a gray, rainy autumn day when your boyfriend is far away, your friends are all out of town, the only privacy you have is in an unheated room, and you have more leisure time than you know what to do with? I put on my shoes, slip into my raincoat, and grab an umbrella. Then I ring the neighbor's doorbell. An ancient couple lives there with a black Labrador who is almost as old as they are. Not too long ago, I talked to the old man over the garden fence, and he told me that their dog, Sniff, doesn't get enough exercise. I offer to take Sniff for a walk.

Half an hour later, my shoes are caked with mud. In Gatingstone there are several public trails that date from the Middle Ages. One of them runs closely behind the Lanes' house. I've wanted to explore it, but what I hadn't anticipated—and learned the hard way—is that these paths can be a bit treacherous, passing through dense vegetation, over hedges and ditches, and straight across freshly plowed fields. Sniff finds the whole experience quite exhilarating. As old as he is, he is suddenly revived and happily pulls so hard on the leash that I have to jog behind him.

As we walk, I think about Ethan. What is he doing in this crappy weather? Is he hanging out with friends? Visiting a museum? Reading a book? If so, which one? What does he do in his spare time? I realize that I really don't know much about this man that I like so much and desperately want to be with. He rarely talks about himself, but this mysterious aura makes him even more appealing. Ethan already knows so much about me. He has me figured out, really. He knows that I can be spontaneous, reckless, and sometimes quite naïve. I hope to win his heart despite my shortcomings.

I bring Sniff to the front door. When his owner sees him covered in mud, she cries, "Oh!" and rushes off to fetch a towel. She says good-bye without a word of thanks. I can understand why. Now what? I decide to go to the library, so I carefully pack my laptop in a waterproof case. I'm looking forward to getting online. I wonder if Alice has an Internet connection.

As I enter the library, the gray-haired gentleman behind the counter lifts his head, eyes me over his reading glasses, and nods shortly before becoming engrossed in his book once again. I find an open desk in a secluded corner and throw my coat over the back of my chair. I open my laptop and immerse myself in the Internet. First, I sort through my e-mails, most of them spam, then delete them after reading them.

I write an e-mail to my parents mentioning that I hope to move soon. Then I Google Alice Hunstead. It can't hurt to do a little research on someone you plan to live with. I discover that Alice made a big career change when she resigned from the police department: she now owns a trendy perfumery right on Bond Street. The home page is quite elegant and high-end. Not bad.

Then I go to Facebook and find the usual variety of posts and messages. My German roommates uploaded some party photos. I recognize our common living room. Marc is curled up on the couch with an unfamiliar beauty, waving a bottle of beer. A few people are dancing in the background, and I recognize Lisa among them. They seem to be having a ton of fun. I browse through more pictures of laughing, dancing people. All this is making me a little bit homesick; I seem to be missing out on a lot. It's not exactly party central here in this English village's small library. Maybe I should ask Catherine whether she wants to go dancing with me in London. But I'm reminded that Ethan's into neither dancing nor demonstrations of wild exuberance. I need to put more effort into acting grown-up and sedate.

"Go ahead and dance, girl," I whisper to Lisa's photo. "Your pimple-faced dance partner can't hold a candle to my Ethan."

All at once I hear the familiar *ping* that someone wants to chat. An instant message appears at the bottom right-hand corner of the screen: *Hi, Lea! Nice to see you on here. You okay?*

I freeze. Oh no! The message is from Jens. My fingers hover over the keys. Should I answer or quickly close the page? My mood softens on this gray, lonely day. I type, *Yeah, really good. And you?*

He types, *:-(Guess why?*

Now would be the time to break off communication, but before I know it, my fingers type, *No idea.*

He types, *Ha-ha*, followed by a link. I click on it. It's a picture of a couple on a punt on the River Cam. The boat and the weeping willows along the bank are reflected in the water, and the couple is kissing.

I write, *As if! Ha-ha! Keep dreaming.*

Several links follow at lightning speed. Where is he getting all this? One leads to the Hohensyburg Casino home page. Another is a photo of a stretch limo at night; you can see the reflection of neon lights on its highly polished paint job. Another link goes to the Italian restaurant where we had our meal. Another shows a picture of bare feet. I smile. One leads to a *Wikipedia* article on St. Peter's Church in Cambridge. He sends the message, *I will, too. And nobody can stop me.* Then he logs out of Facebook.

I sit and stare at the screen for a while. Although I didn't really want to chat with him, I'm sorry he's gone. For one moment I hadn't felt so lonely on this long, gray day. It's sweet that Jens collected so many links about us, and a shame we're just not a match.

I shut the laptop and look at my watch. I've been here for several hours. Time to go home and change clothes. I'm visiting Alice this evening, and she's expecting me in half an hour. On the way to Walnut Cottage, my growling stomach reminds me that I didn't eat breakfast or lunch. When I unlock the door, Abby rushes in from the kitchen.

"Where were you for so long, love?" she asks me excitedly. "We were worried sick. Glen wanted to call the police."

Glen, who is asleep in his armchair, lifts an eyelid now and smiles at me sleepily. Then he goes back to sleep. I really don't believe Abby's last statement, but nevertheless, she's really stressed out. She's literally wringing her hands. "Imagine if something terrible were to happen to you—what would your parents say?"

Oh man! This is getting to be a little too much for me. When I was in Lancaster, I partied till the wee hours of the morning. And one night during my semester in Turkey, a drunken local grabbed me on my way home from the disco near the river. I hit him so hard he fell flat on the back of his head, much to the amusement of his drinking buddies. Meanwhile here in this sleepy town, my landlady worries about me because I'm not home by seven o'clock in the evening.

"Abby," I say patiently, "you forget that I'm old enough to look after myself. If you had actually called the police, they would have burst out laughing."

But Abby looks at me worriedly. "I like to know when to expect you home, then I wouldn't have to panic."

I don't reply and go up to my room. I put on a nice skirt and blouse and comb my hair. When I go back downstairs, Abby comes out of the living room. "Are you going out again? Glen, she's going out again. It's already quite dark," she frets.

Glen mumbles, "Bye, dear. Have a nice evening."

I quickly close the front door. Through the single-pane windows, I hear Abby scolding her husband. What would she say if she knew I was going out to inspect my new accommodations?

The streets of Gatingstone are completely deserted. Everyone's at home, probably watching TV. You can see the bluish light flickering through the curtains. The church bell rings in the middle of the dreamy silence, and a car occasionally passes by. The smell of cabbage and roasts hangs in the air, which makes my stomach growl again. I know the way to Weaver's Mews quite well. I used to pass the entrance to the little residential street when I walked from the Seafields' house to school. It is lined on both sides with cute little houses that are new but tastefully emulate the village's older style. I quickly find Alice's house—it's the second one on the right. Climbing roses twine themselves around a small arbor, and I read a porcelain sign with the words "Rose Cottage" in an ornate font in the inviting light of the door lamp. I press a shiny brass button and hear a melodious bell and high heels clicking on the floor to the front door.

Alice opens the door. She is wearing a flowing dress with a pink floral pattern that deftly conceals her curves. It's a bit like my Laura Ashley dress from Cambridge.

"Good evening, Lea," she welcomes me. "How nice of you to come! Come in quickly, and hang your coat on the coatrack." She smells of very expensive perfume—*probably from her shop in London*, I think.

Alice leads me from the entrance hall to the living room. It's not big, but it's very tastefully decorated. It's the living room of a single woman with discriminating taste. The wall-to-wall carpet is a soft green, which complements a casual pink and green floral sofa and two armchairs. The fabric matches the carpet perfectly. Silver picture frames and candlesticks sit on two low end tables made of some sort of precious wood. Beautiful engravings hang on the wall—landscape scenes, probably of Essex County. In a corner of the room is a round table with a spotless white tablecloth. It's already set with dishes and cutlery.

"I've prepared us a little something for dinner. I hope you haven't eaten yet," Alice says graciously, and returns from the kitchen with a fragrant quiche. My mouth waters as she serves us each a piece and pours Bordeaux into tall wineglasses. I take in the scene, wide-eyed with amazement. What a contrast this is to the Lanes' tiny, swelteringly hot living room with its booming television. Everything here is quiet and peaceful, tasteful, and comfortable. The scene is reflected in the large lattice windows, which most likely look out on the garden. Baroque music from a CD plays lightly in the background. It sounds like Vivaldi.

Without thinking, I say, "You have no TV at all."

"Oh, yes, I do," Alice says. "I just keep it upstairs in my small office. A television's pretty ugly, don't you think? It would totally spoil the nice atmosphere in here."

I know how that goes.

"Unfortunately, Maura isn't here this evening," she says. "It would have been nice if you two could have met."

"Oh, she moved out already?"

"Pretty much. She has a boyfriend who's moving back to Ireland with her. Oh, what can I say?" Alice sighs. "He's a terrible guy. Maura has completely changed since she hooked up with him. She used to be such a nice girl, neat, polite, and friendly. Since she's been with Ron, she's like a different person. She's sullen and moody, and she leaves a mess when she makes jam sandwiches. The other day the whole stairway banister was sticky with jam. I asked her to clean it up, but after three days she still hadn't done it, so I wiped it up myself. Honestly, I'm glad that she's moving out now. I would have given her notice, anyway."

"Oh, I'm sorry to hear that," I say courteously. In my heart of hearts, though, I know this development is to my advantage. If the upstairs is as nice as this, I'm moving in as soon as possible.

For dessert, Alice serves a big portion of vanilla ice cream with raspberry coulis, whipped cream, and meringue cookies crumbled on top. "This is naughty but devilishly tasty," she says, and winks at me. I think, *So much for eating like a bird. A bird's stomach would explode after this!*

After dinner, I follow Alice upstairs. She shows me the room where Maura lives—for a little while longer, anyway. Everything is predominantly blue-gray: carpet, furniture, curtains. It's lovely. The bathroom is also blue-gray. Unfortunately, there's no shower, but I'm gradually becoming more accustomed to English bathrooms.

"This would be your bathroom," Alice says. "Mine is here across the hall, next to my bedroom." She shows me her bedroom, decorated in dusty pink and pale green, and her spacious private bathroom with its sunny-yellow tiles. "So, what do you think?" she asks.

I exhale joyfully. "It's beautiful! I can easily imagine living here."

Alice opens the door to her office, which has a low leather couch, a TV, and a desk. "Good," she says. "Come sit down, and I'll get us a little champagne. We'll toast to your becoming my new tenant. I'm thrilled!"

When Alice comes back with two glasses and a bottle, she says, "So, what's your story?"

I furrow my brow. "I don't understand."

"I mean, do you have a boyfriend, maybe back home in Germany?"

I blush. "Not really, but there is someone . . ."

"Here in England?"

Damn it, she's interrogating me like the Lanes. It's a bit irritating, but I don't want to destroy the good mood. "There's someone I'm potentially seeing. It could become more serious."

"How nice," Alice says. "I didn't want to pry. After all, it's none of my business." *Exactly*, I think, *thank you*. She continues, "I just want to clarify something in advance. You need to know that I won't tolerate any gentlemen callers. I'm a single woman and have to watch out for my reputation. On our street, people are usually discreet, but I don't want to provide any fodder for the village gossip mill."

I nod, although I'm secretly disappointed. Now that my romance with Ethan is heating up, a pretty blue-gray bedroom would be perfect.

Alice looks at me sternly. "And that holds for when I'm in London and you are here alone. On account of my business, you'll be alone here quite a lot. Generally, the house is at your disposal, but if you want to invite a girlfriend for lunch, you have to prepare for it yourself."

"Sounds good. I look forward to the peace and quiet. I'll definitely be able to study better here than at the Lanes'. Do you have Wi-Fi?"

"Yes, of course," Alice says. "I'll write the password down for you. It's Rosealice."

I lean back into the soft, tufted sofa and take a sip of the champagne. *What a lucky girl I am*, I think. I take this as a sign that better times are ahead. After about an hour—and another glass of champagne, which makes me a little dizzy—I take to the dark streets of Gatingstone, thinking about the best way to convey the news to the Lanes. It won't be easy.

. . .

The next morning, I decide not to waste any time. Better to make it short and sweet and take the old folks by surprise rather than turn it into a long, drawn-out affair.

I wait till we sit down for a lunch of cold chicken and salad at the camping table. Glen has put in his false teeth for the meal and looks a bit more dignified and not so sunken and defenseless. It feels fitting, given the gravity of the moment. After we finish the meal, I dab my mouth with a napkin and take a sip of water. I clear my throat before I say, "Once again, an incredibly delicious meal, Abby. Thank you!"

"I'm so pleased you liked it, love," she says.

"It's just unfortunate that soon I won't be able to enjoy your wonderful cooking," I say.

"Oh, that's not for a while yet," she says. "I'll get to whip up many good meals for you before your safe return to your parents next summer."

"I'm afraid not," I say, my heart pounding. I feel terrible. "I'm moving out in two weeks."

Abby freezes on the spot, completely stunned. She drops her cutlery onto her plate with a loud clatter. "Did you hear what she said, Glen?" she finally blurts out.

Glen leans forward, holding a hand behind his right ear, and says, "Eh?"

"She's moving out," Abby says.

"Eh?" he says again.

"She's moving out!"

Glen gazes at me, obviously confused. "Why do you want to move out, dear?"

"I found new accommodations here in the village. They're less expensive," I say.

Abby gazes at me in desperation. "But . . . but . . . You can't just move out. What are we going to do, then?"

"You can search for a new tenant," I suggest.

Suddenly, something unexpected happens. Abby becomes furious. "Search for a new tenant? How can you say that? It isn't that easy! It's impossible to find someone that quickly. It can take months and months! And what should we live on in the meantime?"

Glen reaches out to her, trying to calm her down, but she pushes his hand away irritably. "So this is the thanks we get for all the trouble that you've put us through. Do we really deserve to be treated like this?"

I'm beginning to get fed up with this. Ethan was absolutely right when he said that the old couple interfered too much in my life. Our relationship should have been a strictly professional one between renter and landlord, but they obviously have come to consider me a kind of substitute daughter.

"You've taken advantage of us," Abby cries. "Yes, indeed! You've practically eaten us out of house and home. There wasn't anything about feeding you lunch in the rental agreement. Your behavior is typically German. A nice English girl would never have the audacity!"

Abby's unexpected anger upsets me. I stand up, stare them down, and say coolly, "I always paid my rent on time and in full. For this reason alone, I would have expected to be treated with respect. Even under the current circumstances, I don't see why it should be any different. I see that I'm no longer wanted here, so I'll move out immediately and relieve you of my presence."

I go upstairs, drag my luggage out of the closet, and start to throw my clothes in the suitcase. Glen interrupts by gently knocking on the door. I open it a crack and ask, "Yes?"

"You shouldn't take it personally, dear. She loves you like a daughter."

"That may be so, but enough is enough," I reply.

"Why didn't you tell us you were so strapped for cash?" he asks. "We could have renegotiated the rent."

I place my hands on my hips and gaze at Glen sadly. I can't bear to tell him face-to-face that his house is small, drafty, and uncomfortable, that every night I freeze to the bone until I finally fall asleep, that his blaring television brings me to the edge of despair, and that it drives me crazy to eat on a small, rickety camping table every day.

But I can tell him one thing. I say, "Abby's maternal instincts are driving me around the bend. I'm not used to being treated like a little girl. She's smothering me."

Glen immediately understands what I mean. He says, "Oh, there's nothing you can do about that, dear. That's just how she is."

"I know, but that's why I have to get out of here."

He looks at me with sad, puppy-dog eyes. "It's a pity. We're going to miss you. Abby is sitting downstairs crying." Then he turns and walks away.

I didn't mean to make her cry. Should I run downstairs, apologize, and agree to stay? But I can't. I don't want to have to deal with the same problems. Also, her angry, poisonous words about Germans are still ringing in my ears. If anybody needs to apologize, it's Abby.

I finish packing, then look around the room and under the bed to make sure I don't forget anything. I put my house key on the bed, close the bedroom door, carry my luggage downstairs, and leave the house.

Way to go, Lea, I say to myself sardonically. Outside, it's cold and windy. To make matters worse, it's starting to rain again. Now what? What should I do? Maura doesn't move out for another two weeks. I fish out my phone and call Alice's cell phone.

"Hunstead." The voice sounds cool and distant.

"This is Lea," I say. "I'm in kind of a tricky situation."

"Lea! Hello." She sounds significantly warmer. "What kind of tricky situation?"

It spills out of me, and poor Alice must endure my entire tale of woe. She listens patiently, then says, "The solution is perfectly clear. You must move in immediately. You can sleep on the couch in the office. Pick up the house key at the neighbors' to the left. They have a duplicate key so they can water my flowers when I travel."

I'm overwhelmed with gratitude, but Alice interrupts me. "I must go back to work now. Sorry, Lea. We'll see each other this evening. If you want, you can cook something. Look and see what you can find in the fridge." Then she hangs up.

I haul my heavy bags through the drizzle to Weaver's Mews. Fortunately, Alice had the presence of mind to call her neighbor, so she's already waiting with the key. I let myself in, put my luggage in the hallway, and go into the living room. I sit down on the beautiful sofa and look around. Once again, I notice how pretty and tasteful everything is. It's perfectly quiet until a blackbird trills in the garden. The garden is small but well kept, and there is a terrace, which looks like an Italian garden with red terra-cotta pots. Autumn flowers—bright asters and chrysanthemums—are in bloom. A small lawn ends at the brick wall of an adjacent house. A climbing vine covers the wall.

I sigh. I feel so wonderful here. I feel sorry for Abby from the bottom of my heart, but one thing is crystal clear: Ethan was right. She did me no good. I'm glad he pointed it out to me. It was high time to move out and start afresh. In the future, I need to listen to what Ethan says. His discernment is impressive. I wonder what he'll think when he returns from Cambridge and hears that I followed his advice so quickly. Will he recognize it for what it actually is, a declaration of my love for him? I think about how he reacted to my offer to join me in the dreadful broom closet. I remember his words about "our first night together." They sounded so incredibly promising.

A noise at the front door startles me. Someone's coming in. Who can it be? Did Alice come back from London early because of me? I suddenly feel like an intruder and quickly jump to my feet. A young woman stands in front of me. Although she's small, her tight sheath dress shows off her lush curves. English girls use way too much makeup for my taste. Under lashes thick with mascara, her green eyes flash with surprise when she sees me.

"Hello. May I ask what you're doing here?" she asks, not very affably.

Then it hits me. "Hello, you must be Maura. Alice told me about you—you're her tenant."

"True, but it's still not clear who you are."

Her harsh tone repels me, but I answer, anyway. "My name is Lea. I'm your replacement."

Maura raises a narrow, plucked eyebrow. "Are those your bags at the entrance?" I nod. She scowls. "Then I must disappoint you. You're too early. In case Alice has forgotten, I'm not moving out for another fourteen days. That's the deal. I sincerely hope you two aren't planning on showing me the door before then. Bye, it was nice to meet you." Her face says the exact opposite. She turns around and disappears. Considering how small she is, she stomps upstairs rather noisily.

I swallow. Oh my goodness! What's the matter with her? She doesn't come off as very personable at all. I let myself fall back onto the sofa. I no longer feel very comfortable here. Now I feel as if I'm in the waiting room of a doctor's office. I pull the book I'm reading out of my purse, but I can't focus on the text. I remember what little information I know about this strange Maura. She was once nice, but because of her new boyfriend and his influence on her, she completely changed. Alice said that she'd planned to give Maura her notice, anyway, which doesn't surprise me now—not one bit. What kind of weird boyfriend would change her from a nice, approachable girl to such an obnoxious person? I shake my head.

Then it occurs to me that I should get off my high horse. Didn't I let the Lanes push me around? Didn't I become a different person, little by little, under their influence? It's a good thing that I have a boyfriend—well, almost—who's good for me and has a positive influence on me. I can only imagine how much better everything will be when we're actually together. Wow!

I read until the natural light in the living room is no longer sufficient, and my growling stomach reminds me that Alice proposed that I cook something. I decide to do exactly that. I can show her how grateful I am for her offering me refuge so last minute and not leaving me out on the street. There's not much in the fridge except for a withered head of cauliflower. I pull open a drawer and find a block of cheddar cheese, and in the fridge door I find an open carton of cream from our dessert yesterday.

Impulsively, I tie on an apron and get to work. I steam the cauliflower in salt water and find a cheese grater. Twenty minutes later, it smells like cooked cauliflower. A delicious cheese sauce is bubbling gently on low temperature. I sprinkle the sauce with salt, pepper, and freshly grated nutmeg, then turn the stove off. I find a slightly stale baguette in the bread box and bake it in the oven until it's crispy. With everything finished, I set the table in the living room for three people. I untie my apron and wait.

It doesn't take long until the key rattles in the door again. Alice comes rushing in, throws her purse on a table, places her high heels underneath the coatrack, and removes her thick gold earrings. "I can't wait to get rid of these things each evening," she says, rubbing her aching earlobes. Then she wrinkles her nose and sniffs. "You've really done it! You've cooked something! Today is my lucky day." She beams at me in a way that warms my heart. For the first time since I entered the house with my luggage, I feel welcome.

"I'll run upstairs quickly and freshen up. Then we'll eat. It smells so fantastic," she says, and disappears.

I pull the baguette out of the oven, slice it up, and put it in the bread basket.

Less than two minutes later, Alice is back downstairs. "I notice you set the table for three people," she says. "Is Maura here? Have you already met?"

"I suspect she's upstairs in her room."

"Maura," Alice calls up the stairs, "time to eat!"

An uncombed head appears above the railing. "Go ahead and eat without me. I can't stand cauliflower—the entire floor up here stinks! I'm leaving soon, Ron's picking me up in half an hour."

Alice presses her lips together as if she would like to reply but forces herself not to. Wordlessly, she removes one of the place settings and brings it into the kitchen. She returns with two wineglasses and a bottle of ice-cold Chablis. She turns the corkscrew with a vengeance, as though she's imagining that the cork is Maura's head.

"It's better this way," Alice says. "She would have only ruined our meal with her sour attitude." She pours a drink for each of us, then lifts her glass. "Welcome to Rose Cottage, Lea. I'm very happy you're already here. I think we'll be quite comfortable."

I pass her the bowl of steaming cauliflower. "It's just unfortunate that Maura doesn't think so."

Alice scrutinizes me closely. "Oh, so she's already made that clear to you?"

"I'm afraid so, yes. On the other hand, I can understand her position. After all, she's paying full rent and has to share the bathroom with me for fourteen days. Plus I'm hogging the TV room."

Alice waves dismissively. "Oh, she'll calm down when I give her back half the rent and you pay me the other half. Then she'll realize your presence isn't a complete disadvantage." She tastes the cheese sauce and rolls her eyes with pleasure. "Mmm," she says. "If you were a man, Lea König, I'd marry you on the spot. It tastes even better than it smells. I feel like this is the beginning of a whole new era."

"Could be—I just love to cook. It bothered me a bit that Abby ruled the kitchen at the Lanes'. It never would have occurred to her to let me near the stove. I don't believe that she knew I can cook at all."

"That's pretty mindless of her," Alice says, reaching into the bread basket for a piece of baguette to dip into the sauce. "You have free rein here. You don't know how tired and hungry I am when I get back from London, and then I still have to cook! By the way, feel free to go grocery shopping at my expense and just present the bill to me afterward."

"And Maura? Does she cook?"

Again, Alice makes a dismissive gesture. "Oh, her! That would have been nice. Her boyfriend isn't bringing a housewife into his life, believe me. I don't know what he sees in her. They probably have great sex, that's all." She sounds pretty resentful. I decide not to push the subject.

After dinner, I clear the table and wash the dishes. Alice disappears upstairs and takes a bath. I hear the front door close. Maura has apparently gone out, as she said she would. I carry my bags upstairs into the small office, also called the TV room. It's not really worth unpacking at this point—there's no closet space at my disposal. On the couch, Alice has laid out two pink sheets, a pillowcase, a quilt, and a pillow for me. I make my bed and watch a little TV. Then I open my laptop, enter the Wi-Fi password, and browse the web for a while. Nothing exciting is happening on Facebook. I don't see a green dot next to Jens's name, so no chatting with him. He didn't send me a message, either. Wistfully, I think, *It doesn't take very long for people back home to forget all about you.* It doesn't matter. I'm pretty tired, anyway.

Alice pokes her head in and wishes me a good night. Then it's quiet in Rose Cottage. I turn off the light and listen to the distant traffic on the main road. I quickly fall asleep—without my hot-water bottle. What luxury!

Chapter 9

For the remainder of autumn break, I do more studying than I did the whole time I spent with the Lanes. I also sleep in. Each morning I wake up when the blackbirds begin to sing in the garden. I know the house will soon be mine and mine alone. Though I'm still half asleep, I hear water running from the bathroom taps as well as the urgent pitter-patter of my roommates' feet while they prepare for their day. The front door slams twice in a row, first Alice and then Maura setting off for work. I stretch out luxuriously, turn onto my side, pull the blanket over my ears, then fall back asleep. No one bursts in with a cup of tea to "pamper" me.

I then eat a leisurely breakfast, propping open my book next to my plate. Eventually, I get dressed and tackle a bit of housework. My rent is very affordable, and I want to show my appreciation. *Had I known my financial situation would improve so suddenly, I could have spent another week in Cambridge*! I think. I'm a whirlwind of activity. I didn't scrutinize every corner of the house during my first visit, but now, from the sharp-eyed perspective of a diligent housewife, I realize there's a ton of work to be done. I roll up my sleeves and have at it.

I start in the downstairs guest bathroom. I wonder whether the cleanliness standards in England aren't a couple notches lower than they are back home. In the bathroom sink, decades-old lime deposits have formed around the faucet. I polish and scrub with detergent and plenty of elbow grease until the lime completely disappears and the basin shines like new. Then I tackle the toilet. Next, I vacuum all the carpets throughout the house. Every day, I seek out a new task, whether it's ironing the linens or cleaning the windows. The work is fun, and the physical activity clears my head. I no longer feel like a spoiled child like I did at the Lanes'. Instead, I feel like a self-confident adult who helps keep up her shared living space.

On Friday, I go shopping, and each evening I have a meal ready for Alice. Maura comes down to have a bite to eat with us only once. Alice is thrilled by my contributions. She praises my diligence, which spurs me on to do other tasks. It's actually quite clever of her. She openly expresses what I secretly think. "Your people are so neat and clean. We could learn a lot from the Germans. I'm glad you're my tenant."

When Maura overhears her comment, she grimaces and leaves the room. There's a lot of negative energy between us, and I have the feeling she thinks I'm a troublemaker. Through little comments and gestures, she insinuates that I have no business being here and treats me like a cuckoo that's made herself at home in a foreign nest, displacing the actual residents. Everything I put out on the shelf under the mirror in our shared blue-gray bathroom ends up in the bathtub. That said, I suspect that Alice is pitting her against me. Occasionally she praises me in Maura's presence so emphatically that I can only assume she wants to get back at Maura. Despite everything, I feel much more comfortable at Rose Cottage than I did with the Lanes.

On Friday evening, I borrow Alice's bike—naturally, I left the one that Glen fixed up for me at the Lanes'—and bike to the Seafields'. Melissa welcomes me with open arms and urges me to stay for dinner. I do so quite gladly. When I tell the family that I moved, they congratulate me.

"Don't take this the wrong way," Melissa says, "but staying with the old couple wasn't the best place for a student to learn proper English."

I open my eyes wide. I hadn't thought of that at all.

Melissa laughs when she sees my surprise. "Indeed, it's true. The Lanes are simple people; she was a cook, and he was a truck driver. They don't exactly speak the Queen's English. You've become accustomed to a lot of 'Glen and Abby' expressions. Did you notice that they use 'good' instead of 'well' as an adverb? That's a big mistake. I could mention a bunch of other examples."

"Why didn't you tell me?" I ask.

"Well," Melissa says, "you seemed to be quite comfortable there. Nevertheless, Lea, this is just between you and me. I don't want you to quote me. It's true, but it sounds terribly snobbish."

I'm pensive. "Even though I left there under less than ideal circumstances, I think it's good I got to know such simple, humble people. I believe you should acquaint yourself with all classes of society in a foreign country, even people you wouldn't normally socialize with."

"Thanks to us, you get an inside look into the world of the English native," Morris says wryly. "We're conceited snobs who think that our neighbors on the other side of the Channel wear pointed helmets and run around screaming, '*Achtung*,' when they're not leaning over tables loaded down with beer and wearing lederhosen or a dirndl."

I look at him seriously. "But that's exactly how it is in Germany."

Everyone breaks into uproarious laughter.

"And what was it like in Cambridge?" Melissa asks.

"Wonderful," I say.

"What did you do there? Did you visit some of the colleges?" she asks.

"A pity that I wasn't there," Morris says. "As a Fellow at Trinity, I would have taken you to the Master's Lodge. You could have gotten to know the real Cambridge. You haven't really lived until you've gone to a dinner there."

"But I did go," I say.

Everyone stares at me in disbelief. "What? You? How is this possible? With whom?"

I blush and say, "One of the teachers at school took me."

Linda lets her fork drop just as she is getting ready to put a bite of food in her mouth. She says sternly, "With whom?"

"Oh, it's not important," I say. "In any case, it was great."

But Linda won't let it go. "It was Mr. Derby, wasn't it? Otherwise you wouldn't be blushing."

Darn! Why am I blushing? It's really none of her business.

Melissa notices my embarrassment and says, "Linda, it's not proper to interrogate our guest."

"I need to know," Linda says stubbornly. "Somebody needs to look after Lea."

"Very funny," her father says. "First you need to look after yourself. It's really none of your concern who Lea chooses to socialize with. She is an adult woman and can decide these things for herself."

"Mr. Derby is a chauvinistic asshole," Linda says. "Lea is much too good for him. He'll only make her unhappy."

Melissa has had enough. "Linda, I don't want to hear such language at our table. Whomever Lea chooses to spend time with is up to her. She's got a good head on her shoulders."

"Thank you, Melissa," I say. Then Morris changes the subject, and Ethan no longer comes up. As I spoon my dessert, I wonder, *What's the matter with Linda*? Why would she say something so mean about Ethan? Is she maybe a teeny bit jealous? It's the only explanation I can think of for her outburst.

On Saturday morning, Alice and I enjoy a late breakfast alone. Maura stayed overnight with her boyfriend. To repay me for the last few days of chores around the house, Alice cooks a classic English breakfast, complete with stewed tomatoes, little sautéed sausages, and poached eggs.

Afterward, as we chat comfortably over a cup of tea, Alice suggests we take a little trip. She wants to show me some of Gatingstone's environs. She's aghast when I tell her that the Lanes didn't take me to the neighboring village, where Glen always purchases chicken feed from a farmer ("You and Abby can take a nice little trip there sometime," he used to say), or to Basildon, where they did their weekly grocery shopping at the large supermarket. I did become quite good at helping them heave the heavy shopping bags out of the car, though.

"That's unacceptable," Alice says. "You have to see some of our beautiful countryside before your year in England is over."

The front doorbell rings, and Alice flinches. Unlike me, she's still in her robe. "Lea, I can't get the door right now. Can you see who it is?"

I eagerly jump to my feet and go to the front door, carefully cracking it open a bit. I look out. What I see takes my breath away, and my heart instantly begins to pound like crazy. It's Ethan. I take a step back and look at him.

"Ethan," I whisper. "Is that you? I thought you were still in Cambridge."

Ethan grabs my shoulders with his powerful hands and looks me right in the eye. "I couldn't do it," he says. "I couldn't take it. I've been thinking of you constantly. I left early this morning. I went by your house, and the old couple told me you moved out. At last, I've found you."

Alice stands up and calls from the entrance to the living room, "Good morning! Whoever you are, please come in. I guess you're the young man Lea's told me about. Would you like a cup of tea? I can make a fresh cup; it will only take a second."

But Ethan shakes his head violently. "No, thank you. I came to kidnap Lea. Lea, go to your room and pack a few things. I want to take you to Thorpeness."

Alice sighs. "Thorpeness! How heavenly romantic. Oh, to be young again. How I envy you, Lea."

I'm unfamiliar with Thorpeness. Is it some sort of destination for elopers like Las Vegas or Gretna Green? Do I really want Ethan to kidnap me? *Oh, yes*, I think, *I want this very much*. On my way to the TV room, my heart is pounding with excitement and joy. Ethan came here because of me, and he wants to spend the weekend in some famously romantic place. I rummage through my suitcase, my hands trembling. I wonder frantically what I should pack for a romantic weekend. Crap! If only he'd warned me, I would have bought some seductive lingerie and a ravishing nightgown. I should just tell Ethan that I can't go right now; I have to prepare first. But that would be the dumbest thing I could possibly do. My excitement pushes aside any uncertainty about my wardrobe. Ethan can't be without me! Ethan longs for me the way I long for him! Life is so beautiful! After grabbing the bare necessities—after all, it's only for one night, since school starts on Monday—I hurry downstairs with my bag.

"Too bad, I was looking forward to a trip with you, Lea," Alice says. "But when I look at your boyfriend, I absolutely understand that I cannot compete." She gazes at him with undisguised admiration. It occurs to me that she may have a higher opinion of me after meeting my handsome admirer.

Ethan looks fantastic, as usual. He didn't shave this morning (maybe because he couldn't wait to come?), and the slight shadow on his cheeks makes him look more masculine than ever. He follows me with his eyes, as if he were a hungry animal and I his prey. It's more than thrilling.

After we drive off, Ethan glances at me. "Well, that is quite an improvement over your old accommodations. I'm amazed how quickly you took my advice." He smiles. "Good girl!" He places his hand on the back of my neck and rubs it gently. I feel a shiver go down my spine.

"I got lucky," I say. "I met Alice on the train ride back from Cambridge, and she made me an offer. But without your advice, I never would have thought to take advantage of it. I'm glad you forced me to see how much the Lanes stifled me."

We stop at a traffic light, and Ethan gazes deeply into my eyes. In his deep, velvety voice, he says, "Dearest Lea, if you're smart, in the future you'll only let yourself be pampered by one person—me."

The light changes to green, and Ethan must pay attention to the road again. I'd give myself to him gladly, body and soul. To hide my insecurity, I say, "Tell me where we're going. I've never heard of this Thorpeness. Where and what is this place?"

"Thorpeness is the successful product of one man's active imagination," Ethan says.

Great, now I'm no wiser than I was before. "Whose imagination?"

"A certain Glencairn Stuart Ogilvie."

"A certain who?" I start to giggle—it sounds so funny.

Ethan looks at me with irritation. I bite my lip and immediately stop giggling. After all, I want to act more grown-up.

"That's really the man's name," he says. "Ogilvie lived at the turn of the century. He must have been a tremendously clever fellow. Although he was a lawyer by profession, he designed trains the world over, which made him fabulously wealthy. He purchased a considerable piece of land along the coast of Suffolk, where he built a vacation villa for his employees and relatives. They spent entire summers there."

I try not to look too disappointed. Warily, I say, "It sounds a bit like Disney World. I can't imagine it would be that romantic."

Ethan says, "Just wait." Nothing more. In any case, he doesn't mention an express wedding or anything of the sort. That's all right with me. I mean, I'm crazy about him, but I don't know him well enough to marry him . . . yet. Or maybe I would. When would I ever get another opportunity to meet such an awesome man?

We head north. Luckily, the rain of the last few days has cleared, and we're having magnificent autumn weather again, just like the day we drove to Cambridge. Again we wind our way through quaint, little villages, and I gaze happily out the window. Ethan and I are on the way to a romantic weekend. It's so exciting! To think: a few days ago, I was just a passenger hitching a ride. Now the whole purpose of our trip is to spend time together. I can't believe my luck.

After a while, Ethan turns to drive east toward the coast. Although the landscape is flat, when we briefly drive up a hill, I can see the sea stretching into the distance. I feel as blissful as I did the first time I saw the ocean on one of my childhood trips to Denmark. Ahead of us lies the fishing village of Aldeburgh. We are soon driving north again, this time along the coast. Now the sparkling sea accompanies us on our drive. I can't take my eyes off it.

Ethan says, "You're doing it again."

I check my hands. No, I'm not chewing on my fingernails—I quit for Ethan's sake. "What?" I ask.

"Are you checking me out?"

I laugh. "No, I have to look past you to admire the sea."

"A pity," Ethan says. "We're almost there, by the way. And did I tell you I regularly donate blood?" Huh? Why is he telling me this now? This man is full of surprises. He looks at me and adds, "So you don't have to worry."

It suddenly hits me. I realize that he's basically trying to tell me that, although he's slept around, he doesn't have AIDS. I think of how we'll be alone together in our hotel room tonight, and my heart beats faster. How considerate of him to reassure me!

A short time later, a cluster of houses appears ahead of us. As we approach, I realize that we're headed into another fishing village.

"I thought Thorpeness would be relatively modern," I say. "This doesn't look modern at all."

"That is exactly what makes Thorpeness such an attraction. Ogilvie wanted an old fishing village, so he built one himself. Every single house in Thorpeness fits this concept."

We drive through the village. I'm amazed—it's not like Disneyland at all. It's just perfect. I feel like I'm in a historical village dating back centuries. The slightly crooked cottages crowd around a small lake with ducks and rowboats. A very strange house, built atop some sort of tower, is situated by the lakeshore.

I point at it. "That looks very Disney-like to me. What kind of strange building is that?"

"That's the famous House in the Clouds. The building was formerly a water tower. It was no longer needed, so Ogilvie made it into vacation rentals."

"It looks crazy, but also quite lovely."

Ethan slows down and pulls up in front of a wood-frame building. It's much larger than the small houses beside it. Above the entrance is a sign that says "The Dolphin Inn."

"We're here," he says. "This is the end of the line."

End of the line? What a curious thing to say. I'd rather think it's the beginning of something new—for me, for us.

We get out and stretch our legs. Although it's a beautiful autumn Saturday, there aren't too many people on the road. I bet all hell breaks loose here in the summer.

"This Ogilvie must have been a very special person," I reflect. "He obviously was a man of strong character. He knew exactly what he wanted to do, then did it. Quite impressive, isn't it?"

"Yes, such people exist," Ethan says. The corners of his mouth twitch almost imperceptibly, as if he finds my remark kind of funny. I look askance at him; he's staring at me with intensity. Then I understand. He's thinking how he wants me. At this thought, I become warm all over. Ethan puts an arm around my shoulders. I feel a bit like I'm his captured prey and he's taking me into his cave. If it were anyone else, I'd be furious; but when I'm this close to him, I feel as though I'm melting.

We enter the hotel, and a friendly host rushes up to us. "You must be the Derby couple," he says. "We spoke earlier, Mr. Derby. It's lovely that you've come to visit us. Welcome!"

"The Derby couple" sounds good. Lea Derby. Not too bad. As the host turns to lead us up to our room, Ethan winks at me and smiles. I smile back. The Derby couple follows the host to a spacious room on the second floor. It has giant lattice windows with wide, low windowsills and overlooks a radiant field and a colorful autumn forest. The view is unbelievably beautiful. The carpet, wallpaper, and curtains are color coordinated in warm golden tones. A magnificent autumn bouquet is set out on a table to greet us. Behind a white wooden door with a playful brass handle is a lovely bathroom, complete with a claw-foot bathtub.

The host hovers nearby for a moment. "Do you like it?"

I exhale. "Yes, very much! I'm sure we'll be very happy here."

The host nods briefly and mentions the mealtimes and the excellent dining options they offer. Then he disappears.

Ethan turns me toward him. "How can you be so sure of that?" he asks coyly.

I'm flaming red. "I didn't mean it like that," I stutter in embarrassment.

"Oh, I think that's exactly what you meant, dear Lea," he says gently. "Now we'll see if we can make that happen."

He takes my bag and puts it on the floor. Then he calmly and purposefully starts to undress me. I stand there perfectly still and let it happen. My heart is beating so violently it feels as if it might burst out of my chest. On the surface, Ethan seems cool and calm, but I notice that his fingers are shaking and his breathing is erratic, so he really isn't very calm at all. *Lea König*, I think, *what a dream come true that you can get such a reaction out of this beautiful man*! The thought excites me even more.

After he takes my clothes off, he again eyes me with that hungry look of desire. I close my eyes and feel how cool the room is. I wait. Ethan whispers, "I will now remove this exceedingly tasteful bedspread, dear Lea, and pull the blankets aside, so you can lie down. I want to see your beautiful body stretched out on the bed. You think this room is so perfect, but I first need to see you lying there before it will be completely perfect for me."

Ethan is an Ogilvie type of guy, I suddenly think. He is self-confident and knows exactly what he wants. I find it so insanely erotic it makes me dizzy. With trembling legs, I walk over to the bed and lie down. The sheet is cool underneath me and smells like lavender. The autumn sunlight streams through the window and touches me with its warmth. I'm no longer quite so cold.

Ethan unbuckles his belt and quickly strips. "Your skin is like gold in the sunlight," he whispers. "Everything is now perfect."

I close my eyes and wait. My eyelids glow red from the sun. I don't know whether I want this moment of unfulfilled passion to last as long as possible, or if I want to finally give in to my longing for him. He comes to me like a wave breaking on the beach. I'm carried away by the force of the wave and let myself become completely immersed in it. I feel how he lets his hunger become more powerful and merciless. I don't mind; it's exactly what I'd been waiting for. I, Lea, am having sex with my dream man, and my body responds passionately. We briefly rest before we give ourselves over to desire again . . . and again. Finally, we lie side by side, completely exhausted.

Ethan holds a lock of my hair against the light. He smiles and says, "You're taking good care of it. Good job, keep it up." Then he lies back and is silent again. He's a man of few words. He doesn't comment on what just happened between us. He's very cool instead.

I feel pleasantly tired and pull the duvet over my naked body. I roll onto my side so I can see his profile. He's so handsome; I'd like to seduce him. I haven't had a chance to pounce on him like he did. What would he say if I initiated sex? Gently, I reach out a finger and stroke his angular, stubbly chin. I slide it down over his neck, his chest, and on down . . .

Ethan grabs my hand and squeezes it. "Enough, Lea," he says. "I want us to get dressed and stroll through the village. Then we'll eat here at the inn."

"Agreed," I say, springing to my feet and heading to the bathroom.

"Lie down again," Ethan says. "I'll go to the bathroom first."

I hesitate. "Why?"

"Because I said so, Lea."

Okay, I think, *that works, too.* I lie down and snuggle under the covers. I hear the purr of Ethan's razor and doze off.

Ethan stirs me awake. "Get up. And please be so kind as to not leave any hair in the sink when you're done. So many women do that, I think it's a nasty habit."

I smile at him. "Of course not. I feel the same way." While I get ready, I consider that one of the things I love about Ethan is how he states what he wants so clearly. He doesn't beat around the bush. He says right from the start what he likes and dislikes. It is so refreshing how honest he is. I furrow my brow. He said "so many women," and I'm secretly curious how many women he's been with. I catch myself wondering whether he was satisfied with my performance, considering his experience. I tell myself it's dumb to think that after such a passionate time. We had great sex. It was good.

And yet it gnaws at me. Was Ethan satisfied with me? Will we continue to be lovers, or was that it? Did he push my hand away because I didn't really fulfill his expectations? I forcefully brush my hair, as if I could brush the disturbing thoughts away. But it doesn't help. Brush in hand, I peek out of the bathroom at Ethan. He is sitting on the edge of the bed, concentrating on tying his shoes. I put the brush aside, walk over to him, sit in his lap, and kiss his forehead.

He takes me by the waist and shifts me over onto the bed. "Lea, what are you doing? I don't appreciate being attacked."

"Sorry, something simply came over me. It's your own fault for being so handsome."

"Okay," he mutters and turns to his other shoe, as if I am some sort of annoying mosquito. Around him, I always feel small and helpless, while he seems so strong and sure of himself. It turns me on.

"Now if you would stop all this nonsense and get dressed perhaps," Ethan says.

"Sure," I answer. Then I burst out, "Do you think I'm good in bed?"

Ethan looks at me with astonishment. "What a typical question coming from you. How fitting. An airhead is an airhead. You're a grown woman, Lea. Answer the question yourself."

Oh great, I think, *I'm as much in the dark as I was before.* "Okay, fine," I say, and look directly at him to monitor his reaction. "I'd say I was good."

Ethan now stands up and shakes his head. "Oh man, Lea. Let me tell you something—you weren't good at all! I was the only one who did anything. But I don't ask myself whether I am good. Because I'm an experienced adult, I know exactly how ridiculous such self-doubts are. We had sex, and the sex with you was very good. That's all that counts, right?"

He said the sex with you was very good, I say to myself. Hurray! I needed to hear that. I breathe a sigh of relief. Now that that's settled, I can be happy and relaxed about the rest of the weekend.

Half an hour later, we are strolling arm in arm through the narrow streets of Thorpeness. I am delighted. The village is wonderfully British—each house has its own character and its own lovingly tended garden. Eye-catching wreaths or glass beads hang in the windows, and there are pots filled with lavender or autumn asters by the front doors. Benches invite you to relax and chat. The houses have quaint names like Fisherman's Cottage, The Widow's Den, and Poppy House. I can't get enough of it. I read them aloud and comment on them. Ethan seems satisfied; as always, he is silent. Then he says, "Maybe you shouldn't squeal with such excitement, Lea. Not all people in Thorpeness want to participate."

I pull myself together immediately. He's right, of course. We complement each other so well. Although there are not many tourists around, I occasionally notice women admiring Ethan. It's so exciting. Ethan is my lover—this tall, good-looking man with his broad shoulders, narrow hips, and gorgeous curls is mine. I feel like I've grown two inches taller with pride. I'm sure everyone envies me.

In the evening, we return to the hotel. In the best English tradition, we are asked to wait at the bar until our table is ready. The bartender asks us if we want an aperitif.

I open my mouth, but Ethan cuts in quickly and says, "Two sherries, please."

"Whoops," I say cheerfully. "My companion is mistaken. I'm in the mood for a mimosa, if you don't mind."

"I don't mind at all," the bartender replies. "I can't deny the wishes of a beautiful young woman." He selects a bottle of champagne, pours it into a glass, mixes it with orange juice, and hands it to me.

I giggle at the compliment. "Thank you," I say. "I believe I know why he ordered for me. He was afraid I would order a malt whiskey again."

The bartender raises an eyebrow. "And what would anyone have against that?"

"Because it's not a proper drink for a young woman. Apparently, I must renounce it for the rest of my life. I imagine it's not proper for old women, either, just old men."

The bartender laughs and says, "I could easily believe that you will never age. Some women stay beautiful forever."

Again I giggle. He's a charming man. I like that the English are so relaxed and humorous, not uptight like most Germans I know. I turn around to see whether Ethan's amused, too. But he looks like he always does, maybe even a bit more serious than usual. He probably didn't catch the gist of our lively banter.

We are led to our table, and the waiter brings us the menu. "We'll take the mussel soup and the steamed plaice," Ethan says.

I decide not to be obstinate this time and concede to him, although I really love to browse menus. Maybe I would have rather eaten the smoked mackerel, if they have it. I love smoked fish. But Ethan is my host. If he wants to make the decisions, then he can do just that. He didn't seem very pleased when I rejected the sherry and ordered something else.

While we wait for our food, Ethan leans over and gazes deep into my eyes. My heart beats faster. His gaze always does that to me. His eyes are so wonderfully brown and expressive. "What happened earlier wasn't nice," he says.

Oh! What does he mean? I wince. Does he mean that the sex wasn't . . . ? I exhale, and he continues, "I mean earlier at the bar."

"What exactly?" I ask.

"Your unbridled flirtation with the bartender. I thought you were going to stop this kind of unseemly behavior."

Oh yeah. He's right. I fell back into my old habits. I lower my head and stare at the tablecloth. "I agree, Ethan, that wasn't good. I'm sorry, my mouth sometimes has a mind of its own and says things I don't want it to say. But I promise I'll work harder to be better."

"Okay, Lea. While we're at it, let me tell you something else. I can't stand it when you flirt and joke with other men in my presence. As your partner, I should have the privilege of your undivided attention. I feel as if I'm carrying on with some sort of floozy."

I sigh. Of course. Ethan has again pinpointed something I must address. I love him and him alone. It's true; I send out mixed signals when I joke around with other men. I look at him earnestly.

Ethan softens up a bit. "Don't get bent out of shape about it. We'll work on it together. We're already on our way. You told me in Cambridge that you appreciate my honesty. I think that's a good foundation for a relationship."

I nod vehemently. "That's exactly what I think. I'm so thankful that you give me such good advice."

"You're a lovable thing," Ethan says warmly. "It's a lot of fun to be with you." I feel his hand on my knee under the table. He softly massages my thigh.

"If you keep that up, we'll have to cancel our meal and go back to the room right away," I murmur.

"Okay, let's go," he says, his eyes gleaming.

I laugh rather loudly but keep it under control. Thankfully, no one turns around to look at us. *Be ladylike, Lea*, I say sternly to myself. "Unfortunately, we can't do that," I say. "I'll die of starvation."

The waiter soon comes with our meal, and we dig in. Ethan is so wonderfully noble and discreet. He doesn't speak much, so I while away the time observing the other guests and looking around the restaurant. The entire hotel is decorated in a historical style with lots of antiques. We could be a couple living in the nineteenth century, if it weren't for the fact that we're both wearing jeans instead of a long frock coat for him and a floor-length dress for me.

"Isn't it wonderful that we live in modern times?" I say.

Ethan looks up from his soup and says, "What do you mean?"

"I'm just so glad to be with you, and you with me—like you said before."

"And what does that have to do with modern times?" He looks at me as if I'm not very bright.

"Think about it—a hundred years ago, our being together would have probably been a huge scandal. My father would have probably had a duel with you, or we would have had to travel to Gretna Green so you could make an honest woman out of me."

He smirks. "What possesses you to come up with such things?"

"I do it all the time," I say. "I majored in English literature of the eighteenth and nineteenth centuries, and the novels of the period often involve scandals like that. In *Pride and Prejudice*, Elizabeth Bennet's world collapses when her younger sister takes off with a man. In George Eliot's *The Mill on the Floss*, the heroine is shunned by society because she's alone with a young man on a rowboat that drifts out to sea, where they are picked up by a fishing boat. Tess in Thomas Hardy's *Tess of the d'Urbervilles* has an extramarital affair." I'm completely wrapped up in the topic. "Should I tell you what happens to her in the end? Have you read the book?"

Ethan shakes his head. "Honestly, I don't find it very interesting. The stories sound like something out of a dime-store novel."

I feel like he threw cold water on my face. My beloved novels! The crème de la crème of English literature like dime-store novels? *Okay, I tell myself, it's Ethan's right not to be too interested in English literature.* Not everyone has a soft spot for it. I've been really into this subject for a long time. *Actually, most guys aren't into this kind of thing*, I think in an attempt to console myself.

"What do you like to read?" I ask.

"Oh, sometimes hunting or car magazines," he says. "I don't need anything else."

Of course! I should have thought of it myself. Real men read hunting or car magazines. That's Ethan. I'm mollified. Although . . . "I wish I could get you excited about literature," I say. "You can learn so much about people from books."

Ethan rests his spoon against the edge of the bowl, blots his mouth with a napkin, and reaches for his wineglass. "Lea, don't get mad at me, but I've always hated literature. It's all just fantasy and silly crushes." He sees the hurt look on my face and adds, "But it's nice that you have fun reading it. Even if your degree ends up being useless, you'll have a nice hobby with which to pass the time. That's good."

Of course, I can't expect him to share my enthusiasm—definitely not. I silently turn to my food. Sometimes I do wonder if my degree is practical. Maybe I should have studied something more hands-on, like architecture. But to do that, I would have needed to know math, and I was always quite hopeless at it in school. I'm a little bent out of shape that Ethan thinks so poorly of my intellectual pursuits. Maybe other people feel the same way. Maybe they pretend to be impressed just so they won't hurt my feelings. Maybe Jens only visited the museum in Cambridge with me because he has a crush on me. I'm gradually becoming aware of a pattern: the more time I spend with Ethan, the more I admire him. My self-image was probably quite inflated. Good. Ethan is helping me keep my ego in check. I was definitely arrogant and conceited.

Later we climb upstairs to our room. Once inside, I wrap my arms around his neck. "Ethan?" I say.

"Yes?"

"Do you know that I love you?"

He smiles disarmingly at me in a way that warms my heart. "I already assumed as much, otherwise you wouldn't have come to Thorpeness with me."

"I had no other choice. You marched into Alice's house and said"—I lower my voice to a low grumble—"'I came to kidnap Lea.'"

Ethan laughs. "Of course. I knew exactly what I wanted."

"That's exactly why I love you. You're so strong and self-assured. Next to you, I feel so small and insignificant, like a tiny mosquito."

Ethan fumbles with the buttons of my blouse. "Come on, little mosquito, off to bed," he murmurs in my ear.

The next morning we stay in bed late—we can't keep our hands off each other. After breakfast, we go to the beach and walk along the sea. We're silent most of the time. Why not? It's nice to be quiet. You can hear the sound of the waves, the chirping of the sandpipers, and even the rustle of beach grass in the wind. It's really beautiful. That said, the silence takes some getting used to. I usually talk quite a lot, but whenever I broach a subject with Ethan, he only murmurs in response or doesn't react at all. That's okay, though. Normally I chatter nonstop. It will be good to learn how to be calmer and more thoughtful. Calm, thoughtful people seem more profound, like Ethan.

Later, when I'm packing my bag to go home, I sigh loudly.

"What is it?" Ethan asks. "Are you in pain?"

"Yes," I say. "My heart aches. We had such a wonderful weekend. I'm sad that it's coming to an end."

Ethan doesn't respond, but I'm sure he feels the same as I do. On the trip home, my heart gets heavier and heavier. Ethan will drop me off at Alice's, and what's going to happen after that?

As we drive past the sign to Gatingstone, Ethan says, "I'm glad you don't live with that old pair of control freaks anymore. Alice isn't so old-fashioned. I think she's happy you're with me."

"Absolutely," I say.

"Certainly she wouldn't have anything against my visiting you there."

"Definitely not," I say happily. Then it hits me, and I add rather sheepishly, "You can only come over during the day, though. She has pretty strict house rules."

Ethan doesn't say anything, but I see his jaw tense as if he's upset about it.

I say quickly, "Maybe I could visit you sometime in Brantwood?"

"That wouldn't be smart. I don't like to bother my roommates with my personal life. The apartment is quite small."

How terrible, I think. How in the world can we spend more time together under these circumstances?

"Don't worry your sweet, little head, mosquito," Ethan says. "We'll find a way to be together. You'll see."

When we arrive at Rose Cottage, he leans over and kisses me very intensely. His hand wanders underneath my blouse. I push it away gently. "Don't make this any more difficult for me than it has to be," I say. Then I kiss him, grab my bag, and jump out of the car.

"See you soon," he says. Then he starts the car and drives away.

Chapter 10

Catherine returns from Brittany relaxed and refreshed, and, naturally, she wants to resume our usual activities.

"Are we going to play tennis again? That would be so cool. The weather is great. How about Thursday?" she asks me during our lunch break on our first day back at school.

"I can't. I have a date." Actually, Ethan needs new hunting boots, so I'm accompanying him on his shopping trip to Colchester.

"Whoa! A date!" Catherine exclaims. "Is there something I don't know?"

I struggle a little; then I confess: "Yes, I'm seeing someone."

Catherine is pleased. "How great! Who is it? Where did you meet him? You have to tell me everything."

We're in the school cafeteria, and the noise is deafening, as always. "Here?" I say. "Impossible!"

"Okay, then, I'll come by your place this afternoon. I want to check out where you ended up, anyway."

Just then Ethan walks by our table. He doesn't look at me—we've decided not to advertise our relationship—but in passing he glides his hand briefly over my shoulder, his fingertips stroking my neck. No one would have noticed if I hadn't turned beet red under Catherine's sharp gaze. Crap! The slight physical contact and my reaction don't escape her attention.

She says immediately, "Is it him? Are you seeing Mr. Derby?"

I nod. I admit, I'm a bit proud of it. Ethan is the most sought-after bachelor around, and I'm with him.

I expected Catherine to squeal or go pale with envy. Instead, she just looks dumbfounded and shakes her head. "I can't believe it. You—with him? Don't you know what everybody says about him? He's an incorrigible womanizer!"

"Oh, that's absolutely not true. People say that just because he's so good-looking. People always think that about handsome men."

But Catherine isn't convinced. How can I convey to her what a wonderful man he is? I'm still thinking how to say it—I can't just tell her that sex with him is over the top—when Catherine jumps up to clear away her plate.

"I personally can't suffer him one bit," Catherine says, standing over me. "He cut me off before autumn break from one day to the next. Now he ignores me completely."

I look at her, totally perplexed. "Why would he do such a thing? You must be mistaken." Maybe Catherine begrudges my happiness. Maybe she's a little jealous. I'll always have to live with this type of thing as Ethan's wife.

Catherine bends down and says in my ear, "Oh no, I'm not mistaken, Lea. I can tell you exactly when he cut me off. It was the night he took me out on a date and I told him quite clearly that I wouldn't sleep with him." She straightens up and walks off, her head held high. I'm thunderstruck.

On the way home, I brood over her words. What kind of a strange story is that? Did Catherine make it up? I can't believe what she said is true. Unless it went something like this . . . Ethan must have invited her on a date out of politeness. As a foreign student, she's a little lonely.

Exactly. After all, she made crêpes for everyone. The date was a small thank-you for her efforts. That is so typical of Ethan. He's a gentleman through and through. He must have noticed that Catherine felt attracted to him. Maybe he knew about her boyfriend and didn't want Catherine's hopeless crush to ruin things for them. Ethan obviously had no interest in Catherine at that time because he was already totally interested in me. I know this from our evening at the pub when he whispered such sweet nothings in my ear. Catherine sensed his coldness toward her, and because she liked him very much—how could a woman be with Ethan and *not* like him—she said something snide, like she wouldn't sleep with him, anyway. That's when Ethan decided, in keeping with his well-bred manners, that it would be better for them both if he gave her a wide berth in the future.

Poor Catherine! I feel so sorry for her. It's hard enough to be rebuffed, but then to see how happy I am with Ethan? I hope it doesn't hurt our friendship. I really like her a lot. I hope she'll still come by this afternoon.

When she does, I'm so pleased that I put extra effort into making tea while she admires the living room.

"It's really great here," she says approvingly. "Much brighter and more comfortable than at the Lanes'."

"Yes," I say. "And in a few days I'll even have my own bathroom." I tell her how I ended up moving and about the fight with the Lanes.

"Frankly, I wondered how you stuck it out for so long," Catherine says. "I couldn't have survived a week. They smothered you so much."

"It wasn't *that* bad," I say. "They meant well. But now that I live here and I'm independent again, I feel really great. Ethan was the one who suggested I move out."

Catherine stiffens when I mention his name. What an ass I am! I wasn't going to bring him up. I don't want to hurt her unnecessarily. I only did it because my head is so full of thoughts about him these days I'd really prefer to talk of nothing else.

Catherine measures her words carefully. "Lea, I respect the fact that you are seeing Ethan. I also respect the fact that you have a different opinion of him than I do, but don't expect me to talk about him with you. I don't talk about Christian incessantly."

"Sorry," I say. "You're right." I quickly finish setting the table and bring in the cake and teapot. As I pour the tea, I say, "Let's talk about something else. How was Brittany?"

"Super nice! I was so happy to see my family again—and my boyfriend, too. I'm going back home again for Christmas. I'm really looking forward to it. I must admit, I sometimes get terribly homesick."

I say, "I do, too, but I think it's a shame not to use time off to explore when you're abroad."

"Yes, you're right, of course," Catherine says, "but I also miss my loved ones. I figured out a great solution for spring break. My older sister is coming to England during her Easter holidays, and we're going to see Cornwall together. It's supposed to be really beautiful there—I always wanted to visit. My sister is going to drive, we'll travel up the coast and stay at a vacation rental."

I sigh. "That sounds so heavenly."

"You're invited," she says. "It would be so fantastic if you could come. Inez is going, too."

I blush and sheepishly say, "I don't know whether that will work. We—I mean, I,—may have other plans then."

Catherine stays cool. She bites into her cake with relish and says happily, "You don't have to decide immediately. We've got a couple months."

As we eat and sip our tea, we chat about all sorts of things. Then there's a pause, and Catherine looks at me thoughtfully. She suddenly asks, "Are you really okay?"

I roll my eyes. "Why do you ask that? Of course! I'm the happiest woman in the world!"

"Don't take this the wrong way, but you seem so subdued, as if you're under some sort of strain."

I look at her with puzzlement. What does she mean?

"I'm trying to find the right words," she says. "Usually you're so lighthearted and easygoing. You laugh about everything. But today you seem so different. Did something happen with your family?"

"No, nothing happened," I say. "You're imagining it. I'm still the same old Lea."

"Good," she says. But for the rest of her visit, she continues to give me strange looks, as if there is still something about me that bothers her. As we say our good-byes, I wonder whether she's trying to spoil things with me and Ethan a little. Maybe she wants to make sure I'm not that happy because she's jealous. That wouldn't be very nice of her, but I'll overlook it. I don't really have many friends in Gatingstone, and I would miss her terribly if we had a serious falling-out.

The next night all of us teachers meet up at the pub. Ethan and I don't sit next to each other, and I'm glad. His physical proximity would excite me too much, and everyone would see how crazy I am about him. Yet everyone seems to sense what's going on, anyway. People exchange furtive, knowing glances. Did Catherine say something? Maybe—I didn't ask her not to.

"How was Cambridge?" Anne asks me. "I see Ethan delivered you there in one piece."

I regale everyone with stories about my visit, including the chaotic house. Everyone seems quite amused. Ethan is silent, then at one point exclaims, "Our Lea is crazy! Everyone knows that staying with a bunch of students is bound to be a mess. Listening to you, Lea, you seem proud of your experience. But admit it, you're guilty of creating that situation."

The others are naturally eager to hear Ethan's reasoning. He smiles and says, "Lea let her hairdresser arrange her accommodations."

Our table roars with merriment. I laugh a little, but I really don't think it's all that funny. Hopefully, they don't all think I'm some sort of airhead.

"Don't let it bother you, Lea," Ethan says. "In English, we say, 'live and learn.' You're still wet behind the ears, so let the wind blow on them until they dry."

Although he looks at me tenderly, I'm a bit upset. I consider myself an adult, but Ethan obviously sees things differently. To be honest, I'm not so sure of myself anymore. All at once, I feel really small and helpless. I'm glad I have such a confident boyfriend; maybe some of his confidence will rub off on me. As a precaution, I'm silent the rest of the evening and just listen to the others chat. Catherine stares at me quite intensely, then looks away quickly when I catch her eye. What's on her mind? Perhaps she's thinking, *I'm so much prettier than Lea; I don't understand why Ethan prefers her over me.*

As it gets late, our lively group gradually leaves the pub. Only Ethan and I remain.

"You're not mad at me about earlier?" Ethan asks gently.

I know what he's referring to, but I act as though I don't. "About?" I ask.

"How I had a little fun at your expense."

I shake my head. "It was still a nice evening. I think a person ought to be able to laugh at herself."

"That's very kind of you. It's just that you are so terribly childish and naïve, my little mosquito." He puts his arm around me and pulls me to him. "When and where can we meet again?" he whispers in my ear, giving me goose bumps.

I shrug. "I don't know. It's your call."

"How about if I come by your place after school? I saw a door hidden in the back of the garden."

A chill goes through my body. That would be risky, even if it does make me tingle all over. I decide against it. "I don't want to give Alice any reason to kick me out," I say. "I really like living there. Besides, Maura could catch us."

"Well, I'm looking into a small country inn for the weekend," Ethan says.

When we leave the pub, Ethan pulls me into the shadows away from the streetlights. He kisses me so passionately it takes my breath away.

"Good night, mosquito," he says, and disappears.

Mosquito. Ethan uses it as my nickname, and right now, it seems quite appropriate. I feel like a small, buzzing mosquito that must constantly swirl around Ethan in order to survive.

On Thursday, we are going shopping in Colchester. Ethan rings the doorbell at four. Before I make it downstairs, someone lets him in. Apparently Maura has the day off from work. I hasten my steps and storm past Maura to throw my arms around Ethan in an attempt to kiss him. It occurs to me that Maura should see we are together right away. You never know.

"Hello, Ethan!" I say.

Ethan hugs me quickly, then pushes me away. His eyes glide over Maura's lush curves. She throws her auburn hair over one shoulder and appraises him boldly. Ethan's gaze remains on her in a way I do not like at all.

"Come on, sweetheart, let's go," I say quickly. "The shops aren't going to be open for much longer, and we have a long drive ahead of us." I've never called him "sweetheart" before. I feel his look of irritation burn through me. Uh-oh.

In the car Ethan is silent for quite a while. Only when we're on the highway does he finally say something. "Lea, I think we have to clear something up. I don't like public displays of affection. Also, I don't like it when you call me 'sweetheart.' It sounds so cheap."

I hang my head. I did something wrong—again. Crap! Sometimes I wonder how long Ethan will be able to put up with me. Will he finally get fed up with me and ditch me? I'd only have myself to blame for my misery. Sometimes I act like a spoiled child. Why don't I think before I do such stupid things?

"I'm sorry, Ethan," I say. "It just slipped out. But since you call me 'mosquito,' I'd like to have a pet name for you, too."

"Ethan's a lovely name. I think you should just stick with that," he says.

I can understand. Ethan *is* a beautiful name. Perhaps nicknames are a little derogatory. At the Lanes', I'd gotten used to being called "love," but maybe I shouldn't have. Maybe they wouldn't have smothered me so much if I'd forbidden them to call me that from the outset. Under certain circumstances, keeping your distance is definitely better. But I do feel a little put out when I think that Ethan wants *me* to keep my distance. We're a couple. I wouldn't do anything that would hurt him. I love him too much for that. Should I tell him that? Right here, right now? I decide against it. I respect his position. Maybe I'll succeed, little by little, in convincing him to let his guard down. I'll definitely need to be patient.

Ethan finds his hunting boots quickly. He knows the style he wants and where to find them. Later, he says, "I'd like to get you something nice for coming with me. What would you like?"

"Oh, we don't have to do that."

"Come on."

"Then I'd really like to browse a bookstore."

Ethan snorts. "I thought you girls liked new clothes or shoes. That's what I would have expected."

I look at him sternly. "I'm not 'you girls,' Ethan. I'm an educated woman who wants to learn more."

"You don't have to do that," he says. "I like you the way you are. Once I marry, my wife won't necessarily have to work."

My heart skips a beat. He said, "Once I marry." That sounds electrifying. It's the first time Ethan has spoken to me directly about marriage. Is it possible that I'll have the insanely good luck to spend my entire life with him? How wonderful would that be?

Ethan continues, "You don't have to clutter your little mosquito brain with so much learned stuff, Lea. Come on, let's go shopping for some jewelry. How about a pretty necklace?"

He gazes at me so imploringly that I surrender. I can go to Colchester by myself to search for a book, or I can buy one on the Internet. I won't refuse a necklace from my boyfriend. We find a small jewelry store, and the seller sets a velvet tray with several necklaces on the counter. My eyes fall immediately on a pretty silver chain whose links are fashioned in a way that catches the light. I start to point it out, but Ethan grabs a totally different necklace.

"We'll take this," he says. The seller nods with pleasure. The chain is made of gold and is much more expensive. I don't like it—it looks too pretentious. Filigree jewelry is much more to my taste.

"Does it have to be that one?" I ask. "I prefer silver."

"Silver is too cheap," Ethan says without compromise. "Anyway, gold suits your skin tone better."

I give in. He's probably right, as usual. I'll just have to get used to the new chain.

When I get home later, I examine myself critically in the mirror. The necklace really doesn't suit me, and on top of that, it cost three times as much as the one I wanted. How annoying. I should have insisted on my preference. Now I have to wear it even though all my other jewelry is made of silver. Before leaving for England, I'd had my ears pierced, and my entire collection of earrings is silver. I can't wear a gold necklace with silver earrings. How stupid would that look?

Sighing, I pick up my favorite earrings—small, delicate hoops—and put them in my jewelry box.

On the weekend we drive to a country inn called The Three Lions in the nearby village of Stock. Of course, it doesn't take long before we jump into bed. Ethan can hardly wait. It's so exhilarating! His passion rolls over me again like a wave. Afterward we lie there, exhausted and happy, just like we did in Thorpeness. Apparently my worries that I wasn't good in bed were completely unfounded. We're perfect together. It's like a dream.

At night, I listen to his regular breathing after he falls asleep. I'm still awake because something rankles me. Of course, I think it's really great that he's so wild about me—I'm wild about him, too. But I'd prefer if we could take things a little more slowly and be more tender with each other. I wish he'd engage in a bit of foreplay—he wouldn't have to do much. Ethan rushes into sex like a gladiator who is sure of victory. He's certainly not plagued by any doubts in this regard. I wonder whether I should share my wishes with him. I don't want to offend him or be misunderstood. Will he think that I'm trying to criticize him? That's the last thing I would want to do. I would never criticize Ethan; I love him too much. No, it's better to just hold my tongue and wait. Maybe once things calm down and we get into a bit of a rhythm, he'll start to be a little more sensitive to my needs.

Weeks become months. Ethan and I meet regularly, usually at the same inn. Word eventually spreads that we're a couple. It's no longer a secret we have to hide from the villagers and the school. I'm quite sure everyone envies me.

I'm trying to prepare for my exam, but for some reason I'm not motivated. It's strange, because I have plenty of peace and quiet. Maura moved out, and Alice is usually away. I have the whole house to myself, yet I have to force myself to study. The exam becomes a necessary evil—something to get through, nothing more.

Christmas is fast approaching. In the village and throughout Essex, colorful Christmas lights hang everywhere. The first snow falls. The more ubiquitous the Christmas decorations become, the more I long for home. Ethan must celebrate Christmas with his family; Alice is going to her brother's in Cambridge; and, of course, Catherine is going to Brittany. I have absolutely no desire to hang around all by myself.

I call my parents and tell them that I want to come home over the holidays. I believe my mother literally jumps for joy while we're on the phone.

"I thought you wanted to stay there until the summer," she says.

"I thought so, too, but I've changed my mind. I want to celebrate Christmas as usual, at home with you and Dad."

My mother is very touched. "That's fantastic! I'm very happy. Do you hear that, Wilhelm?"

My father mutters something in the background.

"Lea," my mother tells him. "It's Lea. She's coming home for Christmas."

He mutters again.

She adds, "I'm going to get you an especially nice gift as a reward for coming home."

I smile. "That's not necessary."

"No, we already have an idea . . ."

I'm not looking forward to revisiting my childhood. Under Ethan's beneficial influence, I feel more grown-up and calmer—exactly as he wished. Wistfully, I think this might be the last time I'll celebrate Christmas with my parents. Who knows what will happen in a year? Maybe Ethan and I will have already begun our life together. It could happen.

When my parents pick me up at the airport in Hannover, I feel like an alien on a new planet. Everything seems so strange to me. Around me, I hear scraps of German and read German signs. For a moment, I even see my parents through the eyes of a stranger, as if I'm seeing them for the first time. My mother has a new hair color; apparently, she's started to color her gray hair. My father has new eyeglasses, which somehow make him look wiser, but also older. His hairline has receded a bit more. They throw their arms around me and hug me tightly, as if they never want to let me go. I hug them back.

On the trip to Bielefeld, I remain silent as I look out the window. The countryside along the autobahn looks so different. Were there always so many hills and valleys? In the distance, an evening haze hangs over the landscape. It hasn't snowed yet. The trees stretch their bare branches to the leaden sky. As a child, I was always fascinated by the picturesque silhouettes of the dark, leafless treetops. Here, unlike in Essex, rows of stately trees line the avenues.

"Lea, you're so quiet," my mother says. "Are you tired?"

"Hmm," I say.

"How was the flight?"

"Good."

"Anything interesting happen on your way here?"

I consider her question. Yes, there was an amusing incident with a woman who at the last second realized she was sitting on the wrong plane . . . But my parents probably wouldn't be very interested in that.

"Nope," I say. I lean my forehead against the cool window and look out dreamily.

After about an hour, we're home. My mother has decorated the house beautifully. Strings of Christmas lights glow merrily, and a thick fir wreath with round red ornaments hangs on the front door. My father carries my suitcase up to my old bedroom. It feels kind of strange to be here. I've matured so much during my time in England. Am I really the same Lea to whom this shabby teddy bear belonged? Is this my *Pride and Prejudice* movie poster? What compelled me to hang it up? The film wasn't all that great. Strange. Usually after a long absence—like after my time in Turkey or Lancaster, for instance—I immediately feel at home in this room. Now it seems as though nothing belongs to me. Perhaps I've finally become a grown-up under Ethan's influence. I feel so detached from the things that once belonged to young Lea.

My father puts my suitcase down. "Welcome home, my love," he says. "Mama says dinner will be ready in half an hour."

I nod. He leaves, pulling the door closed gently behind him. I throw myself on the bed and stare at the ceiling. There's my old butterfly mobile, which I made from paper in elementary school. It sways to and fro in the warm air coming from the radiator. A wing from one of the butterflies tore off years ago. I remember I gave it a name—Halbi, or something like that. I made up stories about how the accident happened and how Halbi would be healthy again.

I suddenly jump up, rip the mobile from the ceiling, and throw it in the trash. Without Ethan, I feel like Halbi, missing a wing. What he's doing now? Does he miss me at all? Does he miss me as much as I miss him? I'm used to Ethan being at the center of my world. All of my thoughts revolve around him and him alone. Should I call him? I'm sure he'll want to know I arrived okay. I could just send him a text, but I desperately want to hear his deep, velvety voice in my ear.

I dash downstairs to get my phone. My mother, who's setting the table, smiles warmly at me. "Do you have to use the phone now? Don't take too long, dinner's almost ready."

"Okay, okay," I mumble and go back up to my room.

The phone rings for quite a while. I almost give up when Ethan answers. In the background, I hear loud voices, laughter, and glasses clinking.

"Hi, little mosquito," Ethan says. "Did you arrive all right?"

"Yes, I just wanted to let you know."

"Great, thanks."

"Do you have a little time to talk?"

"Actually, you caught me at a very bad time. Theo and I are at a pub with a couple of friends. I can hardly hear you, it's so loud in here."

"Okay," I say.

Ethan almost hangs up, but I exclaim quickly, "Stop!"

"Yes? Is there something else?"

"I already miss you terribly."

Ethan laughs briefly. "Well, I hope so, my little mosquito!" Then he hangs up.

He doesn't say one word about missing me, too. Well, he was at a pub, with his brother and his friends—female friends?—sitting around him. Under these circumstances, Ethan would rather bite off his tongue than whisper sweet nothings in my ear. I can understand that. I throw myself back onto the bed and stare at my phone. I gained nothing by making that phone call—I feel almost the same as I did before. A tear runs down my cheek, and I wipe it away angrily. *Lea!* I scold myself. *You want to be an adult, so pull yourself together now. Don't cry. What would your parents think?* I blow my nose and wipe my eyes, then go downstairs.

My mother has prepared the meal with such love; I feel like the prodigal son about to feast on the fatted calf. She serves my favorite ham and cheese. She even bought a pomegranate; they are so hard to find, and I've always been quite crazy about them.

"Mama, everything looks so lovely," I say. "Thank you."

"We're just so pleased to have you home." She beams.

I look at my pleasant surroundings. The house is well heated. I can see the garden from the big window. Dad turned on the outdoor lighting, and I see the first snowflakes gently dancing in the light. In the dining room, we sit down at the large cherrywood table that belonged to my grandparents. Everything is comfortable, tasteful, and spacious. I think about the difference between our home and the Lanes' cottage. When I remember their camping table, I have to smile.

"What's so amusing?" my father asks.

"Oh, nothing," I say, reaching for the bread basket and taking a slice. I don't think my parents would be terribly interested in my anecdotes. They would think their daughter was pretty dumb to rent a room with such terrible living conditions. It would be embarrassing. My parents exchange glances, but say nothing.

After a while, my mother says, "I'm sure you've made some new friends there in England." She looks at me as if inviting a response. She wants to know if I have a boyfriend. Should I tell them about Ethan? No, I'd better not. What if we break up? Then it would be better if my parents never knew anything about him in the first place. Anyway, I'm an adult. My relationships aren't really any of my parents' concern. If we decide to marry, they'll know soon enough.

Instead I say, "I befriended a nice girl from Brittany. Her name is Catherine."

"Oh, lovely! Brittany is so beautiful. Maybe you can visit her there one day."

"Yeah, maybe."

And that's how the days go. I just want to relax and enjoy being back home, but my parents want to chat and gossip with me. I have nothing I want to share with them. I want to be left alone so I can think about Ethan. We phone each other almost every day, and every day I feel feverish until the moment I hear his deep voice. Unfortunately, our phone calls are relatively short and dull. Ethan—my gentle, understated Ethan—is just a very taciturn man, and it's even worse on the phone. During one of our brief conversations, he apologizes to me and says, "I hope you understand it's a sign of my great affection for you that I call you at all, mosquito, because I hate to talk on the phone."

Meanwhile, my words spill out like a waterfall just so he doesn't hang up. I talk and I talk. Ethan then sometimes wearily says, "Dear Lea, must you tell me everything now? We can pick it up again when we're together in Gatingstone."

It doesn't escape my parents' notice that I'm on the phone so often. "You and the French girl must be very close," my mother comments.

"Yes," I say, and change the subject.

The days go by quickly, and soon it's Christmas Eve. There's a small, flat package for me under the Christmas tree. My parents look on expectantly as I unwrap it. It's the special gift my parents promised me. I hold it in my hands, extremely grateful and happy: it's a brand-new smartphone. I have an old cell phone, and although it's pretty practical, I can't get on the Internet with it.

"We also set up a great contract for you," my dad says. "It covers both Germany and England at a flat rate for an entire year."

That is so amazing! It's exactly what I've always wanted—and needed. I can now send messages to Ethan to my heart's content—plus I can e-mail, chat, Skype, and take and send photos anywhere. I throw my arms around my dear parents and thank them profusely.

"I'm glad we got the right thing," my mother says. "It's hard to know what will make you happy these days." Her last sentence sounds a bit fishy, and I'm not the only one who notices it. My father seems shocked, too.

Bright-red splotches appear on her cheeks. This has been happening since she went through menopause, but usually only when she drinks a glass of red wine. "Oh nonsense," she says immediately. "I didn't mean it like that!"

But my father furrows his brow. His forehead is very high, so there are quite a lot of wrinkles. "No, Elsa. Now that you've mentioned it, you should stand by what you said." He turns to me. "We are both worried about you, Lea."

My mother nods.

"About me? How come?" I ask in amazement.

"We have the impression that something's bothering you," he says. "You've changed so much since you went to England."

I give them a puzzled look. "Changed? In what way?"

"Sweetheart, don't take it the wrong way, but you're uncharacteristically quiet and withdrawn. What happened to your usual lightheartedness? Where's your sense of humor?" my mother says.

"Did something happen to you in England?" my father asks. "Are you unhappy there? Maybe you should cancel the rest of your trip abroad and just come home. You could continue your studies in Münster after Christmas. No one would hold that against you."

What's wrong with them? Why are they harassing me like this? This is terribly annoying. I'd like to just say good night and retreat to my room, but that wouldn't be fair to them. It's Christmas, and I know they've been looking forward to my visit. I can't do it, especially after they've given me such a generous gift.

I think about how to best explain my change in personality. With a sigh, I realize they probably won't stop worrying until I tell them about Ethan. "You're definitely wrong about that," I say. "I'm not depressed. On the contrary, I'm incredibly happy."

"Oh?" my father says. He doesn't seem very convinced.

"Why are you so happy?" my mother asks.

"I met my dream man in England! His name is Ethan, and he's a teacher at the same school where I work. He loves me, too. Everything's incredibly awesome and wonderful!"

"Aha," my father says, and looks at my mother with a perplexed look on his face.

"I can still remember how happy I was when I met the man of my dreams and he told me that he loved me," my mother says. She smiles lovingly at my father. "But in my case, everybody noticed that I was radiating happiness. I became pretty silly and high-spirited—everything seemed so easy and carefree. The world was my oyster!"

"Oh, yes, I remember," my father says. "You were irrepressible. Nothing could upset you, and everything made you laugh."

I look at her. What do I say now? The Thomaner Choir Christmas CD, which we play every year when we exchange gifts, is playing in the background. "Rejoice, rejoice!" the boys jubilantly sing in their highest falsettos. How fitting.

"Just because that's the way it was with you doesn't mean that's how it is with everybody," I finally say. "With me, it's just different. My love for Ethan has a different effect on me. It's made me quieter, more contemplative, and more satisfied. That's okay, right?"

Again, my parents exchange glances. "I'll be honest with you," my mother says. "I liked the fun, lively Lea better." Her voice falters. "I miss her."

Oh, darn it all! Now tears are glistening in her eyes—and it's Christmas. Maybe this has something to do with menopause. I once read in a women's magazine that menopausal women cry more easily.

My father puts a reassuring arm around her shoulder and says, "Now, now, Elsa!" He turns to me. "If you're saying you're happier, Lea, we have to take your word for it. But—don't take this the wrong way—you don't look very happy."

I shrug. "I'm sure it's because I miss my sweetheart so much. I can't explain it otherwise. He has such a calming influence on me. He doesn't like it when I act like a clown. He prefers that I act like a grown-up. I'm learning a lot from him, rest assured."

But my parents don't look reassured at all. I decide to change the subject and say, "Aren't you one bit curious what I got for you? Unwrap your gifts already!"

The rest of the holidays aren't really fun. Although my parents hit the jackpot with the smartphone, I mostly mope around missing Ethan. My parents pick on me and speculate about things that aren't true. All my friends and acquaintances are with their families and apparently have no time or desire to do something with me. I have a feeling that since I live abroad, I'm out of sight and out of mind. I do have fun hiding away in my room with my phone, though, working my way through the owner's manual. Of course, I should be studying for my exam, but I'm not really motivated.

I download apps until my smartphone's memory protests. I rush into the city to buy a bigger memory card so I can download more stuff, like reading material for my exam. I notice that I can read it quite well even on the small screen. Maybe I should ask for an e-reader for my birthday. Then I could give away my many paperbacks and travel lightly. I would have preferred something like that from Ethan. I finger the gold chain around my neck. For the money that this stupid necklace cost, I could have bought at least three e-readers. But Ethan definitely would have refused to give me something like that. Sure, it wouldn't have been the most romantic gift in the world, but it would have been the perfect gift for me.

I log on to Facebook to see what all my friends are doing. One of my friends has changed her relationship status from "Single" to "In a relationship." I can do that, too! I update my profile. If only I had a photo of Ethan—it would create quite an uproar among my friends. Ethan also has a smartphone. Now I can chat with him as often as I want. As soon as I install the program, we can have at it.

Right before breakfast, I text him that I miss him. I take a photo of our Christmas tree, which still looks really good even after almost a week, although the needles are starting to drop. My mom keeps cautioning us that we should be careful not to bump into it. I send him links to exciting YouTube videos I discover while surfing the net, quiet things about hunting and stuff. I'm sure he'll be interested in them. Ethan puts up with it every day for exactly five days, and then he calls me. This is rather unusual for him. Most of the time I have to call him first.

"I'm glad you got a smartphone for Christmas," he begins the conversation. "I'm happy for you, but could you use it a little less, please?"

"Why? I thought you were happy about it."

"Dear little mosquito, I can't go anywhere without my cell phone ringing and vibrating constantly. It's too much. My friends make fun of me when we're at the pub. Would you be so kind as to give it a break?"

Phew! Now I am really frustrated. Now that I can finally be in constant contact with him, he doesn't want it at all.

Ethan realizes I've fallen silent. "Mosquito, we'll see each other again in a few days. Then we won't need to talk over the phone. I'd like a break from your bombardments."

"Does that mean that I should only call you once a day?"

"Yes, that's what it means."

Okay, great. Out of frustration I start playing a game on my phone. It's really great. There are colorful candies scattered across the screen, and you can shoot them with various weapons. It gives me a tremendous feeling of satisfaction when they shimmer and explode. Once I set my mind to a task, I'm quite relentless. It's why I'm such a good student. But now, instead of reading or studying for my exam, I spend my time on the game. I'm working my way up, level by level. It's quite entertaining. Every morning I wake up and play a few rounds. I take my phone with me to breakfast, put it next to my plate, and keep going. When my parents watch TV in the evening, I curl up in my favorite chair and play until my eyes burn.

My mother says, "Lea, don't you want to get together with your friends while you're here?"

"Nope," I say. "Why? I'm quite cozy here with you two. Am I disturbing you?" I turn the volume on my phone off so I won't bother anybody.

"No, of course not," she says. "But your recent activities seem extremely solitary, don't you think?"

"Huh," I mumble. "I'm just using my smartphone. Isn't it great?"

Shortly before New Year's Eve, I log on to Facebook and see that friends from my dorm are planning a New Year's Eve party. I'd love to go dancing. Every New Year's Eve, my parents watch the old comedy show *Dinner for One*, then the usual music programs. Shortly before midnight, my father opens a bottle of champagne. They toast each other, take a sip, and kiss. Then they hit the sack. I refused to participate in this tradition years ago; there were always a thousand more exciting things going on. But this year I could comfortably kill the time until midnight with my smartphone. After all, I'm already at level 48. It would be nice if I could crack level 50 to ring in the new year.

But I decide to drive to Münster. The Portuguese student went home for the holidays, and my roommates assured me I can sleep in my old room.

"Will you be very sad if you have to celebrate New Year's Eve without me?" I ask my parents.

"No, not at all!" they both say, almost simultaneously.

"On the contrary," my father adds. "You've always been so crazy about parties, we'd be worried if you didn't go!"

I understand. They're still concerned that there's something wrong with me. Well, they're going to have to get used to the fact that I've taken a giant leap into adulthood thanks to Ethan.

On New Year's Eve I stand on the street in front of my dorm in Münster and look up at the façade. It reminds me of the moment I got out of the limousine after my strange trip to Hohensyburg. Even I wonder about myself these days. Look how I've been wasting my time on childish bullshit recently! I'm glad that Ethan knows nothing about it. He would find it highly questionable; that's for sure.

I ring the bell, and Marc and Lisa come to the door immediately. They greet me effusively.

"Hey, stranger!" Marc says. "How are you? Long time no see. What's up?"

"Everything's okay," I answer.

Lisa pumps me for information right away. "I saw you changed your relationship status on Facebook. Tell us more!"

"Yes, I found the man of my dreams," I say confidently.

"Wow! Congratulations! When's the wedding?" Lisa laughs.

"Go ahead and make fun," I say. "That possibility isn't totally out of the question."

"So should we look for someone else to rent your room when Sophia goes back to Portugal?" Marc asks.

I say simply, "Maybe, who knows?"

I help them prepare for the party. We drape streamers, chill the champagne, and fill bowls with crispy snacks. The first students arrive around ten. We turn up the stereo and start dancing. It's getting more and more crowded. Heavens! Have these two invited everybody in Münster? I have to admit, although I think of Ethan with a guilty conscience, the party is really fun. I should be sitting in a chair somewhere, staring wistfully into the distance and holding a damp tissue in my hand. But I love to dance too much. It's the first time I've had the chance since the memorable party in Cambridge. I'm sure no one there is as wild and boisterous as I am. It's almost as if I developed a thirst for dancing that desperately needs to be quenched.

Just when I take a break to get something to drink, Jens appears in front of me. When he sees me, he smiles in joyful recognition. "Lea! Hey, how great to see you here! I thought you were in England."

I look around for the fastest way to get away from him, but the room is so densely packed I'm practically pressed against his chest. I recognize the scent of the cologne he wore in Hohensyburg. It doesn't smell half bad.

"Hello, Jens," I say too curtly. "Who invited you?"

He winces. I'm a bit ashamed of myself for being so rude. He was so nice to help me out of my predicament in Hohensyburg, and things weren't all that bad in Cambridge, either. So I say, "Sorry. That wasn't very polite of me. I'm glad to see you again, Jens."

He starts beaming immediately. When he looks at me like that because he's so obviously happy to see me, something inside me thaws a little, and I feel warm inside. I don't know how that happens. I'm definitely not cold. In fact, it's quite stuffy and hot in here. And yet . . . I can't quite put my finger on it. I probably drank too much. The alcohol is flowing quite freely. Everyone in the room has a bottle or glass in hand. Some people have indulged in other substances, too, but I leave those things alone.

Time marches on, and soon the hour is upon us. Everyone stares at their watches or their cell phones to see the moment when the old year finishes and the new year begins. "Five . . . four . . . three . . . two . . . one . . ." Our voices rise to a crescendo, and we cheerfully cry in unison, "Zero!" Everyone then shouts, "Happy New Year!" and hugs. Suddenly, in all the tumult, Jens wraps his arms around me. "Happy New Year, Lea," he says. He's not loud and obnoxious, but gentle and insistent. Then he gives me a kiss—not on my forehead or cheek, but directly on the mouth. Is it my fault or his? His lips linger significantly longer on mine than necessary. What should I do? Normally I would be obliged to give him a resounding slap in the face because he so shamelessly exploited the chaotic moment. But . . .

When the kiss is over, Jens looks at me guiltily. "I don't know what came over me. I'm sorry, Lea. It won't happen again."

After such a lame excuse, I *definitely* should slap him, but here's the problem: I feel the same way. I don't know what came over me. Cross my heart, his kiss was pretty good. And Jens is such a nice guy I even buy his protestation of innocence.

"It's okay, Jens," I say. "Don't worry about it. Come on, let's dance some more."

Just as we start to dance, Lisa swings past us with her partner. "I saw that," she says, teasingly wagging her finger.

"What?" I ask.

"Your kiss. I couldn't believe my eyes. What does that say about your committed relationship, Lea?"

I could strangle her. Furtively, I look at Jens to see his reaction. Apparently he hasn't been on Facebook much this week, because he obviously doesn't know. I should have told him the truth. Now, because he got zinged by the likes of Lisa, I don't have to.

He abruptly lets go of me. "Crap!" he says. "If I had known, Lea, I wouldn't have kissed you like that. I think I better leave now."

And he's gone. Over the heads of the other dancers, I see his shoulders droop as he goes to the door, grabs his jacket from the closet, and disappears. I feel so sorry for him. I really like him. I like how he's funny and cheerful. I can't remember the last time I had so much fun. We joked and laughed—it was almost as fun as the time we went to that restaurant in Hohensyburg. Yes, I do have a boyfriend, and he still is the man of my dreams. But it gives me no pleasure to hurt Jens.

Ethan. It occurs to me like a bolt of lightning that I totally forgot to call him at midnight. I take my smartphone out of my pocket and stare at it. It's already twelve thirty. What will he think of me? I look around. It's too loud for an intimate conversation, even in my room.

I slip into my coat and hurry out onto the street. With trembling hands, I find Ethan's number. While I'm waiting for him to pick up, I curse myself. What is wrong with me? Why did I let Jens kiss me? *It's probably because I miss Ethan so much*, I tell myself. I would have kissed anyone so I could pretend it was Ethan.

He doesn't pick up. Maybe he's at a New Year's celebration and it's too noisy for him to hear the phone ring. I send him a text. Up in the apartment, I push my way through the dancing couples, go into my room, and lock the door. I take off Sophia's bed linens and put them on a chair, and then I spread my sleeping bag on the bed. The bed smells of a strange, heavy perfume—something exotic. I lie on my back and stare at the ceiling.

As I fall asleep, something occurs to me that makes me stop and think. Jens's kiss wasn't just good; it was wonderful. It wasn't pushy or demanding. He made me feel like a queen, as if he were a humble knight currying my favor. I know it sounds corny, but that's how it felt.

Chapter 11

Only a few days later, I'm headed back to Stansted Airport. School starts again on Monday. Half my time in England is already over; summer vacation starts in June.

My parents don't want me to go. At the airport in Hannover, my father takes me by the collar of my winter coat and looks at me earnestly. "Lea, if you need to come home . . . if something happens that makes you want to leave . . . just tell me. I'll come pick you up—with the car if I have to."

"Oh, Papa," I say. "What are you thinking? I'm fine. I'm excited to get back to England and Ethan. You two should just look out for yourselves!"

My mother hugs me mutely and wipes away a tear. *Menopause is making her very sentimental*, I think.

On the plane, I put my phone on airplane mode and play my game as if possessed. I'm on level 102, which wasn't easy to get to; the game is pretty tricky. Ethan is picking me up at the airport, so when I land, my heart pounds with excitement and joy. I can hardly wait to get through baggage claim and see him. Of course, everything is especially slow, and my luggage is the very last one of a million bags to arrive on the conveyor belt.

Ethan towers over most people in arrivals, so I see him before he spots me. Oh, what a wonderful boyfriend I have! His brown eyes wander over the crowd, searching for me. He impatiently pushes his curls away from his forehead. I let my bags drop, rush forward, and throw my arms around him.

Ethan takes me by the shoulders, pushes me away a little, and looks at me reproachfully. "Are you falling into your old habits again, mosquito? A lady doesn't pounce on a gentleman in public."

I laugh. "And you're the same old Ethan. You must admonish and educate me once again. Hooray! All is right with the world."

But Ethan doesn't laugh. He looks at me with irritation and says, "Come on, let's go. The parking meter will expire soon." He grabs my suitcase and marches off.

I trot next to him like an overeager puppy. Uh-oh. I've fallen out of favor again. How annoying. I've screwed up our beautiful reunion with my foolishness. I would never have guessed Ethan wouldn't like my enthusiastic greeting.

"I'm sorry, Ethan," I say sheepishly. "You're right. It's only because we were apart for so long. You just have to have a little patience with me. I'll get used to everything again."

He turns around and gives me one of his rare smiles. "All right, my little mosquito. We'll straighten you out." He takes my hand, and we walk side by side to the car. As soon as we're inside, he leans over and kisses me forcefully and demandingly. I immediately feel like I'm melting away.

"So what are we going to do now?" I whisper.

"I'm taking you home, what else?" Ethan says.

I sink into my seat with disappointment. But Ethan laughs and says, "Just kidding, mosquito. I reserved a room at The Three Lions. You didn't think you could escape from me that easily, did you?"

We fall into bed quickly and passionately. It's beautiful, as usual. But after Ethan falls asleep, I'm wired. I take out my new phone and play my game. I turned off the ringtone, so when a text comes in, the phone vibrates: *I know I have no right to ask, but I would like to know whether you arrived safely in England.*

Oh great. Now Jens is stalking me over the phone. Where did he get my number? I quickly type, *Agreed*, then, *Yes*, and hit "Send."

Jens sends me a picture of a finger pointing at a sad face.

I send a thumbs-down icon.

Jens sends a question mark.

I send the most evil, annoyed-looking face on the emoji keyboard. That works—he doesn't answer. Good.

I keep playing my game. The current level is pretty difficult. Only two more levels to go . . . I can do this . . . I think I've got it this time . . . Hurray! Ethan's large hand suddenly covers the screen, and the game ends. That sucks. I was so close to conquering another level.

"It's extremely unnerving when you play on the phone while I'm trying to sleep," he says crossly.

"Sorry," I say. "I was so excited I couldn't sleep. I'll turn down the display so you won't notice."

"What are you doing, anyway?"

"I'm playing a really fun game. I was just saving a little rabbit from a chocolate lake where he'd gotten stuck."

Ethan moans. "Not only do I have to deal with students messing around with those things at school, now you're doing it."

"Ethan, I'm really good. Imagine, since Christmas I'm already on level 112!"

Apparently, Ethan is unimpressed. "Lea," he says—I've come to realize he only calls me by my real name when he's angry with me—"I really don't give a flying fuck what you're playing and what level you're on. Turn the stupid thing off and go to sleep this instant!"

Grinding my teeth, I put the phone down. "Okay, Ethan. Sorry."

He turns onto his side and looks at me, supporting his head with his elbow. "Tell me, Lea, are you ever going to grow up? Will I always have to deal with your childish whims?"

"No, you won't have to," I say. "Go back to sleep. I'll be a good girl now. Good night."

He dozes off again. My fingers itch to pick up the phone from the nightstand and continue to play, but I let it go. Perhaps I am overdoing it a little with the games. Besides, I don't want to annoy Ethan. I love him too much to do that. Everything is as it should be. He is the strong, smart, and sensible one, and I'm his little mosquito. I feel safe.

We fall back into our old routine. On the weekends, Ethan and I meet up somewhere. During the week, we don't have much time to see one another because we are busy preparing lessons or correcting homework. The school is satisfied with my work and allows me to lead class more often. I'm having fun and love the challenge. I'm especially proud of myself when I occasionally get feedback from my students that they enjoy my lessons.

Ethan laughs at me. He thinks I shouldn't make anything of it. "The students are nice to you only because they know you're just an assistant. There's nothing at stake for them. What do you think would happen if you were their regular teacher? They'd probably make mincemeat out of you."

That logic doesn't make any sense to me, though. When I was a student, it was the reverse. The students harassed the substitute teachers, exactly because there was nothing at stake for them. When the students liked a substitute teacher who motivated them to finish their lessons on time, he was held in high esteem even among more experienced colleagues. But I've given up talking with Ethan about these things. It's not important enough to fight over.

Inez, Catherine, and I continue to go to our class in Brantwood to prepare for the Cambridge certificate. We'll be tested at the end of February. After our last lesson before the test, we sit down together rather wistfully at the pub where we've gone after every class. We still laugh about the first time we came here, when the owner didn't want to serve me because he thought I was too young.

"Do you remember all the wise pronouncements we made?" Inez says after she takes a long drink of her beer. "Lea, you announced that you wanted to stay single for a long time, and that a dream man was impossible to find."

"Ha," I say. "That's right. And now I found him, and he's much more than I would have ever believed possible."

Catherine looks at me thoughtfully. "I remember something that you said at the time, too, Lea."

I wave her off dismissively. "Seems to me I was talking a lot of nonsense that evening."

But Catherine continues, "It didn't seem like nonsense to me then, and it doesn't seem like nonsense now. I remember you said you could never be with a man who treated you like a child and didn't respect you. Do you remember? I told you about Christian and how he treated me that way."

"And has he changed over the last few months? Did your plan work?" Inez asks, interested. She tucks her long hair behind her ears and looks at Catherine eagerly.

Catherine sits up straight. Her big, beautiful eyes widen. "Oh, yes, very well indeed," she says. "Christian is extremely impressed that I'm successfully making my own way in England. It's incredible. Things have become so much better between us. He no longer looks down on me but instead treats me with respect and even admiration. That's how I always imagined our relationship. It's a partnership now."

"It's the same with Ethan and me," I say with satisfaction.

"Really?" Catherine says dubiously.

"Of course!"

Catherine lowers her eyes and says, "I'm sorry, but I don't see it that way."

For a moment, I think I didn't hear her correctly. What is she talking about? I really like Catherine, but I'm starting to feel a bit annoyed. "Well, then, please explain it to me," I say.

"Lea, I see how Ethan treats you when we're at the pub or out together," she says.

"Yes, he cherishes me. Ethan is a perfect gentleman."

Catherine persists. "If Christian treated me like Ethan treats you, I would shoot him on the spot."

What in the world is going on? What is the matter with her? Then it hits me. "Catherine, could it be that you're a bit jealous? I really am starting to think you have a crush on him."

"I *what*? That is ridiculous! Ethan is very handsome, and any woman would feel attracted to him of course, but . . ."

"But what?"

"But I have Christian. I love him and only him." Catherine hesitates, as if she's not sure she should say more. "Ethan is so condescending and disrespectful to you, I don't understand how you put up with it."

I wince as if she just slapped me in the face. "Have you gone crazy? Where do you come up with this stuff?"

Catherine leans forward and says, "I have eyes, Lea. When you two are together, you stare at him like a lost little puppy. You don't even dare to open your mouth. When you do make a remark, he puts you down and acts as if you are too stupid to exist."

I feel rage beginning to boil inside me. I have the urge to say something very nasty and bitter.

Inez puts a hand on my arm and says, "That would explain some things."

I turn to her. "Oh, so now you want to add your two cents? Are you both conspiring against me?"

"No," Inez says. "Of course not. Calm down, Lea, and just listen. You're our friend. We don't want to hurt you any more than you'd want to hurt us."

I cross my arms, lean back, and hiss, "Well, then, let's get it all out, Inez. What do you mean by 'that would explain some things'?"

Inez puts her glass down and looks me right in the eye. "Maybe the way Ethan treats you is why you've changed so dramatically."

"*I've* changed?" I snort in disbelief.

"Yes, you have," Catherine says.

"In what way, pray tell?"

"Only six months ago, you were the personification of *joie de vivre*," Inez says. "It just bubbled out of you. Your attitude was contagious—you infected everyone around you."

Catherine nods. "And you were so strong and confident, I envied you and secretly wished to be more like you."

"But I'm still the same," I say rebelliously.

Catherine raises her eyebrows and gazes at me silently.

Inez clears her throat and says, "No, you're not, Lea. You've become a quiet, passive gray mouse. You don't tell jokes, and I get the feeling you try hard to suppress your emotions. Quite honestly, you don't seem to be very happy."

"I can explain that," I say, "but you're probably not really interested. You've already made up your mind."

Catherine seems hurt. "Lea, don't be that way with us. We mean well, really. Good friends should be able to tell each other the truth, right?"

Inez adds, "Sometimes, good friends *have* to tell the truth. Ethan is not good for you, Lea. It worries us."

Catherine puts her hand on Inez's arm. "You don't have to put it so bluntly, Inez."

I try to sort out my thoughts. I want to explain how I've changed to my "well-meaning" girlfriends. "On the contrary, Inez," I say. "Ethan has been enormously good for me. He's had only a positive influence on me. Before I met him, I was just a silly, naïve girl. I laughed about every stupid thing. Every person I met always told me that. I was a big pain in the ass." I pause to take a big gulp of beer and continue. "Ethan set me straight and helped me act more sophisticated. He taught me how to behave elegantly and unpretentiously. And in the meantime, I've become very pleasant company for him. He says so himself. We are quite comfortable together."

Catherine says gently, "*I* liked you better before. I never found you to be a pain in the ass."

"Yes, Lea, I'm sure he feels comfortable with you, I can totally believe that," Inez says. "That's because he's molded you into exactly what he wants you to be, and you let it happen."

I slam my glass on the table. "I've had enough of this! I don't need to listen to this nonsense. You two can sit here and talk trash about me for a while longer, but I'm leaving. Good night!" I shove my chair back, grab my bag, and storm out.

When I look over my shoulder, I see how baffled they look. But I'm the one who has every reason to be baffled. What is the matter with those two? How do they come up with such completely unfounded and absurd statements? My eyes burn. They have pushed me to the point of tears. I'm glad I left them when I did. I don't want to give them the satisfaction of seeing me cry. Foaming with anger, I wait at the bus stop. They're saying exactly the same bullshit my parents did over Christmas. They all have some nerve. Do they think the world revolves around them?

But something starts to gnaw at me. A horrible thought occurs to me: what if they're right? The thought freezes me on the spot, and I rub my upper arms. *What if how you've changed for Ethan has been to your detriment?* a nasty, nagging voice says. Oh nonsense. That can't be. If that were the case, other people would have said the same thing. And I'd feel out of sorts and unhappy, which I don't. Although . . .

Inez's and Catherine's words make me think back to the time before I met Ethan. Is it really true that my former *joie de vivre* was childish naïveté? *Lea, you of all people know that is not the case. You know that you had very real reasons to be happy*, the voice tells me seriously. I shut up and decide to listen. The bus arrives, and I step in. Although it's almost spring, it's still dark already, and I can't see out the window. Instead, I'm confronted with my own reflection. I stare at my large, unhappy eyes. My inner voice continues, *You know there's some truth to what your parents and your friends are saying. See for yourself whether it's true or not.*

Oh, shut up, I think. There is only one way to find out. I need to start paying attention. If Ethan is really trying to change me, as Inez claims, I'll notice it. I admit, my perceptions are somewhat clouded in Ethan's presence. People call that "love." But I'll just have to be a little bit more observant.

The opportunity arises sooner than expected. Ethan wants to introduce me to his family—that is, his widowed mother. She lives in a former vicarage in a village called Sternham, west of Aldeburgh. Ethan's father was a pastor. His successor moved into a new rectory, so Ethan's mother was allowed to stay in the old building after her husband's death.

On the ride to Sternham, I'm churning inside, but I find it thrilling that Ethan wants me to meet his mother. Everybody—and I mean everybody—knows what this could mean. I think Ethan is sealing our fate. Very soon I could be a bride at the altar at Sternham's village church. I should be excited, but for some reason my enthusiasm has dampened a bit. Since that evening in Brantwood, I can't stop thinking about what my friends said. I might have just ignored the whole thing if it hadn't been for the fact that the same thing happened with my parents over Christmas. Phrases and sentence fragments surface like ghosts, harassing me:

Lea, you're so quiet.

Sweetheart, don't take it the wrong way, but you're uncharacteristically quiet and withdrawn. What happened to your usual lightheartedness? Where's your sense of humor?

Did something happen to you in England? Are you unhappy there?

I ask myself the same question: *Am I unhappy*? No, of course not. I have the best boyfriend in the world. Okay, let's rephrase the question: *Am I completely happy*? That's more difficult to answer. If I'm going to be totally honest with myself, the truth is it's very tiring being Ethan's girlfriend. I constantly get the feeling that I'm not good enough for him.

Last night I played my favorite game before falling asleep. The game is rather taxing, and I've had to be tough and patient to work through each level. Sometimes the game feels too hard for me, but because I'm so persistent, I stay with it. Occasionally, a task is so insanely hard I get mad at the stupid game and whoever made it. Sometimes I lash out in a stream of curses; other times the game rewards me with a sense of accomplishment.

It occurs to me that being with Ethan is also like playing a game. With him, I never feel relaxed or casual. I always feel like I have to fight to keep his love and attention. It's a heavy burden to bear. It's possible I do seem exhausted to my parents and friends. *But it's all worth it*, I tell myself.

It's a balmy spring day, and we've rolled our windows down a bit. Ethan's curls are blowing in the wind. I look at his perfectly chiseled profile, his angular jaw, and his straight nose. He's still my dream man.

As usual, Ethan is quiet. Something suddenly occurs to me. "Can you please stop at a flower shop somewhere, Ethan? I'd love to buy some flowers for your mother."

"That only occurs to you now?" he asks. "You've known for days that we're going to Sternham."

The underlying message is: Lea, you're disorganized. Anybody else would have already purchased flowers. Half of me says, *I'm sorry, I'll do better next time.* But before I open my mouth, my other half speaks up: *It's not very nice of Ethan to put you down over this. If he is really the gentleman you think he is, he shouldn't think twice about stopping at a flower shop.*

But this thought seems so horrible, mean, and disloyal that I say, "You're right, Ethan. I should have gotten a bouquet in Gatingstone. I'm sorry to trouble you with it now."

"I'll be damned if I'm going to stop somewhere now," Ethan says. "When you plan things so poorly—and you do that quite often, Lea—then you must face the consequences."

Wow. I gulp.

Ethan glances at me. "Mosquito, if I constantly have to cover for all your mistakes, then I'll spoil you and you'll never become the woman you can be."

That doesn't make me feel better. I feel worse than ever. Thanks to my friends, I'm much more perceptive today. Usually, I wouldn't have recognized the latent cruelty of his words, which is that I'm far from good enough for him. There's obviously still an enormous amount to overcome in our relationship. There are clear parallels between this and my frustratingly difficult game. But who says I have to always be deferential and swallow what Ethan says? I try a new tactic.

"Ethan," I say, "if you were in a similar situation and you accidentally forgot something, I would help you out, you know that."

Ethan shakes his head. "I am never, ever this disorganized, my dear Lea."

This cuts me to the bone. *You're not that perfect,* I think to myself and retort, "You know I love you, but you make mistakes sometimes, too."

The atmosphere grows tense. "So you're lecturing me now?" he says.

I sigh. I might as well keep going. "That would only be fair," I respond. "You just lectured me." The little voice inside me adds, *Every time we're together.*

Ethan pulls off to the side of the road. He shuts off the engine, turns to me, and stares. "Lea, what is wrong with you? Why are you being so nasty to me? Could you please stop it and be your usual sweet self again? I don't see why I should let you criticize me."

I stare at the road in front of us. A bird chirps in a nearby tree, and the trees are already full of green buds. I love this time of year. It's so full of hope and promise. Although it breaks my heart, and I know that I'm risking a lot, I say firmly, "Why not? Why can you criticize me, but I can never criticize you?"

Ethan's face darkens. "Because I know more than you do, Lea. I'm older and have more experience. It's my right to point things out to you. You are like a freshly hatched chick. You still have eggshell behind your ears. What do you know about the world?"

I must look pretty shocked, because Ethan's voice softens. "Look, little mosquito, we get along beautifully. Why should anything change between us?"

Yes, why? Gradually the feeling steals over me that we get along so beautifully only because Ethan calls the shots, and I always do exactly what he wants me to do. There is so much I could say right now in response, but I bite my tongue and say, "It's okay, Ethan, just keep driving. Your mother will wonder where we are."

Ethan starts the motor, puts the car in gear, and takes off, tires squealing. He seems to be hopping mad. I realize it's the very first time I've ever talked back to Ethan—and I did so relatively gently and quietly. His violent reaction shakes me up. This much is becoming clear to me: if I want a nice, mutually respectful relationship with Ethan, like Catherine has with Christian, then a lot has to change. I suddenly realize that Ethan doesn't respect me one bit, while I look up to him way too much. The idea creeps me out. So, where do we go from here? The best thing to do is just wait and see.

While Ethan drives, I think about how it came to this. Why have I only just now noticed what's going on? Have I been that blind? Love is notorious for doing that to people. I know myself quite well. I have qualities that may not necessarily be absolutely praiseworthy but are nonetheless quite useful. I've had them my whole life. For starters, I have the ability to respond flexibly to people and situations. I'm a bit of a chameleon. These animals are known for their ability to adapt to the environment to protect themselves from their enemies, which would devour them. I am an interpersonal chameleon. If a situation appears to be unfavorable or threatening, I adapt so I can fit in. When I was at the Lanes', I implemented this ability wonderfully until I finally found the situation too much to bear. Anyone else would have moved out immediately, but I told myself that the accommodations were practical and made the best of it. It worked great for a while. Often, however, a certain amount of dissatisfaction grows inside me that at some point I can no longer suppress. *Pow*! I attack others quite unexpectedly. What happened with the Lanes was relatively mild in comparison.

And what about Ethan and me? Something bad has developed. Poor Ethan has apparently calmed down again and doesn't suspect anything. All at once, I recognize that I'd become a chameleon again. For Ethan's benefit, I made myself seem small, sweet, inexperienced, and eager to learn—a little mosquito, just how he likes it. But that person has little to do with the real Lea. I repressed the confident, cheerful Lea and forbade her to speak up. I knew the whole time that Ethan would not like the real Lea. It made sense to me because I was terrified of scaring off my dream man. One thing is clear as day: I can't keep up this masquerade. At some point I'll be exposed, because it's as insanely exhausting as a tricky computer game. I just can't take it anymore. I'm worn out and sad. The people who really know me see it.

I've created a big mess. There are only two possibilities now: either admit I'm a fraud and break up with Ethan, or accustom him to the real me in a loving and gentle way. The first would break my heart and, hopefully, Ethan's, too. The second could work, but only if I proceed very slowly. I'm confident that Ethan will come to know and respect the new Lea. I know that he loves me. To help him cope with the change, I'll gradually project more confidence each day. Hopefully Ethan will interpret my behavior as a positive development. Maybe he'll even think his wonderful influence has made me more his equal. Our sex life might even improve as a result; it would be nice if Ethan took a bit more time to satisfy my sexual needs. If that could happen, everything would be perfect. So that's the plan. I'm confident it will do the trick.

Ethan watches the road, ignorant of the plan I've just hatched. I feel sorry for him. It's not his fault at all. He's simply Ethan. He fell in love with a younger woman who looks much younger than her age. He has no way of knowing that I'm really quite sensible and mature. My behavior when he's around hasn't always been very sensible or mature; I admit it. But now I'm going to change that. I wonder if Ethan will even notice. If I'm careful and patient, he might never know the difference when I stop being a chameleon and start showing my true colors. He'll rub his eyes and think that he's probably imagining things, and that nothing has changed that much.

Ethan slows down, and I see a sign for Sternham. I love these villages in Essex and Suffolk. Once again, I am delighted by the colorful cottages, always arranged around a well-kept duck pond. A small, old church tries to look impressive with its massive stone walls, but it's too tiny to succeed. My heart beats faster seeing it. Who knows? Maybe I just caught a glimpse of my wedding chapel for the first time. A wedding in Bielefeld would be nice, too. Several picturesque churches come to mind. They'd all be suitable for a beautiful ceremony, but one in an English village . . . There'd be something so dreamy about it, like out of a Rosamunde Pilcher romance. It would be a dream come true.

Ethan turns into a driveway with a large wrought iron gate. The gate is opened wide, and a sign indicates that the house is the old vicarage, a very dignified residence built of gray stone. It doesn't look as quirky as the colorful stucco houses in the village. The façade is covered with dark-green ivy. It is surrounded by a small garden and, farther off, tall trees.

My heart is pounding faster now. How will my first encounter with Ethan's mother go? These occasions are quite significant! I don't want to do or say anything wrong. I'm going to try to act invisible. I won't make the same mistakes with Mrs. Derby that I did with Ethan. Of course, I don't intend to march into the house with a look-at-me, here-I-come attitude but will carry myself politely and confidently, as if there's no chance she could one day be my mother-in-law.

We step up to the front door, and Ethan grabs the shiny, heavy brass lion's paw doorknocker. He only knocks twice before the door opens. Aha! Mrs. Derby has been expecting us. The first thing I notice about Mrs. Derby is how small she is. She has a petite figure and is dressed in a fine tweed skirt, a pristine white shirt, and a gray cardigan. She looks stylish, partly because she has the same elegant features as my Ethan. Her heather-gray hair is pulled back in a loose knot. Perhaps I expected a cool reception, but this is not the case at all. Mrs. Derby takes my hand gently in her tiny palm and scans my face with her dark eyes, as if she wants to learn everything about me all at once. She greets me warmly.

"Lea, how nice to meet you at last! Ethan has told me so much about you already. Welcome to our house. Come in, take off your coat. Let me show you to your room, and then we'll have a nice cup of tea."

As I follow her upstairs, I wonder why the English always say "nice cup of tea." Everyone, everywhere says the same thing. Funny—it's like how we Germans say "good butter." Is there even such a thing as a bad cup of tea? Probably not.

Mrs. Derby opens the door to the guest room. "Here is your kingdom, Lea. Make yourself at home." Ethan and I have been assigned separate sleeping quarters, of course. He'd already warned me. The room is not big, but bright. The narrow bed is covered with snow-white linens edged with fine lace. I go to the window and look out. There are precisely cut boxwood hedges in the backyard, along with the first daffodils and tulips of the season.

Mrs. Derby shows me the bathroom and returns downstairs. I sit down on the edge of the bed and look around. Whew! It's going pretty well so far. I didn't have to open my mouth once. She seems so dear and gentle I certainly have nothing to be afraid of. I undo my hair and comb it, then neatly braid it. I put on a touch of fresh lipstick, smooth my eyebrows with a wet finger, and go back downstairs.

Ethan is sitting at the coffee table, while his mother flits around and pours tea from a silver pot. Pastries and the inevitable cucumber sandwiches are on the table. I sit very straight and wait till she speaks to me.

"I hear you study English literature," Mrs. Derby says, "and that you want to be a teacher."

"Yes, very much," I say. "I'm very happy teaching at Gatingstone School."

Ethan takes a sip from his teacup, then sets it down. "I've tried to make it clear to Lea that what she's doing now is not real teaching. She's just an assistant teacher, so it won't always be like this. Right now, the students eat out of her hand. And the fact that she's a foreigner has a certain exotic appeal."

He's doing it again. I can't believe he's mercilessly belittling me right in front of his mother. I clear my throat and say, "That would be nice if it were true, but I'm sorry to say I haven't noticed that. I expect my students to be responsible. It isn't always easy, because English schoolchildren aren't all angels. Occasionally I must be quite strict."

Ethan slaps his thigh and laughs. He's not usually so open and cheerful in my presence. "What kind of nonsense are you babbling about, Lea? You, strict? Don't make me laugh. I bet they lead you around by the nose."

Normally I would have lowered my head and quickly changed the topic. But now I decide to put my new tactic into action. I fix my attention on Ethan coolly and say, "Really? How do you know that? Did you hear this from someone?"

Ethan looks at me sternly. He's never seen me like this. "No," he says with determination, "but I know you, Lea. As small and helpless as you always are, you could never hold your ground in front of a class." He shoots me a furtive glance. He seems troubled that I can match wits with him in front of his mother.

I laugh and shake my head. "It's so lovely that you're always so worried about me, Ethan. But I can assure you, just because I'm small and look young doesn't mean that I'm helpless. When the situation warrants it, I can be very self-confident."

Ethan's mother is moving her head back and forth, like a spectator at a tennis match, her brow furrowed. I realize that I need to talk back less; otherwise this visit could end up being quite uncomfortable.

So I say, "But what am I talking about? Of course I can't really compete with such an experienced teacher as you, Ethan."

"That's better, my little mosquito," he says, and calmly sips his tea.

Mrs. Derby quietly says to me, "I have great respect for anyone who can assert themselves in the classroom. I was the village schoolteacher here before I married Mr. Derby. At that time, it was common practice for a married woman, especially a minister's wife, to abandon her profession. I was so happy! I hated that school. My husband literally saved me."

Ethan places one of his large hands over hers. "My dear, sweet mother, I imagine they made mincemeat out of you." I must agree with him. The idea of this small, delicate woman with her soft voice having to face thirty little devils makes me almost melt with compassion.

"Unfortunately, my husband died much too soon," she continues. "Ethan was just fourteen, and Theo was twelve at the time. The boys were fantastic. Without them I would have had a much harder time of it."

As I gaze at Ethan, I feel very touched. This is the first time I've heard these things about him. How nice that his mother speaks about him with such tenderness. It makes sense. Because of his father's untimely demise, Ethan had to take on a lot of responsibility and grow up very quickly.

"It's very chilly in this room. Wasn't the heating repairman supposed to come?" Ethan asks. He jumps up, touches the radiator, and frowns. "It feels stone-cold."

"Oh, I completely forgot," his mother says. She tugs at her cardigan. "I always dress so warmly, I don't notice the lack of heat at all. Sorry, Lea, the heater is defective. But you don't have to freeze. Should I get one of my jackets for you?"

Ethan rolls his eyes. "Mother, I've talked of nothing else for weeks. You've got to do something. You absolutely *must* call them. The repairman only comes when you nag him."

"Yes, yes," Mrs. Derby whispers. "You're right. I'll call first thing on Monday."

Ethan says angrily, "I can't take care of everything from Gatingstone. If I come here next time and it's still freezing, then you can freeze by yourself. You'll only see me in the summer."

Mrs. Derby looks at me apologetically. "You see, Lea, I'm absolutely helpless without Ethan. He can be very impatient sometimes, but I'm so glad he looks out for me."

Hmm. Their exchange is rather disquieting. Ethan used an extremely harsh tone of voice with his mother. Doesn't she realize that? Apparently not. She sits with her hands folded on her lap and looks at her son with admiration.

Now Ethan finds something else amiss. He bends over and looks under the radiator. "There's a ton of dust bunnies underneath here. Tell me, Mother, doesn't Mary Barnsley come twice a week?"

Mrs. Derby says to me, "He means the cleaning lady. A darling soul. She lives in the village."

"And my mother loves her way too much," Ethan explains. "She needs to be more strict with her. She didn't even look under here. She cleans only where she thinks a person can see."

Mrs. Derby sighs. "I'll tell her."

Ethan frowns and says to me, "She says that now. Of course, she won't say anything because she doesn't want to hurt Mary's feelings. Next time we visit, mosquito, pay attention. The same dust bunnies will still be here."

If I were Ethan's mother, I would choke the living daylights out of him. But Mrs. Derby only smiles and looks at her son fondly. Then she says, "What do you want to do now? Would you like to take a walk through the village?"

"I wanted to take the car to the mechanic. I still have the winter tires on," Ethan says. "But knowing you, you'll probably challenge Lea to a game of Scrabble, anyway."

She asks, "Do you like to play Scrabble, Lea?"

"It's my life's passion," I reply.

"Good. Then I'll clear the table, and we can get going." Her eyes dance with excitement.

"Stay there, Mother," Ethan says. "Lea can certainly take care of that."

I gulp. That was totally unnecessary. I would have offered, anyway. And why wouldn't Ethan offer to help as well? It's time to give my new plan a chance again. So I say amiably but firmly, "Of course I'll clear the table. If you help me, it'll go even faster, Ethan."

But my sweetheart says, "That's not going to happen. Washing dishes is women's work. I'm going!" He stands up and leaves the room. Shortly after, I hear his car pull away.

Mrs. Derby looks at me shyly. "It was always like that in this house. The boys didn't have to help with household chores."

Well, great, I think, *welcome to the last century*. My plan to make Ethan more pleasant and less chauvinistic will take a great deal more effort and commitment than I originally imagined. The computer game comparison again leaps to mind. Ambition, commitment, and patience are key, but I have the sinking feeling that I'll feel accomplished way more often playing a game on my smartphone than with Ethan.

In any case, Scrabble is a fun pastime for us. We play round after round. She almost always wins.

"That's only because English is not your native language," she comforts me. "Despite that, you play astoundingly well."

"I could never compete with you, even if I had been born in England," I say graciously.

Mrs. Derby blushes, overjoyed by the compliment. "I'm just crazy about the game," she says. "It's like an addiction. Unfortunately, neither Ethan nor Theo enjoy the game, so I play very seldom."

As I push around the little tiles, it occurs to me that Mrs. Derby is as obsessed with Scrabble as I am with my smartphone game. Apparently, both of us hunger for a sense of achievement and validation. Playing games is a way to get both because we're ambitious and really good at them. Where else would Mrs. Derby get such affirmation in her life? Perhaps with gardening or cooking. I have a dark notion that she doesn't get it from her sons, at least not from Ethan. I've already seen him with his mother. How sad is that?

During supper I feel Ethan's hand creep up my thigh under the table in a rather stimulating way. I blush a little and quickly look over at Mrs. Derby, but she doesn't seem to notice. At bedtime, Ethan and I repair to our separate bedchambers, but only to keep up appearances. It doesn't take long till I hear a soft knocking on my bedroom door.

Ethan comes in. "Mosquito, I've come to pick you up. My bed is much bigger, we'll be more comfortable there."

I don't have to be asked twice. The thought of being under the same roof but down the hall from him, alone in my narrow guest bed, wasn't very appealing. I follow him on tiptoe into his bedroom. Ethan's bed really is bigger.

To Ethan, "more comfortable" apparently means naked, while he, as usual, pounces on me. But this time, I place the palms of my hands on his chest and look at him pleadingly. "Do you always have to go so fast, Ethan?" I ask. "Could we slow it down just a little? I'd love to take a little more time and not just get it over with right away."

Ethan looks at me with irritation. "What kind of notion is that, mosquito?"

"Well, a woman likes it much better if a man takes his time."

"Where did you get that from? Some women's magazine?"

"No, I think it's just common knowledge."

He lifts an eyebrow and looks at me with amusement. "I would really like to know how you come up with these ideas. They're new to me."

Somehow, I come off looking like an airhead. The subject is admittedly rather delicate, so now I feel self-conscious. It's clear that up till now, Ethan's never been bothered by it. I'm not suffering under the delusion that I'm his first woman. On the contrary, women are all too willing to hop into bed with him. And I imagine each considered themselves lucky that he gave them the privilege, so none of them would have said a peep, even if it wasn't a 100 percent positive experience for them. Apparently, in this sphere of his life, Ethan's never heard a word of criticism.

He lies next to me and stares at the blanket. Then he says, "Okay, little mosquito, come on. I want to make everything right for you."

What follows is pretty disappointing. I sense that Ethan's not really into it. Besides, even if his tenderness were more rewarding, I would have still suffered from the knowledge that he would have never dreamed this up himself. Rather, it seems like a nuisance to him. In the end, the sex is great as always, fulfilling and beautiful, but he still could have done a lot better.

Afterward, I lie there awhile, staring at the ceiling. *Oh boy*, I lament. *There's still so much work to do to make our relationship viable, much less perfect. I'm hung up on level 5 with Ethan.* If this were a game, I would be genuinely frustrated. But it's worth the effort so I can spend the rest of my life with my dream man. What more could I want?

Chapter 12

The weekend flew by. Of course, it could have been nicer and more relaxing. Ethan looked at me pensively sometimes, as if wondering what was going on with me. As we drive back to Gatingstone on Sunday evening, I know that my new plan is to blame for the lack of harmony. But I want to try to stay with Ethan, this time on my terms.

The way Ethan interacted with his mother gave me a picture of where I would be in a few years if we were to marry and I stayed submissive, compliant, and self-sacrificing. The whole situation reminds me of Edwin's digging up remnants of the past in his parents' garden. Buried somewhere deep inside me are the remnants of the old, self-confident Lea. They are too precious to just fall into oblivion forever. It's a matter of digging them out, dusting them off, and allowing them to shine once again. But it's ridiculously tiring and gives me a headache. I'm walking a dangerous tightrope. If I proceed too brazenly, I risk losing Ethan.

By the time I'm back at Alice's, I'm truly exhausted. Of course, Alice, like most women, is enthralled by Ethan. "He's so incredibly handsome," she gushes. "Lea, tell me your secret—what does a person have to do to win such a man's affection? I would kill to be that lucky. You must be so happy."

"Yes, I am," I reply listlessly. I turn away quickly, so she can't see my face.

That night I play the game on my smartphone until I'm practically comatose. I make my way slowly up, level by level. If my parents had known this gift would awaken such an alarming game addiction within me, would they have still given it to me? Sometimes I surf Facebook to see what's going on back home. The posts my friends share seem so unimportant and banal to me. Most of the time, I log off quickly to play my game again. Jens continues to initiate contact. He wants to know what I'm doing, whether anything exciting is going on, if I'm happy. He doesn't give up easily. Sometimes I find his perseverance quite touching. Generally, I try to ignore him. Only very occasionally do I write him back a short message, nothing more.

The weather's getting warmer and the days longer. Alice tells me she would be thrilled if I could do a little yard work. I agree immediately—now that the Cambridge exam is behind me, I don't have to study so hard, plus the yard is so small and manageable. I carefully mow and edge the lawn, until Alice says it looks like Priory Park's monastery gardens. I hoe the flower beds until there's not a weed to be found. One flower bed is right next to the brick wall, which borders a neighboring cottage. I remove all the dry undergrowth I can find, gather it in a pile, and throw it in the yard waste.

That evening Alice and I are sitting inside, looking out at the garden and enjoying the fruits of my labor. The yard looks really neat and manicured. Alice suddenly squints and stares at the wall, where a trellis is overgrown with lush vegetation. Well, the vegetation *was* lush; now the branches hang down listlessly.

"What in heavens happened to my clematis?" says Alice. "It's grown so beautifully this spring."

I feel hot and cold all over. I remember the undergrowth I removed this afternoon. The shoots were a strange brown color. "Maybe my yard work didn't agree with it," I say sheepishly.

Alice goes to the window and looks at the mess a little more closely. "I'll be damned," she says. "You practically pulled the whole plant up by the roots."

I follow her gaze and realize that by clearing the undergrowth, the clematis was no longer planted in the ground. Crap. I went overboard with my mania for neatness. I'm completely devastated. "Alice, I'm so terribly sorry. How can I make it up to you? Should I get you a new one?"

But Alice is quiet, and her whole body is shaking. I realize that she's laughing so hard she can't speak. "I call that a really good job," she finally says, wiping tears of laughter from her eyes.

I sigh in relief. *How wonderful*, I think, *that someone like Alice can so easily laugh at my mishap.* I confess that I laugh with her for a while, too.

"Don't worry about it," Alice says generously. "Clematis is a robust plant. It will recover and grow even more beautifully and prolifically than before—unless, of course, you pull it up by the roots again." She starts laughing once more.

"I swear I won't," I say, smiling. Something's nagging at me. How would Ethan have reacted to what just happened? He wouldn't have found it nearly so funny. Presumably, I would have been given a little lecture.

The Easter holidays arrive, and Catherine asks me whether I've decided to come with them to Cornwall. I would love to see Cornwall, but I'm pretty sure I'll be doing something with Ethan. I look forward to the holidays with mixed feelings. I know that I won't feel as excited about traveling with him as in the past. Instead, I'll be tense because I'll be thinking so much about our relationship. Sometimes I feel like he's responding positively to my new plan. It's probably not much fun to hang out with a little gray mouse all the time. But when things are going well, a feeling comes over me that it's only because I'm acting invisible and shutting the real Lea up. I feel like I'm on a long hike, and for every two steps forward, I take one step back.

One night we get into a real fight—our first one ever. Ethan picks me up at Alice's to go out to eat. I wear something especially nice—something a little sexy (but not too sexy), makeup, the whole deal, just the way Ethan likes it. We drive into the country and pull up to an old, beautiful inn, the type found everywhere in England.

As we're sitting at the table studying the menu, Ethan asks me suddenly, "Have you packed yet?"

I look up from the menu in confusion. I was just thinking whether I'd rather have lamb with spring vegetables and mint sauce or a shrimp omelet. "Packed?" I ask.

"Yes, for Wales."

"Wales?" I repeat.

"We're driving to Wales over the Easter holidays. I've already booked a hotel room."

This is news to me. I lay my menu down and look at him quietly. Wales. A few months ago, I would have leapt to my feet and hugged him, but *A*, he's forbidden that kind of "attack," and *B*, I feel like my wishes have been completely disregarded. I would have loved if he'd consulted me first about whether I want to travel over Easter and, if so, where.

I say carefully, "This is the first time that you've mentioned any plan of our traveling together over the holidays."

Ethan looks at me indulgently. "I might have forgotten to mention it to you, but it could also very well be that I did, and, once again, you just weren't listening."

I feel revulsion rising inside me. "Ethan," I say. My voice is shaking, although I try to control it. "You simply can't do that to me. You can't make decisions for me, and you can't always assume I'll be at your disposal. You simply can't take my freedom of choice away from me."

"And why not, little mosquito?" he says, leaning forward with a look of amusement on his face. "Somebody's got to make decisions for you. Somebody's got to take care of things so you don't do something stupid."

So this is what it's come to, I think. Next thing I know, I will be deprived of my rights altogether. "That's not okay. I'm not just some cute insect. I'm an independent adult, and you must treat me like one."

"On the contrary, you *are* cute," Ethan murmurs. "You're so cute, in fact, I have half a mind to give the menus back and get a room upstairs."

This is the last straw. I slam the menu down on the table and snarl, "Great. Let's give the menus back. But then we'll go outside to the car and you'll drive back home to Gatingstone."

Ethan is completely shocked. "What is the matter with you, Lea?" *Now* he calls me Lea.

"I'm sick and tired of you steamrolling me and forcing me to do only what you want to do. I'm sick and tired of you acting as though I'm some troublesome crumb that's fallen on your shirt." My voice is shrill. The guests at a neighboring table turn and stare at us. Ethan doesn't like this at all, but at the moment I could care less what Ethan likes or doesn't like. I have to release my pent-up frustration; otherwise, I might explode. "Something's got to give. Either I have to change, or you, or we both do. But one thing is clear: the way things are between us now cannot continue."

Ethan looks me directly in the eye and says, unmoved, "Good, then I suggest we start with you. We probably don't need to do anything else after that."

That's it. I've heard enough. I spring to my feet and storm out of the restaurant, leaving Ethan sitting at the table. In front of the inn, I pull my cell phone from my purse. My hands shaking, I call a taxi; less than five minutes later, it arrives and takes me back to Gatingstone. As I sit in the back, I replay the scene at the inn over and over again in my mind, like a defective DVD. I can't believe what Ethan said. His words still ring in my ears: "Good, then I suggest we start with you. We probably don't need to do anything else after that." Does Ethan not realize how much I've changed since I've been with him? That I've bent over backward to please him? I can barely recognize myself. I cry quietly. I pull out a handkerchief, awkwardly trying to hide it from the taxi driver. Can somebody please tell me how much more I can possibly change? I don't have the energy or the imagination for it.

At the same time, a feeling of resistance comes over me. Damn it, I don't want to change any more. If I want to change anything at all, I want to go back to the old joyful, exuberant Lea that I was before I met Ethan. I make a quick decision and pull out my smartphone. I write two texts. One goes to Ethan: *Need a time-out. I'm definitely not going with you to Wales.* The other goes to Catherine: *I've made my decision. I'd love to go with you to Cornwall. I look forward to it!* I've just barely sent the two texts when I suddenly feel I made a mistake and would like to take them back. But the old Lea stops me. I distract myself by playing a bit of my favorite game. I'm interrupted twice. One text says: *Hurray! Cornwall is going to be so much fun with you. So happy!* The other one says: *Okay, if you say so.* Nothing more. Great. That is a definitive answer.

The taxi stops at Weaver's Mews. I pay the fare and go inside the house. I feel miserable. Maybe I've just made the biggest mistake of my life. Actually, I've *definitely* just made the worst mistake of my life. I've done exactly what I've desperately wanted to avoid for months. I've turned Ethan against me. Have we arrived at the game-over phase of our relationship? Hopefully not. I love him. No—I'm totally *addicted* to him. Cornwall is going to be horrible. I'll crawl around like a junkie who's had to go cold turkey. I grimly pack my suitcase for the trip. Now and then I have the urge to burst into tears, but all I have to do is recall our fight, then pull myself together and think, *This was the right decision.*

The paradox with Ethan is that he systematically eliminated everything in me that was childish, funny, and easygoing. He wanted me to grow up and be serious as quickly as possible. But now, although he's fairly happy with the results, he still treats me like a little kid, condescendingly and disrespectfully.

I wish Ethan had liked me the way I was from the very beginning and treated me with respect and admiration. This time-out is absolutely the right move. During the weeklong excursion to Cornwall, I'll have time to think about ways I can improve our relationship. Once the trip is over, I'll have a new plan. Everything's going to be okay.

Three days later, a red Citroën pulls in front of Alice's house. I throw my suitcase in the trunk and sit in the backseat. Catherine is in the passenger seat, and a girl with the same light skin as Catherine and flaming red hair is sitting in the driver's seat. She turns around and says, "Hi, Lea. I'm Catherine's sister, Denise. It's so wonderful you're coming with us."

"Thank you for inviting me. Where's Inez?"

"We're picking her up in Brantwood. Then we'll go through London and head toward the coast."

Despite my sorrow, I start to feel happy about the upcoming week with my friends. Hearing the word "coast" lifts my spirits. I love the sea. Tonight I'll probably be on the beach in Cornwall, dipping my feet in the water.

"Where are we going to stay?" I ask.

Catherine says, "I found a place on the Internet. It's a vacation house in Polperro, an old harbor on the bay."

It sounds heavenly. Wales would also have been great, but all I want to do is relax, not stress out over my relationship.

It's a long drive to Cornwall. Luckily, it's Sunday, so we can go straight through London. Otherwise, the drive would be even longer. Denise drives her little Citroën along streets that would otherwise be bumper-to-bumper during rush hour traffic. We marvel as we pass the huge white dome of St. Paul's Cathedral, where Prince Charles married Lady Di. It's surrounded by tall bank buildings. We're soon on the outskirts of London again, but still have four long hours until we arrive at our destination.

After driving for a while, Denise admits she's tired, so I get behind the wheel. I love to drive. In all modesty, I'm pretty good at it. It doesn't take long before I'm used to driving on the left side. I sit up straight and proud. *Ethan doesn't know anything about my strengths*, I think. When we're together, he always drives. I'm not sure he even knows I have a driver's license. Would he ever allow me to drive if we were married? I have a hunch he wouldn't be crazy about the idea at all.

After resting, Denise takes over the wheel again, and I go back to my old seat. I pick up my smartphone and amuse myself with my game.

"What are you doing on your phone?" Inez asks.

Catherine winks, then says, "I think I know. She has to keep in constant contact with her boyfriend."

"How is the irresistible Ethan, anyway?" Inez asks. "What's he doing over the holiday?"

"I have no idea," I murmur as I concentrate on my game.

Catherine and Inez exchange looks. "Does that mean what I think it means?" Catherine asks.

"I have no clue what you mean," I say brusquely.

"Are you two still together?"

I look up with irritation from my game. "Catherine, you of all people should know that relationships don't always go smoothly. Sometimes there are things people have to work on."

Catherine pauses while she gathers her thoughts. Then she cautiously answers, "If you mean that I saw something needed to be addressed in your relationship, then, yes, Lea, I do understand. If you love Ethan as much as I love Christian, then I can only say it's worth it and I wish you lots of luck. I hope you two figure it out. I know what you're going through right now."

I'm quite moved. In the past few months, I've worried that my relationship with Catherine hasn't been quite the same. I'm happy to see that she's so openly on my side. I smile thankfully at her.

"I'm happy I came with you, girls," I say. "You're my dearest friends."

"Now confess what you're doing on your phone," Inez says, immediately lightening up the serious mood.

"I'm crossing the licorice bridge under which a monster lurks," I say. "And, if you must know, a few days ago I helped a unicorn get his horn. I'm quite proud of myself. It was a total bitch."

Now there's no holding back. The mood changes suddenly, and we're laughing so hard we can hardly stop.

Our rental house in Polperro is on a hillside overlooking the harbor. You can see the bay and out to sea. It's breathtakingly beautiful. The house must belong to a sailor. Engravings of sailboats hang on the walls, but apart from that, the furnishings are very simple. There are only two colors, white and blue, so the interior doesn't distract from the fantastic view. Seagulls soar playfully and screech wildly in front of the paned window. Moss-covered steps lead to an overgrown garden, and far below, the multicolored roofs of little houses crowd around the harbor. On the other side of the bay, green meadows stretch across the top of high cliffs, which disappear in the distance.

In the middle of the rustic kitchen is a natural wood table with simple benches. Catherine and her sister brought groceries, which we quickly put away in the fridge and cabinets. Inez wants to prepare dinner, but the rest of us protest immediately. "No," we say almost simultaneously, "let's go down to the harbor."

We walk down over a thousand steps on the way to the village, which we instantly find very charming. Old, crooked houses line the narrow cobblestone streets. Everything is so lovingly maintained. Pots of pansies and daisies sit on narrow windowsills. There are only a few cars since the streets are so narrow. We wander down to the harbor. In the evening sun, it looks as though it is filled with liquid gold, and small anchored boats dance gaily on the waves.

"God, that is beautiful," Inez sighs.

"Come on," Denise says. "Let's walk along the coast a little. Let's see if there's a beach."

As it turns out, there are no wide white beaches of the type our fellow Bretons expected. Instead, we discover narrow coves beneath high cliffs. Catherine climbs over the stones along the cliff that towers over the first cove, washed by the waves.

"I'll be damned," she says. "There are winkles here."

"Excuse me?" I ask.

"She means periwinkles," Denise says as she hurries to her sister's side.

"Hurray!" Catherine says. "Does anybody have a plastic bag?"

Inez has an empty shopping bag in the pocket of her anorak. Both sisters practically rip it out of her hand. They squat on the ground and begin to collect little snails that are suctioned to the rocks.

"Hey! What are you doing there?" I ask.

"Gathering dinner," Catherine says happily.

"You will never, ever get me to consume those creatures," I protest.

Inez, who apparently knows her seafood better than I, says, "Just wait, Lea. They know what they're doing."

Half an hour later, we walk back with the bag containing countless live snails, their shells rattling against each other.

"I'm ready to do this," I say, "but only under one condition: I must have something strong to drink. Otherwise I'll never get those things down my throat."

Denise laughs. "You're just afraid you'll swallow a live one and want to kill them with alcohol. But I assure you I'll cook them at such a high temperature they'll be as dead as a salmon in a fishmonger's basket."

Great, now I'm really queasy. For my sake, we buy a bottle of whiskey. We also pick up a crusty loaf of French bread.

"The one who eats the most winkles can sleep in tomorrow morning," Denise says. "The others must go to the bakery and pick up bread for breakfast."

I'm pretty sure that's a prize I can't win. I suggest that we extend the rule to include whoever drinks the most whiskey.

In the kitchen, Catherine sets a big pot of water on the stove. As soon as it starts to boil, she drops the snails in. Inez distributes plates and paper napkins and cuts the bread, arranging the slices in the bread basket. I open the bottle of whiskey and take a big gulp of liquid courage.

Shortly afterward, we are all sitting around the table, the big pot filled with snails in the center. Catherine's drained off the water.

"What now?" I ask. I have no appetite for snails, but I'm pretty hungry.

"Now we need a sewing kit," Catherine says.

"Huh?"

Inez knows what to do. She leaps to her feet and opens the cabinet drawers in the living room. She comes back triumphantly with a pin cushion.

"Okay, ladies! Choose your weapons!" Denise jokes.

I look on with fascination as Catherine, Denise, and Inez grip their needles. Catherine picks up one of the cooked snails, pokes the needle in the opening, and, with a flick of the wrist, twists out one of the snails. It looks like a little brown rubber spiral. With one fell swoop, it lands in Catherine's mouth. She rolls her eyes with pleasure. "Outstanding!" she says, and reaches for another snail.

Okay, I say to myself, *I can do this*. I take another slug of whiskey—now out of a glass—and reach for a snail and needle. Then I follow Catherine's example. In the end, I eat more bread than mollusks for dinner, but it's all right with the other girls; it means there's more for them. As the pot empties, all of us are pretty tipsy, especially me. Just when I'm thinking I'll have only one . . . more . . . glass . . .

My phone rings. I fumble around for a while before I press the right button.

It's Ethan. "Lea," he says.

"Yes," I say, and hiccup.

"Are you drunk?"

"No." *Hiccup*.

"Mosquito, what are you doing? Where are you? Tell me! I'm coming to pick you up. Damn! I should have known you'd get into mischief without me."

"No . . . No, I'm not." *Hiccup*. "And . . . I'm not gonna say where . . ." I end the call and put the phone on the table. I lay my head down next to it. Somehow, I end up in bed.

The next morning someone wakes me up by whispering in my ear, "You won. We're going to the bakery."

Then I go back to sleep until I'm too cold because someone ripped open the bedroom window. "She urgently needs fresh air," I hear someone say. It smells like the sea and seaweed. A seagull screeches so loudly my skull threatens to explode. After a long time, I work up the nerve to open my eyes. I look out over the sparkling sea.

Catherine says, "How are you, Lea? Are you coming with us?"

"Where?" I moan.

"Over there." She points to the green slopes above the cliffs. "We're going to take a walk."

Denise is waiting in the kitchen with a cup of especially strong coffee, and Inez hands me the bread basket. An hour later, I'm feeling much better. The fresh sea air does me good, and the landscape is breathtaking. We walk on a narrow footpath through the brightly colored broom shrubs blooming with yellow flowers. On both sides of the path, whole fields of violets in full bloom send out an intoxicating aroma. The deep-blue sky arches over the sparkling blue sea. I'm so happy I didn't stay in bed.

Again and again, I stop to admire the view. I take out my smartphone and snap one photo after another. I immediately send my parents one as an e-mail attachment. I post the best ones on Facebook. My friends will see the enchanting place I'm visiting, and because Ethan isn't on Facebook, he'll be none the wiser—although it would be so romantic if he tracked me down and found me. I imagine him bending down on one knee, taking my hand and kissing it, and saying, "Forgive me, my beloved," all in full view of my girlfriends. That would be so wonderful, and so like a Rosamunde Pilcher romance that I would melt on the spot, marry him, and live happily ever after.

But the voice inside me sneers, *Dream on, Lea. You know it's not that easy. There's still a lot to be done. Otherwise you'll end up in exactly the same spot you were in before, and not one step further.* I don't know whether it's my hangover or thinking about my relationship, but I suddenly feel listless and miserable.

Catherine turns around and notices the expression on my face. "Are you okay, Lea? Should we turn around?"

"No, it's okay," I say, and walk with determination.

"You're not exactly happy, huh?" she asks softly.

"No, I'm not."

"Because of Ethan?"

I nod. "Can you share a couple of tricks with me on how you were able to change Christian and make him treat you better?"

Catherine shrugs. "It was actually pretty easy. I traveled to England and stayed for a while. He missed me and saw how well I got along without him, and voilà!"

"Oh, Catherine," I complain, "if it were only that easy!"

"You're doing fine," she says. "You're apart for the time being, and he apparently misses you, or he wouldn't have called yesterday."

I scrunch up my face. "He didn't exactly get the impression I was doing well without him."

"No, he didn't," Catherine says. Her eyes dance, and suddenly she snorts and roars with laughter. I laugh now, too. It does me good. My heart feels lighter in the presence of my cheerful friend.

Then Catherine becomes serious again and says, "You're putting in a lot of effort, Lea. You can't take on all the responsibility for improving your relationship with Ethan. I understand you're head over heels in love with him, but you need to just relax and wait. In my opinion, from the moment you met him, you invested way too much effort and put too much pressure on yourself. Just say to yourself: if things between Ethan and me are good, then everything will be fine, and if they aren't, then it wasn't meant to be."

Her advice sounds so sensible. I take a deep breath and say, "Thanks, Catherine."

"It's okay. Come on, let's walk some more. The others have already gone on ahead."

. . .

I need to do my exam reading, so I've downloaded an e-reader app. But whenever I reach for my phone with the intent to study, I magically end up playing a game instead. While my friends sit around together, cozily reading, knitting, or chatting, my eyes burn a hole through the display, as if the future of the world depends on the outcome of my game.

"You're a bit uncommunicative when you're on that thing," Inez protests. "What are you doing? Are you still stuck on the licorice bridge?"

I grin at them. "Yes. It's terrible. I *hate* this game. Look here, if I don't watch out, the new pieces of chocolate grow, and then it's all over. It's practically impossible to beat this stupid level."

"Someone needs to make a video so that you can see how you look when you play these games," Catherine says. "You're not exactly relaxed."

"Why do you let yourself get so upset over a stupid game?" Denise asks. "Simply uninstall it, and you're done."

I press my lips together. Then I say, "Because I know I can do it. If I stay with it long enough, I can win." I'd like them to shut up so I can concentrate.

The girls become quiet for a moment and look at each other. They seem to be sending each other nonverbal signals, like: *Lea's gone crazy.*

Catherine says warily, "And what are you going to do when you've crossed the licorice bridge?"

I look up and say excitedly, "Oh, then I'll go to the next level!"

"Phew!" Denise says. "And then the next one, and the next... And in the meantime, you'll end up with a stomach ulcer. You're so agitated!"

Inez lifts an eyebrow and looks at me sternly. "Do you know what I think, Lea? You're a game addict. I've heard about it before, but I never saw it in action with one of my own friends. It's kind of creepy."

"Oh bullshit," I say. "I only do it because it's fun and helps me relax."

"At the risk of repeating myself," Catherine says, "you don't seem very relaxed at all."

"Yeah, because I have to concentrate."

Inez looks over my shoulder while I play. Good, now she can see for herself how great the game is and can understand why I have so much fun playing it.

But after a while she says, "You know that it's purely a game of chance, right? It's designed so that you think you're doing something skillful, but in reality those multicolored pieces fall completely by chance."

"That's not true," I say. "Look, if I combine these four here, then . . ."

All at once, little game pieces fall down, blinking and glittering. A message appears on the display screen: "Congratulations! Level complete!" I must confess, it does look as though it was completely random. Not good.

But it doesn't matter. I throw myself back onto the sofa and yell jubilantly, "Finally, *finally*, I've done it! Come on, let's go down to the village pub and I'll buy everybody a beer. We need to celebrate!"

But Inez is unimpressed. She scoffs, "I'm telling you, Lea, it was random luck. I've seen it. I don't understand how you can waste so much time on this shit."

I look at her with dismay. "You really think I'm an addict?"

Denise says, "Yes. You're a game addict, Lea, even if you don't want to admit it. Okay, girls, whoever thinks Lea is a game addict, raise your hand."

Everyone raises their hands and looks at me reproachfully.

Catherine sees I'm shocked by this. "Come on, Lea," she says softly. "I'll make you a deal: uninstall this stupid game right here and now, and we'll buy *you* a drink. What do you think about that?"

I vacillate. This is not an easy decision. I like the game. I love it when the colorful little candies whir all over the screen. I would miss it. Theoretically, I could reinstall it later when I'm back in Gatingstone, but I somehow don't think I'd be able to face myself if I did that. I'm moved that my friends care so much about me and my admittedly ludicrous addiction. I don't want to disappoint them. Also, there's a little voice in the back of my mind that whispers, *They're right, Lea, and you know it. You spend way too much time on this crap.*

"Okay," I say. "I'll do it!"

Everyone gathers around me to look over my shoulder as I uninstall the game. They all sigh in relief.

"Now let's go to the harbor and party!" Inez says. "Come on! Last one's a rotten egg!"

"No," Catherine giggles, "last one's a licorice monster!"

We pull on our jackets, lock up the house, and storm down the steps to the harbor. We find a local fishermen's pub where music's playing and spend a relaxed evening of convivial drinking there. Hours later, we creep up the steep stairs and fall into our beds, exhausted but happy.

The following days of vacation are wonderful. We explore the entire area. One day we take the car on the ferry to the famous St. Michael's Mount, an island offshore that can only be reached during low tide. There's a small town on the island with an old monastery and several old houses. Denise and Catherine are delighted; there's also an island called Mont Saint-Michel back home in France.

We're walking along a path in low tide when Inez suddenly stops, frantic. She calls out in desperation, "Stop, I've lost my contact lens!" We all immediately fall onto our hands and knees and carefully search the ground inch by inch. Wringing her hands, Inez stands by and wails, "Please don't step on it or I'm screwed!"

After a long search, I discover a drop of water on the ground where there is no water. I lick the tip of my finger and carefully tap it. The drop sticks. It's Inez's contact lens.

"I don't believe it! You found it, Lea! You rescued me!" Inez is ecstatic.

I feel as though I've just crossed the licorice bridge. The task—find the contact lens on the much-used tourist path—was extremely tricky, but I did it. Fantastic!

Back on the mainland that evening at Peter's Pub, our new hangout, Inez buys me another drink.

"Something fishy is going on here," I tease after I work through the foam on my beer and take a deep gulp. "First you wean me off one addiction, and now you girls get me started on a new one!"

The next day, Denise pulls me into a small yarn store. "I'm going to teach you something you'll use your whole life," she says mysteriously. She brings two balls of wool yarn and a set of knitting needles to the cash register. "I'll teach you how to knit socks. If you learn how to do this, you'll have every man eating out of your hand. Men love hand-knitted socks."

"Maybe the men in Brittany, where it's cold and windy," I say, wrinkling my nose. "Here in the civilized part of the world, we have something called central heating. Have you heard of it?"

Nevertheless, I sit next to her on the sofa and let her show me how to cast on yarn and knit with circular needles. It's terribly tricky, and occasionally I swear so loudly I startle the rest of the household.

Catherine can't help herself. "You look even less relaxed now than you did when you were playing your game, Lea."

But little by little, I become more adept at knitting. When Denise praises me, I feel a similar sense of accomplishment as I did when playing my game. And when I finish one sock, the other takes half the time. Even better. The pair I knit are obviously too big for me, so I plan on giving them to Ethan to show him that I thought about him the whole time. I wonder if he's thinking about me? Sometimes I get a little panicky. Going solo over spring break was an extremely bold move. Maybe Ethan will use it as an opportunity to break up with me. I'm so happy I'm with my friends, though. They distract me from my worries. Not only that, but I can't help feeling that something positive is happening to me. Day by day, I feel happier and more relaxed.

One day we drive to the westernmost corner of Great Britain, the famous Land's End. Catherine takes me aside and says, "Lea, it's so great to be here with you. You're more like your old self, so funny and quirky. I really like Inez, and I'm close to my sister, but it just wouldn't be nearly as much fun without you."

"Oh nonsense," I say. "You're just saying that."

But Catherine shakes her head vehemently and says, "No, I'm not just saying that, Lea. Inez says exactly the same thing. You exude such a *joie de vivre*, it's really amazing."

That night, I think about what she said before I fall asleep. Is she right? Have I rediscovered the old Lea while on vacation with my friends? Could it be that she didn't really die, but was just waiting until the conditions were right so she could call the shots again? But something in the back of my mind nags at me. If the old Lea is really back, what's going to happen with Ethan and me? Will Ethan still like me if I come back the same youthful and free-spirited girl I was before? *In that case, a pair of hand-knitted socks won't be much consolation for him*, I think cynically.

Chapter 13

Although I uninstalled the stupid game, I'm still not as relaxed as Catherine thinks. Occasionally I pull away from my friends and go on a walk by myself. I stand on top of the cliff and stare out over the sea, which is exactly as far, wide, and mysterious as my future.

We rent some horses. I never really learned how to ride, but Denise, Catherine, and Inez are quite familiar with it. "We'll ride down to the sea," they say adventurously. I suggest that they go without me, but they won't give up. "We'll find a horse for you that's as gentle as a lamb. Every stable has at least one good horse you can ride," they say, but it turns out that the "good" horse likes to dawdle along the way and nibble on vegetation next to the path.

"Oh man! Lea!" Inez calls in frustration. Everyone is waiting on me and my horse yet again. "What are you doing? You have to show him who's boss. You gotta use your heels!"

I sigh. Even horseback riding somehow relates to my current problem. I just can't do it. I can't be tough and kick this poor horse in the sides—I'd rather get off and walk. It's the same with Ethan and me. I should have stood up for myself from the beginning, instead of allowing him to have his way with everything. Sometimes, my heart sinks when I realize it's probably too late to pull the reins in now.

Our vacation is drawing to an end. The weather has spoiled us. It's amazingly warm for this time of year. We decide to make a fire on the beach for our last night. We pack a basket with bread, sausage, German potato salad, and a big jug of hard cider. We each bring a blanket. Well fed and slightly tipsy, we sit around the fire, reflecting on our past and our future. The sea is calm, and our conversation is interrupted only by the gentle slap of breaking waves and the peeping of the sandpipers.

"So what's going to happen, Catherine?" I ask. "Are you definitely going to stay with Christian?"

Catherine smiles warmly. "I think so. Unless he changes when I go back, but that's highly unlikely."

"And you, Inez?"

"I'm still single and hope to stay that way for a while. My ex-boyfriend was so needy, I almost swore off love altogether."

Denise interjects, "But why? You see with Catherine and Christian that people can change if you have a little patience. Christian really has totally turned things around since my sister moved to England."

Inez takes a long drink of her cider, wipes her mouth with the back of her hand, and shakes her head. "I'm happy for Catherine, but honestly, I think that what happened with Christian is a stroke of dumb luck, an anomaly. In my opinion, if two people don't get along well from the beginning, then it's better that they go their separate ways. I wouldn't like it if a guy wanted to change or train me in some way. He should be totally into me, Inez, just the way I am." Her eyes shine brightly, and she adds confidently, "I think that's the least anyone can expect, right?"

Denise and Catherine smile approvingly, but her words stab me in the heart. I know it's not that way between Ethan and me. Maybe he's in love with me, but he's not totally into me just the way I am. That's definitely not the case—Ethan has tried his hardest to change me according to his own tastes because there are so many things about me he doesn't like.

Inez continues, "And vice versa. I don't think it's okay to secretly cook up a plan to change a guy just because you don't like something about him. If I were a guy, I would think it's terribly unfair and quite deceptive."

I feel like I've been caught. That is exactly what I've been planning. I'm working on a plan to teach Ethan not to treat me so poorly. I was so head over heels about him in the beginning I couldn't recognize his shortcomings. Now I view him more critically and want to change him.

Denise looks at Inez skeptically. "If the rest of mankind felt the same way, we would have become extinct a long time ago, Inez. I don't believe a couple can possibly get along 100 percent right from the beginning. There's no such thing as a perfect world—people have to adjust to one another."

Catherine joins in. "Yes, but that only works if you keep the other person's well-being in mind. You have to respect each other, otherwise all bets are off." She pauses and looks at me meaningfully. I know what she's alluding to, but I don't say anything.

Denise throws a piece of wood onto the fire. Sparks fly up, swirling high and vanishing in the black night sky. My friends' faces suddenly flash in the light of the dancing flames. "That assumes that you're totally honest with each other from the beginning and don't pretend to be someone else in order to impress the other person. Otherwise, you have no idea what you're getting into."

Inez says, "But everybody does that at first. People will stop at nothing to impress a potential romantic interest."

I clear my throat and say hoarsely, "But at some point, you have to stop faking it. You can't keep that up forever."

The others regard me searchingly. Or am I only imagining it? I have the feeling this whole conversation revolves around me and my problems with Ethan. It makes me jittery. Are they conspiring against me? Maybe they've all vowed to help me. Who knows? Oh nonsense. I'm acting like I'm a victim or something. Nevertheless, I'm tired of the subject—as if I don't think about it enough already.

I leap to my feet, fold up my blanket, and say abruptly, "I'm cold. I'm going back to the house. You girls can stay if you want to."

"No, we're coming with you," they all murmur. We throw sand on the fire until it dies out, gather our belongings, and stumble over the uneven sand into the night, toward the village.

I walk ahead of them. I want to be alone with my thoughts, which are whirling around wildly in my head, like sparks in the night sky. If it's really true that trying to change your boyfriend is deceptive, then my plan was over before it even started. *Great*, I think desperately, *what now?* What on earth should I do? Continue to play the obedient little mosquito who idolizes Ethan? Get married—if Ethan even wants to marry me? Just the thought of it gives me a stomachache. No, I don't want that anymore. Ethan needs to love me, the real Lea. Otherwise . . .

The more I think about it, the harder it hits me. Something has become abundantly clear to me: I'm addicted to Ethan. And because of my addiction, I've done all the things I promised myself I would never do. I changed myself, suppressed my true nature, and pretended to be someone I'm not.

As I pant and wheeze up the stone steps to our house, I make a solemn vow to myself. I'll write Ethan an e-mail tonight and tell him exactly who I am. I'll ask him to think things over carefully and decide whether he truly wants to be with the real me. I know I'll be risking a lot, but after this vacation, I have no desire to continue with this charade. I've rediscovered my old self and feel happier and more balanced than I have in months. I straighten my back and lift my head. I will never, ever give myself up again for any man in the world.

When we enter the house, everyone finds their usual spot. Denise plunks down on a dining room chair with her knitting, while Catherine and Inez each sit in a corner of the sofa. I curl up in an armchair and begin to compose my message to Ethan. It's incredibly difficult, because I want to find the right words. I keep starting over, erasing everything and beginning all over again. In the old days before the Internet, there would be a giant mountain of crumpled-up paper on the floor next to me. As my friends chat about this and that, I tune out their voices and write:

> *I have to tell you something. When we met almost one year ago, you were amazed by my high-spirited nature and love of life. I think it's important that you know the reason I am the way I am. It's difficult for me to speak about it, so I've always avoided the subject.*
>
> *Something terrible happened when I was still in school. My friend Mia had just gotten her driver's license. I was unbelievably excited about her passing the test, so when she asked me if I would like to join her on her "maiden voyage," I said yes immediately. We started at her parents' house in south Bielefeld and drove toward Münster. To get there, you have to drive over a mountain pass on the edge of the Teutoburg Forest. This road is dangerous because it has so many blind corners. Mia lost control of the car, and we crashed into a tree head-on. She was killed instantly, and I was in a coma for six months. Later, I found out that I'd been given up for dead. Against all odds, I survived. I had a difficult rehabilitation. I had to learn to speak and walk again.*
>
> *The fact of the matter is, I survived the accident. Because of this, I realized deep down how precious life is, and I cherish every moment I'm able to live on this earth. So that's where my high-spirited personality, which you find so "unusual," comes from. Everyone who hangs out*

with me has to put up with it. This unbridled lust for life is a part of me, like my arms and legs. Trying to deny this integral part of myself feels like an amputation. The phantom pain would kill me. Well, think this over, and let me know whether you can put up with me the way I am or not.

That's the whole letter. When I finish it, I reread it at least twenty times. I decide against writing "Hugs and kisses," "Love," or any other meaningless closing. Ethan will see it's from me. I search for his address, hesitate a moment, then hit "Send."

Suddenly Inez springs to my side. "What are you doing on your phone?" she says. "Are you playing another stupid game? Give me your phone!" She tries to snatch it out of my hand.

"No, I'm not playing at all," I say fiercely. "Get your hands off my phone. Hey, give it here!"

We wrestle with the phone for a moment, but I manage to grab it. "Inez, you idiot!" I yell. "If you broke my phone, I'm going to be so mad at you. I just wrote an e-mail, that's all."

Immediately I have everybody's undivided attention.

"A private e-mail," I say emphatically. I turn my phone off and put it in my pocket. "I'm going to pack now, and then I'm going to sleep. I think we're leaving pretty early tomorrow."

As I toss and turn, a thousand thoughts torment me. Has Ethan already read my message, or is he reading it right now, at this very moment? If so, how will he react? What will he think of me? Will he understand what I mean? Maybe I should have made it a little bit clearer to what extent I'd hidden my true self and changed for him. Maybe I should turn my phone on and write another e-mail to explain that . . . This is crazy. I'm so stressed out that I get a raging headache, and I lie awake the whole night.

In the morning, there is no answer. During the whole long ride back to Gatingstone, I stare at my phone. I put it away, then pick it back up again. I think about calling Ethan at a rest stop so I can apologize, but I don't. He got my message, and he can do with it what he wants. It's like I folded up a paper boat like we used to do as children and set it afloat on a little pond. Now I just have to see where it ends up.

When we reach London, a short message comes through: *When will you be at Alice's?*

My heart pounding, I write, *Around three.*

Okay. Nothing more.

We say good-bye to Inez in Brantwood, and then the three of us continue to Gatingstone. As we turn into Weaver's Mews, I see Ethan's car parked in front of Rose Cottage. My heart sinks. What's going to happen? I'm totally exhausted from the long trip. I wish we could just turn around and drive back to Polperro.

"Well, someone can't wait to see you again," Denise says, nodding in the car's direction. Just then, the car door opens and Ethan steps out. He casually leans against the car and waits until we stop. He steps up to pull my suitcase out of the trunk. *He's such a gentleman*, I think to my dismay. He looks unbelievably handsome, as always. I wave good-bye to the girls, then turn toward him and wait. I'm holding my breath.

"Come on, Lea," he says. "Let's take a little walk."

I nod mutely and quickly put the suitcase in the hall. We stroll down a country lane that leads away from the village. Very soon we find ourselves under a clear-blue sky. Larks twitter above us, and daisies, dandelions, and violets are in bloom. We haven't hugged or kissed yet. An almost unbearable tension hangs between us.

Suddenly Ethan stops and says, "What did you mean by sending me that message, Lea? That I don't appreciate who you really are and rob you of your joy for life?"

I look at him directly. "No, not that, Ethan . . . Or, actually, yes." I stiffen and say firmly, "It's true. Since we've been together, you've constantly reproached me for being this way or that way."

Ethan wrinkles his brow. "What do you mean?"

"I'm a cheerful, happy person, hungry for life. I love being silly and boisterous. There's so much that makes me laugh and smile. I know you think that's childish and naïve, but I want to be like that when I'm a hundred-year-old grandma. I always want to have that sense of well-being."

He looks at me sternly, as if he's administering my final exams or—as they say in England—my A Levels. I keep talking because he's finally listening to me. Everything just pours out of me. "I love not being 100 percent perfect all the time. I even like making mistakes, simply because I love being spontaneous and laughing about it afterward."

Ethan looks as though he's boring a hole through my skull. Then he says, "Like when you thoughtlessly got into a car with a new driver and almost got killed? Do you mean that kind of mistake?"

I turn to stone. How can he say something like that? How can he take the confidential information that I shared with him and turn it against me? All at once, it's brutally clear to me: Ethan never really knew, loved, or even tried to understand me. And he'll never be able to, either. He is who he is. I look at my beautiful, wonderful Ethan, completely bewildered. I know that it's finally over. But Ethan doesn't seem to notice, of course. He shakes his head, as if he wants to shoo away a pesky fly.

Then he says, "I thought we straightened all that out, mosquito. I've already forgiven you for everything."

Forgiven *me*? I watch in horror as he takes something out of his pocket and bends down on one knee.

"I'm going to do this the traditional way," he says. Then he takes my hand and says, "Lea König, I love you and would like to ask you: will you be my wife?" He's holding a ring made of tiny, sparkling diamonds.

I'm at a loss for words, but probably not for the same reason as most women. I struggle with my composure. I'm horrified at Ethan's insensitivity and that he would choose to propose to me at this exact moment. I just feel like crying. A month ago, I would have wrapped my arms around Ethan's neck and jubilantly cried "Yes!" Now I just stand there quietly. Ethan is waiting with a self-confident expression, sure that his little mosquito won't reject his proposal. When I don't react, his face grows dark.

I shake my head violently and feel my eyes welling with tears. I turn around quickly and run away. I run down the country lane, my feet beating on the dry, dusty ground, my lungs burning, my heart bleeding, and tears running down my face as if they will never stop. I hurry inside Alice's house, shut the door behind me, and lean against it, panting like crazy until my pulse slows down. Then I go to the kitchen and steal a look through the curtains. After a long while, I see Ethan slowly walk up to his car. He looks stern and at the same time lost in thought. He gets in and drives away. I desperately need a "nice cup of tea" and put the kettle on the stove.

I sit in the dining room, staring out at the spring garden. My tea grows cold. The sight of the withered clematis, which still hasn't recovered from my overzealous pruning, depresses me even more. The weak, little vines sadly hang over the trellis while everything else in the garden blooms and prospers.

"You're the one to blame," I whisper to myself. "Did you have to be so aggressive? You could have been gentler." But could I really have saved our relationship by being gentler? No. After all, Ethan is self-centered and stubborn. It's completely clear to me now.

I look at my smartphone. I could install a nice, little game. My fingers itch. How comforting it would be to see candies whir across the screen . . . I suddenly hear a *ping*, which means an e-mail has arrived. My heart immediately beats faster. Maybe it's from Ethan. Maybe he'll write, "I'm so sorry, mosquito. I want to try to understand you and love you. Don't leave me!"

But the e-mail says:

> Yes, you're right. It was strangely and wonderfully puzzling to me why you radiate such an infectious joy for life, which is the envy of almost everyone you meet.
>
> I love you for confiding in me, particularly since I understand how difficult it was for you to write. I now know the secret behind it all. It makes me sad that you had to go through such a terrible experience. I'm so impressed by how you processed the tragedy in such a positive way.
>
> Why would I want to change anything about you? I think you're simply perfect the way you are, but I believe you've known that for a long time now, anyway.

It is exactly the e-mail that I wanted from Ethan—but it's from Jens. I'm totally confused. How did Jens get a private e-mail I sent to Ethan? Did Ethan . . . ? No, of course not. He doesn't even know Jens.

I open my inbox and click on the "Sent" icon. There has to be an explanation here somewhere. I'm completely flabbergasted now. I sent the e-mail twice, once to Ethan and once to Jens. But how . . . ? I check the time stamp on both outgoing e-mails. They're less than a minute apart—thirty-three seconds, to be exact. I think back to that time yesterday evening, when I sent the e-mail to Ethan. And then? Inez wanted to snatch my phone away. We struggled over possession of the phone. It suddenly dawns on me. During our tussle, the e-mail was sent to Jens, of all people. Blushing at the thought, I scroll through my sent mail. Who else received the embarrassing e-mail? All of my contacts? How terrible would that be?

Thank God. It was only sent to Jens. I read his reply again. And as I read it, I get a lump in my throat. It's so warm and sensitive . . . I shove my phone aside, lay my head on the table, and cry bitterly. I then pull myself together, wipe away my tears, and put my teacup in the kitchen. I desperately need fresh air, so I go outside to the garden. On impulse, I walk over to the reproachful clematis. I need to remove the withered branches and leaves—the sooner the better. But as soon as I touch the dry foliage, I see something. I bend over to get a better look. Little green leaf buds are sprouting from the branches.

"Okay, clematis," I say, "you win."

I long for summer because I'm so anxious to go home. It's difficult for me to forget about Ethan. My time in England is overshadowed by my intense feelings for him. For me, England is Ethan.

On the first day back to school, I remove the heavy gold necklace from my neck. I stick it in an envelope and place it in Ethan's cubby. I put on my favorite earrings. A female student compliments me on them. She says she didn't know that I had pierced ears, and that my small silver filigreed earrings suit me incredibly well.

Ethan doesn't look at me, and I ignore him, too. Occasionally I catch a glimpse of him when we pass each other in the hall. He hurries past me, and my heart bleeds. I look away quickly and continue on, my head held high. After the disastrous proposal, he doesn't trouble himself with me anymore. I'm surprised to see how proud and stubborn he really is.

Alice notices Ethan doesn't come over anymore. "What's going on with your handsome admirer?" she asks. "Too busy with school now?"

I tell her we broke up. "Oh, what a shame," she sighs. "He was really dreamy."

One afternoon toward the end of the school year, I bring a little bouquet to the Lanes' house. It takes an abnormally long time for them to answer the door, and I almost leave. But Glen opens the door, with Abby lurking behind him in the living room.

"I'm traveling back to Germany next week," I tell him. "I wanted to say good-bye to both of you."

Glen's grin is so wide I can see his toothless gums. "How wonderful, dear! We're delighted! Come in, come in."

Abby moves closer to the door. "So nice of you," she says coolly as she accepts the bouquet. She immediately hurries away to search for a vase and probably to cover up her embarrassment.

"Certainly you'd like a nice cup of tea and some dunking cookies," Glen says.

"There's nothing in the world I'd rather have!" I answer.

"She wants a cup of tea and some dunking cookies!" he yells toward the kitchen.

Abby sticks her head out and says with annoyance, "Dunking cookies, Glen Lane? Lea wants a big piece of my angel food cake, and that's exactly what she'll get."

We sit for at least an hour, chatting cozily. A big weight is lifted from my shoulders. Abby tells me about their new tenant, who she found almost immediately after I left—a nice, young interior designer who works for a new hotel in Stock. As I say my good-byes, Abby insists I take half the cake and wraps it up in aluminum foil. She makes me promise that I'll visit them anytime I come back to Gatingstone.

When I make my farewell visit to the Seafields, I take the opportunity to speak to Linda in private.

"You said something once about Mr. Derby," I say sheepishly.

"You mean how he's a chauvinistic asshole?"

"Yes, something like that. Where did you get that from?"

"Everyone at school knows it, unless they're blind or in love with him, as you apparently were," Linda says bluntly.

"But how did you know?" I ask.

"He's always spewing some kind of misogynistic rant. He tells the girls to clean the tables or collect the garbage. What he really means to do is prepare us for his idea of married life. The boys think it's great, of course, but the girls think it's disgusting!"

Catherine is the first among my friends to notice that I've remained the same old Lea even after spring break. She suspects it's over between me and Ethan.

"How are you?" she asks sympathetically. "Are you getting over him?"

I smile at her. "Let's put it this way: I was totally addicted to him. It did me a world of good to uninstall him."

I change my relationship status on Facebook to "Single," and barely a second later, Jens clicks "Like" under it. He offers to pick me up the following week in England, so I don't have to drag my heavy suitcases and my slippery shoulder bag from train to train.

Epilogue

Two years later, Jens and I honeymoon in Cambridge. We stay at a posh hotel in the city, and once again, the weather is simply wonderful. We visit the fantastic collection of ancient Roman sculptures we didn't have a chance to see before. We spend at least an hour at the local history museum. Then we glide leisurely—and carefully—down the River Cam in a punt. At the café, we giggle at the passersby to our hearts' content, and in the evening we go to the Evensong at the King's College Chapel. After some searching, we also find the tiny St. Peter's Church we visited over two years ago and sit devoutly in a pew, holding hands.

"Would you like to ring the bell?" Jens asks.

I laugh. "That's no longer necessary. I'm so happy, I can't think of a thing to wish for."

"Did your wish that one time actually come true?" he asks.

I think about it for a moment, then beam at him. "Yes, completely and totally. And you?"

He throws an arm around me and pulls me close. "My wish also came true, completely and totally."

About the Author

Photo © 2011 Michael Methfessel

Elisa Ellen is an East Westphalian. When she's not writing books, she wanders through the Teutoburg Forest with her husband and dog, reads, gardens, or plays music.

About the Translator

Terry Laster is a musician, singer, former music teacher, and book editor who sang, studied, and translated in Germany for many years. When not translating books or working on her long-overdue historical novel, Terry likes to hike, swim, and jam with her musician friends in Glendale, California, where she currently resides. The mother of four sons, she lives with her youngest child and her tiny Chihuahua.